W9-DBJ-213

Renegade River

Also by Giff Cheshire
in Large Print:

Stronghold

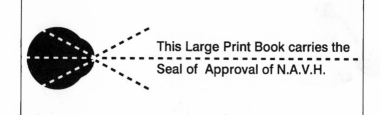

This Large Print Book carries the
Seal of Approval of N.A.V.H.

Renegade River

Western Stories

GIFF CHESHIRE

edited by
BILL PRONZINI

NEW HANOVER COUNTY
PUBLIC LIBRARY
201 CHESTNUT STREET
WILMINGTON, N. C. 28401

Thorndike Press • Thorndike, Maine

Copyright © 1998 by Mildred E. Cheshire and Bill Pronzini
Additional copyright information can be found on pages 387–388.

All rights reserved.

Published in 1999 by arrangement with Golden West Literary
Agency.

Thorndike Large Print ® Western Series.

The tree indicium is a trademark of Thorndike Press.

The text of this Large Print edition is unabridged.
Other aspects of the book may vary from the original edition.

Set in 16 pt. Plantin.

Printed in the United States on permanent paper.

Library of Congress Cataloging in Publication Data

Cheshire, Gifford Paul, 1905–
    Renegade river : western stories / by Giff Cheshire ; edited
by Bill Pronzini.
        p.   cm.
    Contents: The bad year — A mug at Charley's — Strangers
in the evening — Man breaker — Whistle on the river —
Stagecoach Pass — Renegade River — East ain't West — The
road to Jericho — Know your headings — A bridge to the
future — Miracle of Starvation Flat.
    ISBN 0-7862-1031-1 (lg. print : hc : alk. paper)
    1. Frontier and pioneer life — West (U.S.) — Fiction.
2. Western stories. 3. Large type books. I. Pronzini, Bill.
II. Title.
[PS3553.H38R46   1999]
813'.54—dc21   98-43046

Table of Contents

Foreword

Giff Cheshire: Oregon Man

In the years following World War II, the traditional Western story entered a renaissance period. A fresh, forward-seeking group of writers helped it grow and mature from the "bang-bang Western" of the pre-war years — whose emphasis was on furious (and often juvenile) action — into a form in which people, places, and a realistic sense of history were paramount. Chief among these writers were A. B. Guthrie, Jr., Jack Schaefer, and Dorothy M. Johnson. Others of note included Les Savage, Jr., Steve Frazee, Wayne D. Overholser, Clifton Adams, Lewis B. Patten, and Giff Cheshire.

Cheshire had few peers in capturing an authentic flavor of frontier life in the Pacific Northwest, all its grandeur and hardship as seen through the eyes of an impressive cross-section of the region's settlers and empire builders. His knowledge of Oregon history was voluminous; and his talent for blending little-known fact into entertaining fiction, whether historical or traditional, was by no means inconsiderable. These qualities, and his evident love and passion for his native state, make his body of work a small but important contribution to the post-war development of Western fiction.

Gifford Paul Cheshire was born on July 27, 1905, at Cheshire, Oregon — a community near Junction City named for his grandfather who had crossed the plains from Tennessee by wagon in 1852. "I was born and grew up on a diversified ranch [farm]," he wrote in a 1947 letter to *Adventure* magazine. "The little village that bears the family name was the terminal for a wagon freighting outfit and a stopping point for a mudwagon stage. My first job was as water boy on a railroad construction project. During school vacations I worked in sawmills, logging camps, and on harvest outfits. My father simultaneously ran a ranch, a general mercantile, and a construction contracting business. In addition to the grandfather who came across the plains in a Conestoga, another worked West through the gold fields of Colorado, Nevada, northern California, and southern Oregon."

After a period of study at Oregon State University, Cheshire joined the U.S. Navy in 1926. During most of his four-year military service he was assigned to the U.S. Marines and was present during the pacification of the Sandino insurrection in Nicaragua. He spent two years "beating the rugged hills and cañons for *bandidos* or in the roisterous and bawdy *cantinas* that offered the banana republic's only recreation" — and in the process learned what it was like to be shot at by fellow human beings.

Following his military discharge in 1930, he returned to Oregon, worked in a bank, and was married in 1931. Eventually he accepted a position with the U.S. Corps of Engineers. It was while he held this job that he began "turning out authentic but ungrammatical fiction" in his spare time. His first professional sale was made in 1934, to a Western pulp magazine, and he continued to sell sporadically until the war years, when he and his wife, Mildred, and their two children moved to Beaverton, Oregon, a city just outside Portland. By 1944 his output and sales record were steady enough to permit him to write magazine fiction full-time. He remained a professional writer of short stories and novels until his sudden death from heart failure in January, 1973.

Over a twenty-year span from the mid-'Thirties to the mid-'Fifties, Cheshire published some three hundred and thirty short stories and novelettes in a wide range of magazines, among them *Blue Book*, *Adventure*, Street and Smith's *Western Story*, *Zane Grey's Western Magazine*, *Dime Western*, *Doc Savage*, *Ranch Romances*, *Big-Book Western*, and *Short Stories*. The bulk of his output was traditional pulp Westerns featuring ranchers, cowhands, drifters, and lawmen, though his crisp style, well-drawn backgrounds, and flare for creating highly dramatic situations raised even his most prosaic efforts a notch or two above those of most other Western fictioneers. As good as many of his stories of this type are, he was even better when dealing with historical topics, particularly the various facets of water transportation in Oregon and Washington. Dozens of his stories and novelettes have as their settings the Columbia, Rogue, Deschutes, Willamette, Umatilla, and John Day Rivers, and feature the men who traveled and worked on them: river boat owners, captains, pilots, firemen, engineers, gamblers, freighters, ferrymen, steamboat builders, bridge builders. When taken in a body, these stories provide a rich and detailed history of the Northwest's waterways and water traffic in both the 19th and 20th Centuries.

Cheshire turned to the production of Western novels in the early 1950s, as did many of his contemporaries, when the pulp magazine markets began to collapse. His first book-length novel — written in collaboration with Wayne D. Overholser and published under Overholser's Dan J. Stevens pseudonym — was OREGON TRUNK (Avalon, 1950), a richly detailed, fact-based account of railroad building in central Oregon. His first solo novel also carried a name other than his own. BLOOD ON THE SUN (Fawcett Gold Medal, 1952) by Chad Merriman is the tale of a buckskin man and wagon-train guide caught in the midst of a battle between gold-hungry whites and Sioux Indians on the Oregon Trail. Cheshire would publish a dozen paperback originals under the Chad Merriman pseudonym over the next twenty years, including a second collaboration with Wayne D. Overholser — COLORADO GOLD (Ballantine, 1958) which appeared as by Chad Merriman and Lee Leighton, the latter another of Overholser's pen names. Four additional paperback originals and one hardcover novel, all of substandard quality, saw print under the pseudonym

Ford Pendleton. Two other early novels were also published under pseudonyms, one each by Paul Craig and Glenn Corbin.

Under his own name, which he reserved mainly for hardcover novels published by Doubleday and other houses, Cheshire specialized in cattle-country novels. The first of these was STARLIGHT BASIN (Random House, 1954). Approximately fifteen out of his total of thirty-three novels, including some Merriman and Pendleton titles, are formulary narratives of cattlemen versus sheep ranchers, rustlers, unknown enemies, and other cattlemen in conflict over land and/or water rights or for personal reasons. For the most part these traditional "cow yarns" are set in eastern Oregon, though Cheshire also made good use of the Nebraska plains, Wyoming Territory, the State of Washington, the Owyhee country along the Idaho-Nevada border, and the southern Nevada desert. Despite their familiar elements, Cheshire's skill at creating flesh-and-blood characters and an accurate picture of ranch life a century ago imbue his rangeland novels with a realism many other writers could only simulate.

Cheshire's strongest book-length works are those which are solidly based on historical events. STRONGHOLD (Doubleday,

1963) deals effectively, and often power-fully, with the Modoc Basin Indian War along the California-Oregon border. SNAKEHEAD (Ballantine, 1965) by Chad Merriman recounts the hardships involved in the building of a railroad through the Cascade Mountains of Washington. RIDE WEST FOR WAR (Ballantine, 1961) by Chad Merriman depicts the efforts of Southern sympathizers to exploit Oregon mining interests in the early years of the Civil War. Curiously, inasmuch as a large portion of Cheshire's short fiction is concerned with water transportation, only two Chad Merriman novels make use of this theme: ROGUE RIVER (Ballantine, 1962), an action story of gold mining and gun running in the part of Oregon Territory where the Rogue and Illinois Rivers empty into the Pacific, and MIGHTY BIG RIVER (Ballantine, 1967), the tense saga of two pioneer families' harrowing trek down the rain-swollen Columbia on open rafts in an effort to obtain free land being offered in the Willamette Valley.

Arguably, MIGHTY BIG RIVER is Cheshire's second best novel. There can be little question that his *magnum opus* is THUNDER ON THE MOUNTAIN (Doubleday, 1960), a fine recreation of the bitter 1877 war in which the U.S. Army unjustly decimated the Nez Percé after Chief Joseph refused to move his tribe onto reservation land. Cheshire's original title was FROM WHERE THE SUN NOW STANDS, taken from the final words of Joseph's declaration of surrender: "From where the sun now stands, I will fight no more forever." As luck would have it, Will Henry's award-winning and critically acclaimed novel on the same subject and with that exact title was published a few months ahead of Cheshire's. Thus he and Doubleday were forced into a last-minute title change, Cheshire choosing THUNDER ON THE MOUNTAIN because it was Chief Joseph's Indian name. Although Cheshire's version of the Nez Percé atrocity lacks some of the scope and depth of Will Henry's, its abundant merits might well have earned it much wider attention if it had been published at a different time.

RENEGADE RIVER is the first collection of Giff Cheshire's short fiction. In these pages are many, though by no means all, of his best cattle-country yarns, tales of Pacific Northwest waterways, and other kinds of stories. All have the distinctive Cheshire stamp of authentic and colorfully portrayed background, sharp character development, and gripping dramatic incident.

"The Bad Year" and "Man Breaker" are moving tales of the hardships faced by small back-country ranchers and of individuals who, when tested, find ways to overcome personal as well as natural adversity. Both stories first appeared in *Blue Book*, widely considered the perennial best of the pulp magazines for its editorial encouragement of good writing and unconventional storylines. Two other selections also were originally published in *Blue Book*: "The Road to Jericho," an unusual variation on the theme of a wagon train plagued by Indians on the Oregon Trail, and "Stagecoach Pass," an elemental account of a coach driver's struggles to save his passengers when his Sacramento-to-Roseburg stage is caught in a blizzard.

"A Mug at Charley's" concerns a retired steamboat fireman and engineer who makes the most of his last chance to fulfill a lifelong dream — a story brimming with sentiment that manages not to be in the least sentimental. "Strangers in the Evening," which won a *Zane Grey's Western Magazine* award, is a suspenseful narrative of the meeting of a lonely homesteader, a young drifter, and a trio of gold-hungry outlaws on the Oregon side of the Siskiyou Mountains, an area which the author once described as "a lusty and substantial part of the mid-'50 gold boom to which California lays full claim."

One of Cheshire's best short stories published in *Argosy* in 1946, "Whistle on the River," tells of steamboat builders on the Columbia, men and women who live and work in a decaying village "cut off from the world save for the passing steamers." This eloquent historical narrative contains some of Cheshire's most evocative prose. The collection's title story, "Renegade River," has a theme similar to the Chad Merriman novel, MIGHTY BIG RIVER. It vividly depicts the struggles of a wilderness trapper to shepherd a stubborn and wealthy young woman to the Willamette Valley by means of a hastily built raft. The raging rapids of the Columbia River gorge presents one obstacle, a gang of river pirates another, and foul weather a third.

An indolent ferrymaster's rôle in deciding a small-town battle between "the forces of decency" and those of sin and corruption is the stuff of "East Ain't West," a tale enriched by a large measure of tongue-in-cheek humor. "Know Your Headings" is a story Mark Twain might have enjoyed. Its

16

protagonist is a young Columbia steamer pilot, a breed that needed to know their headings "as intimately as a man knows his way around his own house in the dark," and it contains a plenitude of piloting lore.

The final two entries involve the building of bridges in the Pacific Northwest, but that is the only similarity between them. "A Bridge to the Future" is a modern tale of the construction of a huge steel-girder span across Hell's High Cañon, east of the Cascades, and of a young man's coming of age. "The Miracle of Starvation Flat" is an action Western, full of conflict and intrigue surrounding efforts to build a mile-long toll bridge across the narrows between two high-desert lakes in eastern Oregon.

As these dozen stories attest, Giff Cheshire was an accomplished entertainer and a true champion of the rich and varied history of his native state. He is fit company for such other Oregon men of fiction as Ernest Haycox, Nard Jones, James Stephens, and Robert Ormond Case.

Bill Pronzini
Petaluma, California

The Bad Year

I

Through the window at the end of his pillow, Lute looked at the frozen world. From the next room Sherry's voice exploded — "Good God a'mighty!" — and a log dropped hard onto the fire. Sherry cut loose again. He was in the big-beamed living room of the ranch house, and the morning revelation had finally touched him off. Lute frowned, unamused, because this was bad in more ways than one. It was too early in the season, and at any time a freeze on a cow spread could be very bad.

He let his brow crawl down in a scowl as he stared out beyond the tall, thick columns of the portico outside his window. There had been little suggestion of this at bedtime, the night before, beyond a clear, round moon. Now the poplars along the creek, the scattered sage and *chamiso* in the distance, all had the look of ice sculptures, a gusty wind pounding them. Air and sky held the same blue cold above the ruptures of the distant rims.

You won't be out in it, Lute reminded himself, and rubbed off the fog his breath had put upon the glass. This was bad for Sherry for one reason, and for himself for quite another. He could see the huddled saddle band in the corral, drooped, hip-shot, and miserable. Beyond the corral was the slope where he and Sherry had sledded when they were youngsters. At the bottom was the pond where they had skated. He recalled how eager Helen had been for ice and snow to come, and he had got to sharing it while knowing somebody else would be taking her out for the fun.

He grinned at the notion of a grown man and grown woman stirred by icy weather. He knew that, if he were on his feet, he wouldn't give two thoughts to it in the way she did. He would be cursing the devil out of it, as Sherry was. But Helen's eagerness for a chance to skate, which she hadn't had since she was a girl, had got him thinking along that line. Skating was so purely the thing Lute probably wouldn't have again — smooth, simple, satisfying motion.

Another log bounced onto the fire, and Lute called — "Run in the buckboard, kid!" — and hitched himself higher on the pillow.

The edge of the plaster cast caught on it, and he twisted to punch the pillow flat. Within the cast was a back broken some five months before by an outlaw stallion he had tried to ride.

Helen spoke from somewhere. "Neat work there, Sherry. I've added five new words to my vocabulary." Her voice was always warm and spilling over. It was low-pitched and husky, sprung from a well-formed chest. Lute heard her steps as she came down the stairs. "There's strong ice this morning, I bet you. When will you take me skating?"

Sherry answered in a sheepish voice: "We'll have to bell you, girl. But you're welcome to anything out of my vo . . . whatchacallit . . . that you can use."

"I have needed those words," Helen said. "A cow spread is a good place for a girl to learn to express her feelings. And I see I'm having a good effect on you. The word you were groping for is vocabulary. You have a dandy, Sherry, when you just let it rip. Do we go skating?"

"After work maybe, if I don't freeze into a pretty effect outdoors today."

"When's *after work?*"

"I reckon a schoolma'am is just born full of questions. That's *after* I get through doing whatever I've got to do today."

"A neat piece of basic data for a girl to build her plans on. I'll ask Tony."

"Not unless you want your skirt dusted."

Lute flung back the covers, scowling again. He was long and widely built, and his big, meaty hands and arms wore an incongruous pallor. His face and head had the rugged bony structure of the Constants, the craggy good looks. He was very thick in the middle now, and it showed beneath his nightshirt. He had eyes that could glint in quick humor, though they were brooding these days. He had endured all he could take of inactivity.

Big as he was, he had been light and fast as any 'puncher on Pot Hook. At twenty he had stepped into Pike Constant's shoes and made a go of it. He might have built it even bigger than Pike had, save for one day, one hour, one moment, when he had swung aboard the red stallion — the oreana he had caught in the brakes.

Sherry ran the wheelchair in. Except for name, no one would have taken them for brothers. In Sherry, nature had tried to compress the width of Pike with Elvira's small frame. It made him massive in a truncated way, and the devil of it was that the kid was sensitive enough to feel it.

21

Sherry swung the chair against the bed and said: "This is a hell of a note."

"We get it every winter, don't we?"

"Not like we've had it. It's been a hell of a year, and it's going to get worse."

Lute grinned bleakly. "Cheer up. Sometimes our blackest hours come right before a big turn downhill."

He lifted himself by driving his fists into the mattress and twisting until his legs fell over the edge of the bed. He endured the hateful daily moment when Sherry tugged on his trousers for him and pulled on socks and slippers. Sherry went out. Lute finished dressing and rolled to the stand table to wash in the icy water from the pitcher. He combed his hair, deciding he would wait to shave later in the morning, and wheeled out.

Helen turned at his coming, and stood slimly perfect before the fireplace. She was a virile man's counterpart, and knew it. His woman, she might have been, had she not appeared at Pot Hook too late. He had been locked in his prison, paralyzed from the hips down, long before she came.

She smiled. "Good morning, Luther."

"Good morning. So you like this!"

"Of course. It's beautiful."

"So's hell, I imagine, from a distance."

The smile turned into her *gamine* grin. "That's the viewpoint most people prefer, isn't it? With a reasonable detachment." There was a tiny crook in her short nose that spoiled her beauty but perfected her attractiveness. She had wide, brown eyes that snapped when she talked, particularly if she was getting an argument out of someone. Eyes and lips had a way of drinking when she listened to people, and again of spitting them out in quick disapproval. It was hard to picture her in a schoolhouse, which was exactly where she spent a good deal of her time.

It dragged up the good humor in Lute, and he knew she made a point of this when she found him low. They shared something, or had until he realized which way the wind blew. They were steel and flint, in a way, but the sparks they struck had been pleasant.

A door opened beyond the kitchen. Lute heard his mother say — "Good morning, Tony." — and heard the ramrod's genial reply. The big kitchen served both family and bunkhouse dining rooms. Though they had Charley, the hired cook, Elvira Constant had never trusted him out of her sight in the big kitchen.

Tony Minot came through the dining

room and paused in the next doorway. His silken, black hair, softly waving, almost touched the top, and his eyes, black as obsidian, gleamed with a vitality that was like Helen's, a spontaneous and eternal fire. He looked full of supple power, lean and hard-fleshed, competent and confident. Because of something welling in him, Minot had ridden the red oreana, beating it into submission fifteen minutes after it had reared over to crush Lute Constant. Not to avenge his boss, but to beat him — that was the pattern to which Minot was cut.

Minot flicked greetings to the men and settled his full attention upon Helen. "You've got your ice."

"It was a general issue," Sherry said.

"There'll be a good moon tonight," Minot said. "We'll build a fire on the bank. We'll have fun . . . you and I."

"She'll have fun," said Sherry, "but you've got the wrong whatchacallit there."

"Person," Helen breathed.

Tony frowned. "What's that?"

"In this case," Lute said, "it's who takes her skating. I, you, or he."

Minot's gaze came full upon Lute's. Something flicked on his lips and away, and something spilled, deep within the genial, black eyes. "In this case, Lute, I reckon it's I

24

or he." He turned with slack ease and went out.

Sherry's eyes met Lute's. In the same instant Charley, the cook, put the striker industriously to the steel triangle to call the crew for breakfast. Mrs. Constant more sedately called — "Come and get it." — to assemble the family. Lute wheeled in, Helen coming beside him in her long, smooth stride.

Minot's gibe had turned Sherry within himself, and he ate hurriedly, shoved up, and was gone. Plainly embarrassed and turned grave, Helen left soon for school. There were no school-age children on Pot Hook, but it was the nearest place to the school. Since Helen was a town girl and unused to the open country, Mrs. Constant had invited her to stay here.

Lute lingered over coffee, keeping his mother company at the table, for she was a slow eater. A rising anger was kindling against Tony Minot. *You're out of it,* the man had implied. Minot was a top rider, a first-rate ramrod, and he knew that as long as this was so, personal issues would never get him fired.

"Luther," Mrs. Constant was saying, "I don't like what I sense in you."

"What do you mean?"

"You've given up hope. You've turned against Helen. You two hit it off fine when she first came. Now you're trying to turn her to Sherry. That's no go, and Sherry knows it. If you keep it up, you'll turn her to Tony Minot."

"She's grown. She's smart enough to teach school. She's smart enough to see through Tony."

"A hurt woman sometimes likes an exciting man, just because he is exciting. Don't play the fool. The first thing you should do is take a hand in things again."

Lute frowned. "If Sherry's got to take the responsibility, he should have the full say. That's no more than right."

"If you can't run the whole show, you won't even run the curtain?"

"When you've got time to bring me some hot water," Lute answered, "I'd like to shave."

His mother rose from the table. "You're a coward," she said, and went out. She neglected to return with the hot water.

Lute rolled into the living room, more aware than he had pretended of what she had been driving at. She didn't know all that he knew. Nobody could. Through the wide window, he watched the last riders snake mounts from the day band, insert bits warmed especially by the bunkhouse fire, saddle, and ride out. Some carried axes to break the new ice from the water tanks. Sherry and Tony Minot were the last to go, never taking private grudges into the spread's vast and vexatious work. They rode out together.

Lute thought about Sherry. Toward Lute he showed much of the resentment he had always felt toward their father. From the time he was a stripling, there had been a simmering rebellion in the lad. He could not accept a defeat. Pike Constant had been a rough, impatient man, determined to raise a pair of tough sons. Lute recalled the last time Pike had tried to whip Sherry, using a hamestrap and laying it on. Sherry had been in his early teens, starting whiskers. In rising fury he had jerked the strap from his father. "Damn you, Pike, if you can cut it, lick me with your fists!" And Pike Constant had walked away.

Lute drew a calendar from beneath the cushion padding his chair, and fished a pencil stub from the pocket of his shirt. He drew a careful X upon the date of the day before. He was starting the month, and near its end was a date he had circled, the day the cast was due to come off for the second time. There was an earlier one, nearly three

27

months back. It had meant more than the next, for he had still hoped. But something hadn't worked; something wasn't fixed. The broken back was healed; the torn insides had grown back in place. But nerves at the fracture were still out of kilter.

So he was a coward! But there was no real life in his legs; they weren't his. The odd and maddening thing was that he hadn't had this partial paralysis until the first time the cast came off. For some reason, the previous night had been a long, black terror to him. Even the doctor had been puzzled as to why he went completely cold from hips down the moment he was freed from the cast.

"Your weight, I guess," Doc Barnaby had said. "Looks like it cuts something off. We'll have to keep it supported a while yet."

So Lute had gone back into the plaster prison. The very next day he could clamp fingers into the flesh and get the full register of the touch, or shove against the footboards of his chair and make the wood creak. Maddeningly, the restored cast had given him an elating sense of ease; the wheelchair had been a continued comfort to him. And he had crossed off the days until the next trial, not in eagerness, but as a man rations for himself the time left to him before an ordeal.

So he was driving Helen toward Tony Minot! He thought of her first days here, before he had learned what she was doing to him. He was often alone in the house, with the day's full time to kill. Usually Helen came home from school in mid-afternoon, and Elvira Constant had developed the obvious little habit of leaving them together. It had been pleasant, at first. Lute had told Helen about the country and the background of her pupils; how the schoolhouse itself had once served the early settlers as a fort against Indian attack, Pike and Elvira Constant among the defenders. They had played the phonograph, the acquisition of which had been the high point for Pike in his last sick year upon the earth.

Then Lute had made and beaded Helen a pair of fur-lined gloves, and without words she had cupped his cheeks in her hands and kissed him. After that, it wasn't companionship, and it never could be again.

Lute scowled through the window at the cold outside world. *You're out of it,* Minot had said so plainly. Since the man had been completely right, there was no wisdom in this shaking hatred of him. Lute struck the arm of his chair a heavy blow, spun about, and wheeled into the dining room. He got coat, fur cap, and robe from the rack by the door and bundled himself. He flung the door wide and sent the chair rolling out, while he bellowed for Dave, the old roustabout.

Surprised but a little excited, Dave fetched the buggy and team of trotters Elvira Constant used for neighborhood calls. He helped Lute to the seat, and carefully settled the old, buffalo robe about his legs. Lantern-jawed and skinny, Dave had helped Pike Constant found the spread. Too old now to ride, he puttered about headquarters, doing odd jobs, having his own way, freely speaking his mind. He shared an unspoken bond with Lute, for both were active men turned useless, impatient men with time on their hands.

"Don't bounce yourself out," Dave warned, and watched the buggy run out of the yard in a clatter.

Lute disdained the road, heading cross-country, all of which was frozen hard as paving. He drove for an hour, seeing parts of the crew at scattered distances, drawing stares of wonder. Something broke in him; something ran in him that made him want to sing. He begged the trotters for the top of their speed, and they delivered. The buggy skidded as he swung it in the impulsive course of his heated mind, wheels singing upon the frozen earth, and at last he did sing in a surging, unmelodious roar.

At intervals he caught sight of the distant ranch house, big and imposing and white, its massive pillars and portico with its balcony, the touch of local aristocracy Pike Constant had liked. He clipped past one of the many lakes dotting the lowlands, roaring louder. He was an eagle anew upon the wing, a kid on a sled again, himself upright and warm with action. He was straight upon his legs, pulling Helen to him as roughly and fiercely as he needed to, as something told him she would want a man to do.

Consideration for the horses made him draw them down presently. Before swinging for home, he put the rig up a draw onto a lower bench of the Opalcos. Some of the winter feeders were in here. They dotted the expanse, denied grass by the freeze, and would have to be fed from the ranch's precious hay unless a thaw came soon.

Three riders sat bunched between Lute and the animals, and he identified the peaked hat of Tony Minot. Sherry wasn't one of them, and they all had their mounts turned away from Lute to face a rangy steer that stood on spread and stubborn legs, eyeing them. Lute pulled down the buggy without attracting notice, seeing that Minot was quietly shaking out his rope. Minot swung his mount with his knees as his arm whipped up and whirled. The shot loop barely missed the abruptly bolting steer.

Minot cut after it, sending his horse in streaking chase as he shook out the rope again. He angled in, eight hoofs thrumming the hard earth, arm rising and snapping, and then the loop caught. Minot kept his arm raised to prevent the trained cow pony's instant hunker. Horse and steer shot ahead, almost abreast. Minot let the reach of the rope sag on the steer's far side, and he let it drape on down past its rump and shins.

Then he drove at a hard, slanting angle away from the racing steer. The rope tightened and swept beneath it, taking its legs cleanly from under it. In terrific dead weight, it crashed on the frozen ground.

Lute swore, starting the team. Minot swung down lightly to get his rope free. After a moment the steer struggled up and walked drunkenly away, bewildered and hurt, and for no apparent reason. The riders were aware of Lute suddenly, and they brought their horses about as the buggy came up. Minot stepped into saddle again.

He watched Lute's approach with an easy air.

"I'll be jiggered," he commented. "Long time no see . . . out here."

"What'd you bust that steer for?" Lute demanded.

Minot shrugged. "Hell, the critter looked rambunctious. Just figured I'd take him down a peg."

I could fire him for it, Lute thought. *He was showing the others he doesn't give a hoot for Pot Hook's rules. Or any rules.* Lute pulled in a long breath, wondering if Tony Minot had spotted him, after all. But if he accepted the challenge, Minot would have won a round. So good a hand would easily place on a nearby spread, and it wouldn't keep him away from Helen. Nothing kept Minot from a woman he was interested in, be she white or Indian. There had been several Lute knew about who had learned from Minot what that steer must have felt when it tried to stagger up and walk away from it.

Lute drove away.

II

Around three o'clock it began to snow, not heavily, the fine flakes driven on a high wind. Helen came home, flushed and excited, seeing only the promise of fun. The 'punchers drifted in with early darkness, tired and worried, with new troubles ahead. The elation of his ride had by now left Lute, a burned-out depression taking its place. He was back in his wheelchair, weighted into it by his plaster cast.

After supper, Helen brought forth the checkerboard, and Lute knew it was only being dutiful because she had a skating party on her mind. The snow was still fine and light, and so far the wind would have kept the pond swept clean.

Lute shook his head. "Thought you wanted to skate?"

"Can we, in this?"

"Not *we* . . . but you can if you're tough enough."

She gave him the *gamine* grin that so easily came to her mouth. "They call me Hardrock Helen up my way, mister. Too tall to snow under and too torrid to freeze."

"And a match for anything, I take it."

"Why not? At least, we can play until somebody shows up to take me out."

"Who're you betting on?"

She smiled again. "They're both competent fellows, I've found."

She put the checkerboard on the table-leaf slung across the arms of Lute's chair. Sherry came in presently and waited, watching the game. Lute gave Helen the best match he could, but she usually beat him, and did tonight. She had a quick, impetuous mind, a love of gambits that sometimes were headlong and impulsive, but smart. Lute had long sensed in her a delight in daring, and then in beating with dispatch the one who dared.

Minot came in directly from the compound, first having stamped snow from his boots on the side porch. It still dusted his wide shoulders, and twin devils danced in his black eyes. He played a bland study on Sherry's face.

"Forgot to mention it, Sherry, but I seen Pete, that snaggle-toothed 'puncher from Three J, last evening. He'd come down past our line camp. Said Joe Waters is sick up there and can't ride."

Sherry turned grave, his squat body broadening. "You forgot that?"

"Plumb slipped my mind. I'll see about getting a man up there after I've had my supper." Minot went on through the kitchen and into the dining room, unhurried, knowing he wasn't going to have to do a thing about it, that he had neatly dumped the whole responsibility in Sherry's lap.

Skating, Lute thought. *So that's how he means to work it!*

Their eyes meeting, Lute and Sherry traded a long thought. Minot knew that with weather making, Waters had to be replaced immediately. And more than that: Joe was only a kid, a waif picked up by Pot Hook, a button obliged to be a man before his time. If he was sick, he had to be brought in and placed in Elvira Constant's capable hands. A soddy in an open saucer high in the foothills was no place to battle winter sickness.

Minot knew the rules. He had known about Joe that morning, and had probably meant to do something about it until he realized how he could use it against Sherry. Minot played that way, with deadly thrusts.

So he had waited until now, with a sick rider jeopardized, and a storm blowing up. It was incredibly callous, but it was Minot.

When Sherry turned at once toward the coat rack, Lute said: "You can't make it now, kid. There isn't enough snow for the sleigh yet. There's too much for wheels, or will be before you're back."

"I'll make it."

"How?"

"I'll take Judd up to replace Joe. We'll use the buckboard. If we bog down, we can ride the horses on up. By that time, there'll be enough snow. I can bring Joe in on a travois." He spoke with no bitterness against Minot before Helen, but something bleak and dangerous was in his eyes.

Lute saw that Helen was puzzled at first, and then noted with anger that she was amused. She couldn't know what ran beneath the surface, and, though it was beyond her, she had an idea Tony had pulled something clever. The door opened, closed, and Sherry was gone.

Helen showed no surprise when Tony Minot came back presently. He grinned at her. "What do you know? Sherry took it into his head to take a man up there. No sense in that. The kid's probably only got the sniffles."

"We don't make long-range guesses," Lute growled.

Minot shrugged. "Well, no use your wasting a perfectly good evening, Helen. Get your skates."

Lute felt something squeeze his throat when she rose from the bench before the fireplace and ascended the stairs. Minot flung a cigarette into the fire and stared at the flames.

"I don't like your tricks, Minot," Lute said. "I don't like your hand with a rope. Be careful with it, fellow."

"Or what?" Minot asked, without looking up.

"Or I'll kill you."

Minot looked up then. Though he did not speak, his eyes plainly, derisively asked: *What with?* He came about and straightened. He smiled. "You don't look alike, but you Constants are sure two peas in a pod. Your brother made mention of that same thing the other day. A man gets tired of hearing it."

So that was it. So that was what had put this thing upon its sinister tack.

Helen came down, bundled and ready, with her skates across her shoulder. She gave Lute a quick smile and went outdoors with Minot, plainly excited. Lute saw their swinging lantern, their shadows long upon the frozen earth, the light minutely flecked by the continuing snow. Then they were swallowed by the night.

His mother, early rising and early retiring, had gone to her room after supper to sit by her own fire, and Lute knew this was because it usually left him alone with Helen. His anger expanded to include her. A coward, she had called him. What could he do about anything?

He noticed presently that the snow, cutting through the light from the window, had grown heavier. It did not return the skaters from the pond, but it set his mind to a steady worry about Sherry and Walt Judd. But this wasn't a blizzard yet. They knew the country. They probably would make it up there without too much trouble. Sherry would doubtless wait until daylight to start back with young Joe — if Joe was sick enough, which he must be for them to have sent word down.

Presently Lute could see the flickering reflections of a fire Minot had started at the pond, which meant they were not ready to come in. He wheeled away from the window and into his own room. Sherry always helped him to bed, but now a strong revolt filled him. He jerked down the covers and undressed in a deliberately savage clumsiness. He managed to swing into bed and drag the blankets over him. He thought: *I've got to beat that man.*

Lute wakened to hear a high-pitched, screaming wind and to a half dawn that told him they were well into a blizzard. The snow, fine as sand, seemed to blow straight across the windows, and the sashes rattled under the pressure.

At breakfast time they still needed lamps, and Lute knew there would be no riding that day, nor until this blew itself out. Sherry would be pinned at the east line camp — if he hadn't already started back — and no one dared ride out to discover which. Mrs. Constant asked about Sherry and took the news with a small shock on her face.

Helen, though freed temporarily from her school work, was grave and silent. She bent over Lute in the living room, whispering: "Did they get up there, Lute? Did Sherry start back with that fellow?"

"How do I know?" he snapped, all his fury of the previous evening exploding under this morning's strain.

She stepped away. He saw a total surprise on her face, and behind it hurt, and behind that anger. She turned and went up the stairs, and he saw no more of her that morning.

There was scarcely a let-up that day, and Lute often could not see the barns and other structures forming the headquarters compound. In the few moments of clarity he saw snow pillowed deeply on the leeward of the roofs, the other side blown bare. The watering trough in the middle of the yard seemed supported on a pedestal of twisted ice. The saddle band, held in the corral on baled hay, was harassed and dispirited.

The next day broke quiet and clear. Scarcely with full light, Lute was in the sleigh and crowding a wallowing team toward the Opalcos and the east line camp. Old Dave rode beside him, because the undertaking was dangerous for a cripple who, if thrown from the sleigh, would freeze helplessly where he landed. The overstepping horses tangled their feet and floundered. Lute turned them across the wheeling white flat. At distances he could see Pot Hook riders, already out and moving strays back into the protecting foothills.

He reached a place presently where a wide, scuffed trail swung at a tangent across his course, pointing toward a fringe of cottonwoods on the margin of a nearby lake.

Dave swore: "Drift, by damn!"

"Looks like it." Gloom settled on Lute. Drift was the slow stampede of cattle when the underfooting would not let them run, a mass movement down the wind that was their attempt to escape harassment. He swung into the broad path, making a hard, dry swallow in his tightened throat. They went over a rise, and then he saw it. But the cattle hadn't seen it. The lake ahead had just chanced to lie squarely ahead of them, down the wind.

"Let's get on with our work!" Dave growled. "I don't like to see them things."

Lute slapped the reins, and the sleigh ran on, following in the way the storm-whipped cattle had gone in the night. They skimmed through the band of trees, and he swung the sleigh half around to a stop at the frozen lake margin. The scuffed-up trail ran on for a hundred yards to terminate in great jagged upthrusts of ice, refrozen into its present pattern. Lute knew what they would see out there, perhaps some horns protruding from the ice, or a cow's tail frozen like a snake within. The width of the path told of the numbers, the weight that had blindly placed itself upon the frozen lake. It had been enough for a collapse.

"Goddlemighty, Lute, let's get out of here!"

"God Almighty made himself some foolish critters, Dave. If they'd bucked the wind, it wouldn't have happened."

"Who're you to talk?" Dave snapped.

Lute started the team again, swinging north toward the foothills. Dave remained silent and grumpy. But he had asked a good question, and Lute kept turning it over in his mind.

An hour later they sighted a horse and travois, coming out of a foothill draw and followed by a wallowing rider. It was Sherry, bewhiskered and drawn, but relieved at the approach of the sleigh. Young Joe Waters, unconscious and roped, was slanted on the travois. The men made silent greeting. They transferred the sick young 'puncher to the back of the sleigh, where Dave had placed loose hay, and started back to headquarters.

III

For two days the blizzard hung poised in the sky while Pot Hook rode in a kind of controlled frenzy, with ice-clad men forking numb, stumbling horses, plowing through snowdrifts, searching the last, battered foot of the home range. They threw the big herd back into loose cohesion. They tailed up surrendered animals. They stumbled mutely past many an unmoving mound. By the second morning the sleds were transporting hay from the stack yard and scattering it in strategic shelters provided by nature. Until a thaw, the cattle had to be fed. As long as they could be out, 'punchers had to stay ahorse night and day. They rode and froze and cursed; they ate hurriedly, soaked up a little heat, and rode out again.

Sherry, when he showed himself for a few minutes at the big house, had red, black-rimmed, inscrutable eyes. He had a whiskery, chapped, and wooden face. But there was work, and, while this was so, nothing else mattered. Even Tony Minot was a cowpuncher again, doing his job flawlessly. The break in the storm suspended passion, but it hung its heavy hint beside the glowering threat in the sky.

With a patient to care for, Elvira Constant withdrew into a world of her own, a world of quiet vigilance, of hard-won homeopathy, of poultices and cold cloths, herb tonics and unspoken prayer. A frontier woman, she prayed with her hands, her swift body, her endless energy, and she had Helen's willing help.

Lute saw none of them very often, or for very long. The second clear morning, he wheeled out along the path Dave had shoveled across the compound and rattled on the door of the blacksmith shop with his fists. Dave was within, and Lute had seen the smoke of the forge. The old man let him in, helping him up the little ramp from the ground level. He had something going in the fire and returned to it, curious but unquestioning.

The sharp, pleasant odor of burning coal hung heavily in the air, and the interior was warm. A grindstone stood along one wall, and Lute rolled to it. He maneuvered the chair parallel to the stone, which stood on a frame like a sawhorse, and then realized he couldn't make it alone.

"Want to help me aboard, Dave?" he asked.

Dave came over, the look of wonder still in his eyes. He helped Lute swing astraddle the frame and settle himself on the small, iron saddle that formed its seat.

Lute put his weight on a foot, starting the big stone with his hand. A treadle rose against the other foot, and he pushed it down, the other rising. An odd feeling washed up and crested and swept over him. Patiently, weakly, deliberately, he picked up the rhythm — the stone's momentum helping him — supplying the energy required to keep it going. The stone went faster and faster, and he began to breathe deeply through an open mouth. Awkwardly but with climbing joy, he made his static walk.

A weight touched his shoulder presently, and it was Dave's hand. "Reckon that's enough for now. But by God, you run her, boy. By God, you did."

"Yes," Lute said. "By God, I did."

He was spent and panting, far more than he'd expected, when he slumped in his wheelchair again. His legs felt queer, frighteningly queer. He thought: *Maybe I*

46

shouldn't have. Maybe that was bad. Sweat stood on his skin, and he could feel the warm, wet edges of the cast. But it wasn't cold sweat. The panic left him, and he began to feel good.

The first thing every morning, thereafter, he kept this rendezvous with Dave. Each time he could stay longer on the little, iron saddle of the grindstone; each time he was a little more its master.

Elvira Constant brought young Joe out of crisis, pulling him out with her two, small hands. The day she emerged with peace in her eyes, everyone knew without question that all in that particular bedroom was well. She kept him there in bed, but an easing came in the big house. Then the long-suspended blizzard came in, with all its pent-up fury.

With the herd left again to its own devices, the 'punchers loitered about headquarters, keeping to the bunkhouse except to venture forth for chores or to enter the dining room to eat. The storm whipped and howled and choked the range. It made a deadly curtain no man dared to penetrate. Men, out in the blizzard's blast, were like the cattle, lost, numbed beyond reason, driven to windward where lay eventual death. Pot Hook kept indoors under orders, its fate entirely upon the wheel of chance.

It was Helen who suggested a party, on the second storm-bound evening. Minot came over to the big house, without invitation as far as Lute knew. He set Pike's phonograph going, and he lifted Helen to her feet. They danced across the big living room, kicking away the thrown skins, and, because it was spirited music, Helen drew away from Minot and went into a fandango, feeling good, and it was a beautiful sight to see. Minot, his eyes shining, stamped his feet. At this Helen halted, looking around in self-consciousness.

"Why don't we have a party?" she asked. "Why not have the boys in from the bunkhouse? It doesn't help for everybody to be so glum, does it?"

"It's crowded enough," Minot said, and he reached for her again.

Sherry was there, and Lute, with Mrs. Constant off in Joe Waters's room upstairs, providing the company necessary to make him stay in bed. Lute saw Sherry's face pull tight at Minot's remark, and he felt the quick ranklement run under his own skin. But Helen continued to dance with Minot, their two bodies slim and supple, in motion perfectly conformed. Minot changed the records on the cylinder, setting the needle and tin horn back in place, winding the spring, ignoring the two Constants. Sherry did not try to claim Helen in the moments she thus stood free. He slumped in his chair and stared into the fire, and something black and bleak stood out from him.

It was Helen who broke it off finally, smilingly remarking that she was tired. She went upstairs, and presently Lute heard her voice in Joe Waters's room.

Lute wheeled out early the next morning to keep the rendezvous with Dave in the blacksmith shop, along the path the boys kept shoveled in the compound and through a lessening snow. Dave was already there, with a fire started for warmth, and he had discouraged company from the idling riders. Lute had his exercise, the cold drive of determination flogging him this morning.

Sliding from the saddle at last, a shaking impulse took him. He had started to swing to his wheelchair, but he halted halfway and put his feet to the floor. He made a full stand and, with a thudding heart, shifted his weight from his supporting arms and balanced on his feet.

Dave had turned and was watching. "Ah," he said in a quiet voice.

"Get me out of it, Dave!" Lute snapped.

"Cut me out of this damned thing!"

"The cast?"

"The cast."

Dave came over. "Wait a minute, boy."

"Now!" Lute began to strip off his shirt with hands that had turned to tearing, clawing hooks. He flung shirt and undershirt to the floor, and stood with his massive shoulders and arms naked in the shop's pungent heat. Sweat dripped from his armpits and hit the cast. He fought an apprehension that was the most shaking emotion he had ever experienced.

Veto and sympathy mixed in Dave's eyes; then the balance tipped. He got a hacksaw blade and some tin snips. With a decision reached, he showed no more hesitation and set to work. It was a long job, gnawing at the closely conforming composition of plaster and gauze. Tiring, Lute had to put his weight back on his arms, lifting it completely from his legs. He knew his legs were going, with the coldness creeping into them again. Then Dave got his cut made, and his fingers took the new edges and spread them apart, hard. The cast cracked loudly, and Dave dropped it to the floor.

An upshoving constriction came under the ridges of Lute's jaw. He waited while Dave pulled up the draped trousers and belted them, and he slowly let his weight down again upon his slippered feet. They seemed asleep, only his vision registering the touch. Then with an inward, fearful curse, he pitched forward helplessly — to hit the floor before old Dave could catch him.

Without speaking, Dave lifted him and got him into the wheelchair.

"Put it back, Dave!" Lute gasped. "For God's sake, put it back!"

"The cast? There's no putting that one back. And no getting the doc out in this weather. I reckon we went crazy. Just take it easy. I got a leather belt I use on the freight wagon. Maybe it'll help."

"It was supposed to come off pretty soon, anyhow. It makes no difference. Hand me the rest of my clothes."

The dull day wore on. Lute found himself alone in the living room, with Sherry sleeping, trying to catch up on his rest, and with the two women upstairs mostly, keeping Joe Waters company. In mid-afternoon Mrs. Constant descended from the stairs and took a seat near Lute, picking up the knitting she had neglected so long. Her face was deeply fatigued, but Lute saw with a close glance that it was a satisfying tiredness and not depleting. She played her own inspection upon her son's dark countenance.

She asked: "What happened to your cast, Lute?"

He tensed in surprise. "Why?"

"I thought you looked different. I just figured out what it is. Is that what you and Dave were doing in the shop this morning?"

He nodded. "A pair of fools."

Mrs. Constant gave him a sharp, questioning look. "So it still doesn't work. So you still have to have your cast."

For the first time he was humble before her. "Why is it?"

"I don't know, but I've got a suspicion. What hit you wasn't the fact that an oreana crushed you. It was the fact that Tony Minot rode the brute while it was still on its rampage."

"I'll ride that red devil till its heart busts!"

"You won't," Mrs. Constant said, "because I made Sherry turn it loose, and you know it."

"I'll get it. I'll catch it. I'll ride it."

"Why don't you face the real thing, son?"

"What?"

"The fact that you're afraid to get well."

Lute laughed without mirth. "What the devil do you mean?"

"I mean that you're afraid of Tony Minot."

"Bosh!"

"It isn't bosh. You're afraid to come out of your cast. You're afraid to face him on equal terms. He mastered something that maimed you, and it got you."

Lute's hands gripped his dead knees and pressed. "Is that why you called me a coward?"

"Exactly. As long as you wore the cast, you knew you wouldn't have to face Minot. With it gone, your legs have to go dead on you, so you can stay a cripple."

"I've never heard anything so silly."

Mrs. Constant smiled and rose. "Maybe so. I've had to tend a lot of sickness out here, and I've observed a few things. Fears come out, Luther . . . fears we don't know we have. You hate Minot because he did something that smashed you, and because he did it to show you he could. But he knew exactly what to expect from the oreana, and you didn't. Don't forget that."

"I hate him, but that isn't fear."

"Hate is fear, when it's bitter, do-nothing, brooding hate. When you see that, I've an idea things might go differently for you." She went out.

Dave came in presently with the wide,

heavy belt he had mentioned.

"Want to try it, Lute?" he asked.

Lute stared at it, amazed at the physical hunger that filled him for its support. He wanted Dave to strap him into it tightly, then maybe the life would come again into his legs. *You're afraid of Tony Minot. That's why you stay crippled.* He made a motion with his hand. "Take it out of here."

Startled, Dave grunted. "Why, it's only a piece of leather . . . not a snake."

"Take it away!" Lute snapped, and he thought: *I've got to get Minot.*

The snowfall stopped, but the high wind held a freezing blast that swept in from the east, harrying the range and screaming on the corners of the big house. The windows by Lute's bed gave off a low, grumbling rattle, but it was not this that kept him awake. Something clawed at his mind that he couldn't get a finger on, something that was elate and at the same time depressing, so that the effect upon him was a completely wakeful, completely exhausted inertia. He had the dim sense of being on the point of a discovery, of finding something he had long sought, and this baffled him for he was in search of nothing.

The dimmest of moons flung its light

from the blackened sky, and, though he stared through the window, it was with vacant interest. Yet, after sleepless hours, he grew aware that there was something to see out there. A figure had appeared at the edge of the portico. It was Minot's shape, and the man was moving in stealth.

Lute watched him quietly, seeing that Minot carried a rope in his hand, that he was in shirtsleeves despite the freezing wind, and must have just come from the bunkhouse. Minot was moving swiftly now. He had a loop in his rope, and, standing at the edge of the portico, he brought a hand sharply upward, flinging the loop straight into the air. He made four tries, then it did not fall, and Lute knew it had caught upon one of the iron pickets on the portico balcony. Minot went up in a quick hand-over-hand, then the rope was lifted to disappear.

Lute's throat was dry as he flung back the covers and rolled himself to the edge of the bed. He reached for the wheelchair, pulled it into position, and tried to flop himself into it. A cold thought stopped him. Two bedrooms opened onto the balcony, the spare one occupied by Joe Waters and Helen's. Doors and windows throughout the house were strongly constructed. Minot could get in nowhere without help from inside. He must have been fairly sure of getting help, to have risked this venture. Sickness weighted Lute's stomach.

He got his feet on the floor and held himself upright on the edge of the bed. It was a long moment before he heard a swift, light movement down the stairs. Then he saw Helen's slim shape slip past his door, in a robe and highlighted for an instant by the dim, indirect light of the banked fire. He heard her cross the living room, and in a moment a lamp came alight in there. Lute's mouth dropped open when, in the next moment, the phonograph blasted out a martial air.

Helen appeared in his doorway, and her voice was urgent. "Lute? You awake?"

"I am now." Something broke, and he wanted to laugh, to shout and sing.

"I couldn't sleep. Do you mind the racket?"

"Love it!" Lute said.

He heard her gasp. "Lute, do you know?"

"Saw him go up. Girl, I love you, too. We'll keep him there."

"That was sort of my idea."

She helped him into the chair and placed a blanket about his shoulders and another over his lap and legs. She pushed with energy as she wheeled him out into the other room. She left him by the window and went to start the phonograph over again.

"He had the nerve to rap on my window."

"You think fast," Lute commented. "Expect it?"

"Kind of. The night we skated, he hinted he was a pretty fancy, second-story man. I didn't think he'd try it, but a girl gets to wondering what she'd do in such a case."

He grinned at her for the first time in days, and saw the smile begin to tug at her lips. He recalled her checker game, the fires that kindled in her, the delight in outwitting her opponent.

"You wanted a party," Lute said. "By gum, we'll have one." Then he bawled: "Sherry!"

Helen looked uneasy. "Please, let's don't be too mean. Let's keep it between you and me and Tony, shall we?" He liked her for that.

Sherry was already roused, for he emerged from his room down the hall half dressed and grumpy-eyed. "What in blue blazes?" he demanded, viewing with interest the two, night-clad figures before him.

"We couldn't sleep," Lute said.

"Been having trouble myself, the last few minutes."

"Then let's have a party. Bring in the boys."

Sherry swung toward the kitchen, shaking his head but grinning. There is in men under tension something that lets go in pure nonsense if the chance offers, and a moment later Lute heard Sherry's booming voice rousing the crew.

"Blow, wind, blow!" breathed Helen. Her eyes met Lute's, and they were together again.

The 'punchers stumbled in from the bunkhouse, hurriedly dressed, rumpled, and sleepy, but coming quickly awake. They took hold with noisy gusto. If the schoolteacher wanted a party, they aimed to deliver one. Mrs. Constant appeared, concerned for her patient until Joe bawled from above that he wanted to come down. Two men ascended, brought him downstairs, and deposited him on the sofa. The phonograph ran on, and in robes, braids and slippers, the women danced with the men.

If anyone noted the absence of Tony Minot, nobody commented. Nerve-frayed and storm-punished, this was release, and they made the most of it. Even Dave and Charlie joined the fun. Charlie made coffee and cut a cake being saved for the next day. Dave tended the fire, a wicked grin on his lips, and Lute recalled that he had a shrewd head for figuring things out.

Lute kept station by the front window. The full light spilled upon the portico, so that he could see all of it. Though it was well below freezing, though the wind whipped and howled, Minot did not try to slip down. Nor could he get into the house from above without breaking a window, creating a disturbance dangerous to his vanity.

Minot had been thrown on his own rope as hard as he had thrown the undeserving steer, up in the foothills, and by a slip of a girl, such as he had roped without mercy many times. Helen had found the perfect weapon for a man like that — ridicule — or, what was worse, the danger of it. It served the purpose better than fists or guns, and it was Helen who had done it. Lute loved her, and knew he would no longer try to hold back his love.

IV

Helen broke up the party as abruptly as it had started, sending the 'punchers back to the bunkhouse. They carried Joe up to bed and left with grins on their faces, perhaps because of the utter unpredictability of the party, possibly because they suspected more than had been openly admitted. Helen lingered, and, when the room was empty except for the two of them, she blew out the lamp and came to wait beside Lute at the window. Long minutes passed. As his eyes adjusted again to the faint illumination outdoors, Lute saw two ends of a rope run silently down from above. Clutching both, Minot appeared, dropping the last distance. He had doubled the rope about a balcony picket so he could pull it free. He retrieved it, whirled, and disappeared.

"He'll go now," Helen said. "We'll be rid of him."

"Maybe not. But if he doesn't, don't ever

let him get his hands on you."

He turned her, and, as if understanding his need, she dropped to her knees beside the chair. He placed hands upon her and gently kissed her, and, as her lips stirred under his, he let roughness come. She was still and conforming for a long moment, then she rose, and went quickly upstairs.

Lute sat for a while in the semi-darkness, watching the freshened fire begin to die again. Though the kiss had been stirring and what he had wanted since the first, it had not been the deep thing he sought. Something else kept crowding, buried in his mind, and not getting through. He had no legs, and so the kiss had been empty for all its fire. The deflation of Minot's conceit had failed to free Lute Constant.

Tony Minot did not pack his war bag and ride away. The 'punchers, if they entertained suspicions, were too shrewd to show them to Minot, whom they all recognized as a dangerous man. Since nobody laughed, or showed inclination to, Minot stayed on. This worried Lute, particularly when clear weather came and school was resumed. When he could, Lute picked Helen up at the school before all her pupils had left, bringing her home — the old mare she rode

61

to school trailing behind the sleigh. When Lute couldn't, Dave quietly assumed the watch.

Meanwhile, there were objective things to center attention. A Chinook wind brought a thaw, and Pot Hook got its increasing estimate of the year's winter kill. Then a quick freeze put an ice crust upon the range, so that the 'punchers had to ride forth with sharpened calks on their ponies' shoes and hay once more became the herd's sole reliance. There came a day when every work-weary rider knew they were in for another heller. Black clouds ran in over the southern horizon, with a high wind springing up. It freighted a freezing touch, lisping upon the ice-crusted snow.

At noon, Mrs. Constant said worriedly at the dinner table: "I do hope Helen's wise enough to send the youngsters packing and come home. Sherry, you'd better ride over there and tell her to."

Sherry nodded, and it was at that moment that a 'puncher, who had been left with the herd while the others ate in relays, appeared in the doorway to speak a single word: "Drift!"

The newly arrived rider jerked the door shut against the high wind and vanished. Sherry shoved away from the table, jarring it, his chair going over in his haste. Mrs. Constant lifted her hand and let it fall. With a fork raised to his mouth, Lute was poised for a long moment. Sherry had turned and shoved out through the kitchen, yelling at the crew in the bunkhouse.

Lute knew that he could not sit through this one. He bawled: "Charlie!" When the cook appeared, he snapped: "Tell Dave to fetch up the sleigh!" The man ducked away.

Lute was ready and stationed on the side porch when the sleigh came up. The sky had the look of twisted, black hair, and the air was full of powdery snow. It was the cook who brought up the team.

"Where's Dave?" Lute asked, as he swung himself in with the man's assistance.

"Dunno. Not around."

The riders already were scrambling for the corral, snaking out mounts and saddling up, hunched against the bitter wind. Lute saw that Sherry was already on his way, riding with the 'puncher who had brought in the word. He slapped reins and put the sleigh on their track, his breath catching at the slippery underfooting for the horses.

He drove for nearly two miles, the mounted 'punchers overtaking and passing him, for their horses were equipped with calks and his were not. He topped a rise and

63

descended, and ran for some distance down a shallow draw. At its end he swung and went up a defile and through a small saddle in the low hills. He came upon an elevation where he looked down into a big bottom. The herd, self-propelled, had assembled there and was moving, stretched in a thick column far below.

Riders appeared on the flat, scurrying for the point of the slow march. Lute spoke to his horses and started them down. He thought of the day he and Dave had come upon the collapsed ice of the lake, and knew the same thing, on a big scale, was under way here. Drift — the slow stampede — the instinct in bunched cattle to move away from the site of punishment. The resumed wind, the black threat in the sky, had piled upon what they had already suffered to start it. With new snow lightly dusting their hunched backs, they plodded down the wind.

The sleigh skidded on the sharp slant, and once a horse stumbled and nearly went down. Lute perched on the edge of the seat, hunched forward, knowing that if he were thrown out he would be finished, for in the excitement he was not apt to be noticed. He came down off the slant and onto the bottom, then swung the team left to where the riders already were throwing their effort — feeble and battering — against the point of the march.

Men had died trying to halt a drift. Maddened and determined, the plodding animals would brook no interference. They would fight to the death for the privilege of dying in their own way, piled against some impassable barrier. For something, somewhere, would halt them — a stream, a bluff, the blind end of a cañon.

The point had to be turned, and already flying squads threw themselves solidly at the head of the march. The bottom was broad enough to turn and mill them on, if they could be coaxed into it. It was also long, but at a distance of some three or four miles due ahead it gave way to foothills and beyond that the badlands of the Opalco brakes. Guns barked. Men yelled and drove their game little mounts into the stubborn mass. If a horse lost footing, it and its rider would die. Harried, the column moved faster. Calves fell, mothers halted, both to be trampled to a soft, red pulp.

Lute was pulled into a tight knot on the sleigh seat, and he thought: *Is this fear?* He growled, though the wind washed around him and carried the sound beyond hearing. He slapped the reins and sent the horses forward at a careless speed. He swung in a driving arc, curving in against the point, putting the bulk of horse, sleigh, and man into the struggle.

When the slewing team nearly mixed with the outer steers, he pulled it away, reversing the curve, and running well ahead of the column. Again he swung, and now he came in head-on, the racing team miraculously keeping on its feet. He refused to pull them out of it.

In the last split second he forced the oncoming column to part. He noted then that the riders had thrown themselves onto his flanks, coming behind him in a flying wedge. Every man in the outfit was making a ride that the odds said plainly could end only in death. The sheer weight of it, the sheer bulk and determination, split the point. The lead steers fanned out, but only to pass the obstruction. The riders clamped onto each point of the formed Y, hammering it, emptying their guns, beating with their hats, and screaming.

Lute stopped the team in the crotch of the Y, holding it there, forcing the animals to part around him. The Y broadened, its prongs beginning at last to turn back upon the stretched stem. The riders increased their hazing. The column began to lose shape, steers turning now to avoid each other, and at last Lute swung the team about and pulled out, knowing they were starting a mill. That would run them down, a formless turning in a circle, and afterward they would submit to dispersion and herding.

On the sidelines and watching the chaotic movement, Lute grew slowly aware of a striking fact. He could identify the various riders, whipping in and out of the sifting snow. It dawned on him that he had not seen Tony Minot. It puzzled him, and, when he caught sight of Sherry, he motioned to him.

Sherry rode over.

"Where's Tony?" Lute asked.

Sherry, excitement still high in him, frowned with an immense relief. "Why, blamed if I know. He was saddling, but, where he went, I don't know. Lute, you reckon he headed for the schoolhouse?"

Lute swung the team. "Stay with the job. I'll find out."

Fear had him by the throat. Until this morning he had not had time to think of Helen. He remembered the stung, humiliated fury in Minot. He hazed the horses, driving them at a dangerous clip over the ice crust, the fine snow spilling all about him.

He had to pass the ranch house to get onto the road to the school. Just short of the compound, he encountered Dave and realized it was the first time he had seen him since the excitement began. Dave swung up into the sleigh, cold rage in his eyes, and rode in.

"Minot nailed her at the school. I seen him sneaking off and followed him."

Lute's tongue was dry, his throat hurt.

"Minot sent the kids home, and he roughed her up," Dave went on. "But she's got gumption, that one. She was still on her feet when I come in. I had to put a gun on the man to stop him."

Lute let out a long breath. "Where is he?"

"Bunkhouse. I told him to git, but he wouldn't."

"I told him I'd kill him if he tried anything like that. That's what he's asking for. It's all he's got left to save his pride."

"Leave me gun him off the place, Lute. He's a bad one."

"No." Lute swung the sleigh to a stop at the porch, where his wheelchair still waited. He swung into the chair. "Put the sleigh up, Dave."

"The devil you say!"

Lute wheeled into the house, with Dave coming stubbornly behind him. The old man wore a gun, and his eyes were dangerous, but he held himself in.

Lute turned through the kitchen, which was empty, passed through the dining room, and went on into the long, narrow, sleeping building. He saw Minot, half down the length of the room, seated on a bunk. Minot didn't get up, and he had a half grin on his face, and was waiting.

Lute wheeled up to him, at closer look seeing something heated and tumultuous in the black eyes. There were long, blood-crusted scratches on his left cheek.

"Pack," Lute said. "Saddle your horse. Get out."

"The hell you say, Constant!" In the black eyes amusement flickered, and it was mixed with something deep and deadly and ready.

"Get up."

Minot came to his feet. "How you going to fight me? Cripes, what can you do?"

"Give me your hands." Lute lifted his own, the fingers spread, and waited calmly.

Minot understood, then, and he stepped forward with an eagerness showing on his lips. He laced fingers into Lute's, and the black devils were dancing in his eyes.

"Get my throat if you can," Lute said. "If I can get at yours, I'll kill you."

Minot's answer was to come down full with weight and strength. Lute felt the front muscles of his wrists pull into hurting bands. Minot used his height, standing full upon his feet, slanting down his deadly grin. Something had appeared in his face, mixed of confidence and cool relish. Lute heard Dave's growl, but the old man did not interfere.

Slowly Lute got his hands up and turned the grip back on Minot, with the man trying to lift beyond his purchase. Lute tried to pull him down, but Minot's stiffened back was too much for him. Rising on his toes suddenly, jaws clenching, Minot turned and came down with full weight so that Lute groaned involuntarily. The thing that so long had hung on the verge of his awareness got through then, and he saw that it was fear, as his mother had said, fear of Minot, who meant to kill him. The man pressed him down into the chair, his shoulders raised and bulging, a twisted grimace pulling his mouth over onto one cheek.

Then something was released in Lute. Anger shook him, and he put all his strength against the strain of Minot's grip. He got the man's palms turned back, he got the wrists tightened, and kept bending them. Pain suddenly jarred Minot's features. Minot abruptly showed the stark surface of fear himself.

"You damned swell-heads," Minot breathed. "You high and mighty Constants."

"Don't let me get your throat, Minot."

Minot came back on a wave of fury. He fought to lift the purchase to Lute's disadvantage. He rose on his toes, his shoulders high and straining. Lute felt the man's fingers push into the backs of his hands. Lute met it, his own rage cold and unyielding. Minot broke and went down, his knees hitting the floor with a jar. *God,* thought Luke, *I'm standing up!* Minot tried to jerk him out of the chair, but Lute held him, aware that now Dave was steadying it. Lute pulled Minot in, broke grip — and had the throat in his hands. He saw fear in the eyes before him, bald and spilling, as he pressed in with his fingers.

As from a distance, Dave's voice said: "Leave him go. He'll ride now. That's all we want."

Lute released his grip, and Minot fell limply to the floor. Behind the chair and holding it steady, the old man had a quiet satisfaction in his eyes. Lute had sunk back into the seat, and for a long moment he sat quietly, breathing heavily, no longer hating

Minot. *Because I no longer fear him,* he thought. His mother had been so completely right!

"Go on in," Dave said. "I'll throw some water on this skunk and send him packing before Sherry and the boys get in. I'd hate to see what they'd do to him, if they knew."

"For Helen's sake, we'd better keep it quiet, Dave."

"Reckon you're right."

The wheelchair was suddenly hateful to him. Lute placed a foot on either side of the footboards and, using his arms, brought himself to a stance upon the floor. His legs were weak and trembling and awkward, and he knew it would be a long time yet before he could ask full service from them. But he drank in the moment, finding it good. He wanted to walk into the big house. He wanted to walk in to Helen.

Dave sensed it and came over. "You've got a right to a little help at first, kid. Put your arm across my shoulder."

Thus they made a show, stumbling their way down the length of the bunkhouse and into the Constant living room. Two women were there, white-faced, aware of everything, waiting. They said nothing, but Lute saw his mother's hand go quickly to her forehead and fall away. He saw Helen rise from her place, but instead of coming to him, she waited. It seemed a little way to go, now, and he made it.

Whatever signs of mistreatment Helen had brought home had been removed. She stood on the other side of him, with Lute resting an arm upon her shoulder, the other upon Dave's — but on his own two feet at last. It would be a long while yet before he would be his old self, but he knew with quiet satisfaction that it would come.

"It was where you said," he told his mother, and she smiled.

Helen, with her bad hour passed, seemed in natural buoyancy to want to forget it completely. She smiled up at Lute with something of the *gamine* grin mixed into it.

"Shall we sit on the sofa and hold hands?"

He grinned and settled into place beside her. Grinning and batting his eyes at the same time, old Dave went out.

"I didn't dare tell you before," Helen said, "but Tony Minot got caught in something bad the same as you did, the day you both mixed with that wild horse. He thought he'd made a fool of you, but it didn't impress the crew. He told me a little about it the night we went skating, then I talked to Sherry, once. Minot had to beat you, the same as you had to beat him. He had to make the crew acknowledge that he was the better man. That's why he kept crowding trouble, and why he lost his head after I made such a fool of him. He didn't want to marry me. He simply wanted to spoil me for you."

"It's over," Lute said. "He'll clear out."

Minot had left before Sherry and the crew came in from the range. The cow country had its methods of dealing with men who molested women — a staking-out upon an ant hill with eyelids cut away, or the drastic surgery by which young bulls became young steers. Minot knew this. He had saddled and ridden away, no longer interested in signing on at some nearby spread.

Casually, that evening, Sherry began to talk about a replacement for the man.

Lute shook his head. "Do we need a ramrod?"

Something warm and pleased entered Sherry's eyes. "Not if there are two of us again," he said.

"There'll be two of us. It's a long ways to spring, and we're going to catch more hell, but I'm not worried. We've got a fine outfit, and it was proved out there today. If we've got a hundred steers alive, come spring, we'll make out."

Sherry nodded, and it struck Lute that it was the first time he had felt close to his brother in a long time. The old truculence was gone from Sherry's eyes. The kid looked at the floor, then up at Lute, and he had a twisted smile on his face.

"About Helen . . . you're a lucky devil. But I'm glad."

"Thanks, mister." Lute accepted the extended hand and had the answer to the last question in his mind. Sherry, the tough, unblinking youngster, who could never take a licking, was taking one now.

Sherry said: "And another thing. The boys figured out where you had the missing Tony Minot treed the other night. They kept quiet, figuring it was your war. But I reckon they'd like another party, if you and Helen're ready to tell 'em."

"Get 'em!" Lute boomed.

But Sherry was already on his way to the bunkhouse, roaring to turn them out.

A Mug at Charley's

There was a worn two-bit piece in his pocket, and Old Harney's gnarled fingers kept turning it over and over. He was heading for Bert Durbin's store to pick up an end of fat bacon with which to season a batch of dry beans, or, at any rate, he had been. Something had halted him here under the board canopy in front of Charley Bevers's barbershop. Leaning against one of the uprights, Old Harney was careful not to show too plainly that he was looking over the situation inside.

The late Saturday night crowd had gathered there. Captain Tom Cavender was in the chair, with Charley Bevers snipping at his fine shock of white hair. Judge Hooker and Sam Prescott were waiting, together with several of the town's lesser personalities and a couple of men Old Harney did not know. The town was humming, with river men and stockmen and farmers in for Saturday night trading and fun.

Old Harney had always liked the rich, high scents of talcum, shaving soap, face lotion, and hair tonic that filled Charley's shop. Better than that he liked the chinning and joking, the easy companionship of a Saturday night. He turned over the single coin in his pocket once more, the fingers of his other hand stroking the white stubble on his chin. *Hell,* he thought, *I can eat my beans without any seasoning.* Quickly, before doubts could check him again, he wheeled and strode through the doorway.

Everybody turned, including Charley, the barber, and two or three called: "Howdy, Harney!" Old Harney paced to the end of the shop and took a vacant chair in the corner. He flipped a general greeting with his big hand and relaxed.

Mentally he ticked off those ahead of him — six — enough to keep Charley snipping and scraping for a long while. This suited Old Harney perfectly. He could sit here, enjoying himself, probably until Charley pulled down the blinds and locked the door.

Already they had forgotten him. There wasn't anything uppity about this crowd; they'd just gone back to what they'd been jawing about.

Sam Prescott, the banker, looked at Captain Cavender, in the chair, and said: "So you're going to steam up the old *Sophie* again, huh, Cap'n?"

"Come a week from tomorrow. They been after me to take the Sunday school down the river on an excursion."

"Think the old girl'll make it?"

"What do you mean, make it? The *Sophie*'s as good as the day I built her!"

"That's what you think, Cap'n," said Judge Hooker, with a grin. "You're both so danged old you look young to each other."

Old Harney was enjoying it, and his curiosity was aroused. This was the first he'd heard anything about plans to take the *Sophie* out on the river again. He looked expectantly at Captain Cavender, but the old man had pinched up his mouth, trying to think up some retort to throw back at the judge. Old Harney relaxed. He could get the information on that, later. As it had so often in the past, his gaze strayed toward the racks on either side of the big mirror behind the barber chair.

Old Harney had always hankered to have his name gilted on one of the special shaving mugs kept there. It would make a man feel pretty good, he reckoned, to be right up there with the banker and the judge and the old river captain and Van Alden, the druggist, and all the rest of Charley's special friends. But on those rare occasions when he could afford a barbershop shave, Old Harney got lathered out of the plain, chipped mug Charley used for the general trade. A man had to be something extra in town to get on the special mug rack, and Old Harney was the first to admit that this was proper.

The patrons kept coming in. All the seats along the walls were filled, and there was a couple of jiggers, who looked like farmers, standing. Charley was keeping out of the conversation and hurrying, as he always did when he was rushed. When he finished the captain, Charley laid the cloth over the chair and went out to the back room for a minute. When he returned, he bent for an instant over Old Harney.

"Look, Harney, you got lots of time these days, ain't you? I'm plenty rushed. You come back Monday morning when I ain't so busy, and I'll give you a shave for nothing."

"Why . . . why, sure, Charley."

The barber went on back to his chair, and Old Harney climbed to his feet. Embarrassment burned hotly under the saddle-brown leather of his cheeks. He paced back down the length of the shop and went outside. He didn't walk across the street to pick up the bacon, for which he had come to town. He didn't even drift over to the saloon to watch the goings-on there for a while. He went the other way, down past the river landing and on to the little gully, where his shack was.

Charley Bevers had been right nice and friendly in the way he'd made that request, he kept telling himself. Charley liked to get through early on Saturday nights so he could go on to the lodge. Old Harney decided it had been thoughtless of an old loafer like himself to pick a busy Saturday night on which to treat himself to a barbershop shave.

He didn't go back on Monday morning to claim the free shave Charley Bevers had offered him. It was springtime, and Old Harney worked in the vegetable garden he was raising. He did a repair job or two on the little shack. Then he just sat in the homemade chair in front and watched the broad river and the occasional steamboats. He told himself a dozen times that a man didn't have any call to be lonesome when he had his independence and his health, food for his belly, and a shelter over his head come winter.

He did go back to town, though, to see what he could learn about the Sunday school excursion the old *Sophie* was to make, and what he found out got him greatly excited. The old packet had been out of service for maybe ten years, tied up there below the landing. She belonged to Captain Cavender, and he had agreed to fire her up and take the Sunday school kids and their parents on a Sunday excursion down the river.

This was of special interest to Old Harney because he, too, had retired when Captain Cavender and the *Sophie* had. For over two decades he had fired the old girl. And now it stood to reason that if the captain was going to take her out again, he'd want Old Harney below decks, pitching the cordwood into her. He waited, with rising excitement, for the captain to get word to him. But no word came.

The suspense made Old Harney think a lot about the past. Ambition had never crowded him as it had the captain. There hadn't been the slightest jealousy in his heart when Tom Cavender had climbed into a skipper's berth. Later, when the captain had saved enough of his pay to launch his own packet, the *Sophie*, Bill Harney had signed on with him as combined fireman and engineer.

The years were all sort of washed together now, and it was often difficult for Old

Harney to get events laid out the way they belonged. He had had a wife once, but she had died more years ago than he cared to remember, and there had been no children. He had never tried to climb up the ladder of the river hierarchy. Year after year he had stayed contentedly in the boiler room of the *Sophie*. He didn't know if there had ever been what a man could call friendship between himself and the captain. In a lot of respects, they were as different as night and day. Where the captain had saved his wages and worked toward something for himself, Bill Harney had liked to "likker-up" ashore, and risk a dollar on the turn of a card.

So he hadn't had much of a stake when he had come ashore for the last time. He had this shack here, though he didn't even know who owned the land it stood on, and this backwashed gully that wasn't of any use to anybody but himself. But he made out all right, doing odd chores around the town, cutting grass and weeds, fixing steps, and giving storage buildings their annual cleaning out.

In fact, he had got his shack that way. It had been an old chicken house, standing on the back of Fred Plummer's property. Fred had said: "I don't want it, Harney. Move it off my place, and she's yours." It had taken

Old Harney the better part of a summer to get it jacked and skidded and rolled down here to the gully. He'd rigged it up real neat and comfortable with scrub water, old box boards, old pasteboard cartons, and old newspapers. He had spring water of his own, and the best danged view around Westuck. And most of the time he was as tough and strong as he had ever been, that is, when the weather was good.

When Tuesday came, then Wednesday, with no word from the captain about taking the *Sophie* out on the Sunday school excursion, Old Harney decided to expedite matters by showing himself in town. He got his hat and strode up the riverbank, cut across the little flat, then climbed the steep path that led up to the main street.

He observed presently that there was activity around the *Sophie*. He couldn't see anybody, but a water hose crawled around her deck like a giant worm. No smoke came out of the big stack, though. Somebody was just cleaning her up. But somebody ought to have been checking the boiler and the big steam chest and paddle journals. For an instant Old Harney was tempted to go aboard, but some pride held him back.

He stood there for a long moment, looking at her. The captain couldn't have loved the *Sophie* more if she had been a woman. When age and rheumatism took him off the river, he had tied her up, refusing to sell or lease her. She was out of date now, what with all the big, fast packets plying the river. She wouldn't be good for anything but a work boat, and the captain refused to foist this ignominy on her.

The captain didn't show himself on her decks, though Old Harney waited for several minutes. Probably he wasn't even around. Old Harney turned toward the main part of town.

He couldn't locate the captain on the streets anywhere. Nor in any of the stores or other public places. Old Harney strolled up and down both sides of the street, tipping a nod to somebody who smiled and spoke to him now and then but not wanting to stop and jaw. Once he walked to within a block of the captain's big, white house, then with a sudden scowl hinged around on his heel, and headed in the other direction.

He had given it up and was pacing back toward the landing with home in mind, when Sam Prescott hurried out the bank door and called: "Hey, Harney! Just a minute!"

Old Harney turned, his earlier excitement leaping up in him again. The banker smiled at him and said: "I noticed you go by. I been meaning to come down to see you. Can you come into my office for a minute?"

"Sure." The tension went out of Old Harney. Sam Prescott would be one of those behind the Sunday school excursion. The captain probably had just been too busy to get in touch with him. The old man followed Prescott through the bank lobby and into a big private office paneled with black walnut. He took a chair at the end of the desk and watched the banker lower his paunchy figure into a big, upholstered, swivel chair.

Prescott grinned, looking a mite fussed. "I don't relish telling you this, Harney, but you know the bank owns the property on which your shack . . . that is, your house . . . is located."

Old Harney stiffened, alarm going through him. "Yeah?"

"Well, the terminal people have bought it. They're fixing to put up some new wheat elevators. I'd never say anything about you using the property as long as the bank owned it, but . . . well . . . they want it cleared off."

Old Harney swallowed and tried to grin. "Guess I never thought much about who owned it. Kind of a worthless piece of ground. Reckon I sort of figured I'd come by it through squatter's rights, mebbe."

"It's ideal for the grain elevators," Prescott said. There was no question about the banker having a heart in him. He kept trying to grin and his mouth kept twisting out of shape. "So I guess you'll have to vacate it, Harney."

"Sure." Old Harney climbed to his feet. At the door he turned back a moment. "And thanks for all the years I used it."

"Forget it, Harney."

Old Harney went down the street, too bewildered to think clearly. As he passed the *Sophie*'s berth, he saw the captain. The captain saw him and waved but made no beckoning gesture. Old Harney went on down the steep path, across the flat, and turned into the little gully where the shack stood, snugly shaded by willows. He looked at the garden and at the shack and let his gaze travel on to the little sweet-water spring. He turned and looked at the river, seeing it from the best danged standpoint around Westuck.

He had forgotten to ask Sam Prescott how soon he had to get off the property. He tried to comfort himself with the reflection that it would be weeks, even months, before the terminal company could get its new project into the construction phase. Be durned if he was going to rush himself any, uprooting the shack and trying to find a new place to put it.

The rest of the week wore away slowly, but Old Harney kept to himself, and nobody came to see him about the Sunday school excursion. By covert watching, he learned a little, though. The captain was going to take the wheel, all right. And young Danny Trumley, who had worked on the big, new packets, was going to fire her and dish out the steam. Old Harney heard this at the post office on Friday, and on Saturday he saw smoke coming out of the *Sophie*'s stack. Along toward evening she slipped out into the stream for a trial run. Old Harney got out of his chair, went around to the other side of the shack, and fell to work hoeing his garden.

Sunday morning Old Harney tried to sleep late, but danged if his head would stay on the pillow. He was up and dressed and whittling pine shavings with which to start a breakfast fire in his cookstove when the scream of an old, familiar whistle announced that Captain Cavender was taking the *Sophie* out again. Old Harney got his fire going then, and almost involuntarily moved to the door.

Like a proud, old mare back in harness, the *Sophie* came stepping down the channel, pennants streaming, decks packed with waving youngsters, their mothers in straw sailor hats and leg-o'-mutton sleeves, and a few men.

The big *Montrose* was coming up, and the captain ripped her a challenging salute, which the *Montrose* answered respectfully. For a long while Old Harney stood there, big frame erect, eyes gleaming, himself sailing back down a long stream of time. Then, abruptly, weariness sagged him, and he turned to put the old, black, coffee pot on the fire.

There was a long stretch of rapids just off Old Harney's shack site and running downstream. The government work had tamed them a little from what they had been in the old days, but still a packet had to dig in its paddles and snort, pushing up. He could hear the laboring of the *Montrose* as it came on, the *chuff-chuff-chuff* of straining steam. He turned to watch the big stern paddles beating into the roughened water, then swung back to pour batter into the smoking skillet to fry himself a batch of Johnnycake.

Old Harney worked in his garden most of that day, just as painstakingly as if the big scrapers would not be coming soon to turn it under and prepare the site for the new grain elevators. When the afternoon grew warm, he took his ease in the big, leaning chair he had carpentered to his own specifications in front of the shack, his eyes idly on the river. The quiet was soothing, and for a long while he felt a contentment he no longer had a right to feel. Then his eyelids grew heavy. From time to time he lifted his head, batting his eyes, then finally he slept.

He came awake with a start, with a sense of surging to the surface of a vast beer vat, and was aware that evening had come. Then his keen, old ears caught a distant beat of sound, and, glancing downstream, he dimly saw a steamboat entering the foot of the rapids. It was the *Sophie*, coming back from the excursion.

Big frame bent forward, sharp elbows on bony knees, Old Harney watched it, its outline softened by the deep dusk. A disturbance was in him, and at last he straightened. That cherry glow above the stack — it had no business there!

It was hard for him to collect his thoughts so soon after deep sleep, but suddenly he was wide awake. Of course! They were having trouble climbing the rapids. Old Harney could picture it, just as it had been in the old days. The captain would be in the wheelhouse — a mess of town bigwigs with him now — his old hands proudly on the spokes, and he'd be bellowing down the speaking tube for more steam. And that young pup, Danny Trumley, would be sweating in the boiler room, pitching the dry pine cordwood into the old firebox. Old Harney leaped out of his chair as the awareness stabbed him.

He was as much at fault as the captain! He should be hung for holding back stubborn-proud, waiting to be asked to fire the *Sophie!* But he had never thought, no more than had the captain.

Danny Trumley knew how to throw fuel into a firebox, but the modern packets on which he'd worked had automatic safety valves and pumps and all kinds of gauges and doodads to keep the boilers under control. In a boiler room in Old Harney's day a man put steam in his boiler and cylinders and controlled it there with little more than his fire. A man had to know how to build that fire, and when and how to pitch in wood, and exactly how to stoke the great bed of glowing coals and dancing flames to put just the right snort there when the skipper called for it. But not too much!

The alternative sent horror surging through Old Harney. In his time he had seen a couple of boilers let go. They went in a fashion not designed to give passengers, crew, or packet a chance, with midships breaking skyward like the fracturing of a giant stick, superstructure flying and bodies with it, steam billowing, fire leaping.

There was too much fire in the *Sophie*, and young Trumley was apt to put more in her, trying to heave her up the rapids. Old Harney read it all in that cherry glow above the stack.

Rapidly he calculated the time it would take to get himself up to the landing and find a skiff or anything else that would float him down the rapids to the *Sophie*. The answer summed too great. She was about a quarter of a mile downstream, panting against the swift, fretted water, but coming on. Without thinking much what he was doing, Old Harney plunged down the gentle slope of the bank to the water's edge. There he untied and kicked off his old shoes.

There was a tiny, rocky island halfway between himself and the *Sophie*. Swimming hard, the current would just about bring him to it. The packet would pass within spitting distance from it. From there he could flag the captain, warn him, and maybe give him a good piece of his mind. At this point, Old Harney's thought processes ceased, and the stringy muscles of his huge frame went to work.

The water was cold, but not cold enough to be uncomfortable after he had taken a few strokes. He cut straight across, watching the little island below, calculating to get above it and wash down onto it. He had once been an expert swimmer, and now he kept his head above the choppy water without much effort. It never dawned on him that this was far from safe swimming water, that the boils and eddies and undercurrents might trick him lethally even if cramps failed to tie his old muscles into knots.

Yet, he had taken no more than a score of heavy lunges across the current when he realized that it was going to take some doing to control himself properly so as to wash against that tiny speck of rock, sometimes not even visible as he surged to the surface. He was astonished at how quick his breath turned hot and painful in his lungs. He slowed his movement a little then, using less energy. He began to realize that, if he washed past the island, there was little likelihood either of the *Sophie*'s seeing him or of his being able to battle his way back to the shore down there in the rapids. He wished it weren't so dark.

It was going to take a first-rate job of navigating, but Old Harney still believed he was river man enough to cut it. He crowded the worry out of his mind, settled down to slow, powerful movement. The little island was coming at him fast, and he was going to be short of it if he didn't get a wiggle on. An iron will in the old body provided the wiggle.

He caught onto the rocks as he swept past, held there for a moment, lungs laboring, waves washing over him. He realized that it was getting down right dark, and the laboring of the *Sophie* was loud in his ears, seeming to be almost above him. Old Harney lifted himself onto the rocks with a big heave, stumbled to his feet, and plunged to the other side.

The *Sophie* was just below, *chuff-chuffing*, the baneful red shooting a good foot above the stack. Old Harney leaped about, waving his hat, trying to force his tortured lungs to produce a noise loud enough to penetrate the racket from the steamer. They saw him, all right, and stared in astonishment, but it was only the people on the deck.

"The fire . . . the fire!" Old Harney yelled over and over. "Tell that lunkhead kid to draw his fire!"

Sickness rose in him as he realized it was

no use. They could not understand him. And the *Sophie* kept up its straining against the current.

It was a desperate thing that Old Harney did next, its outcome depending entirely on somebody aboard the *Sophie* possessing presence of mind. With the steamer laboring slowly toward him, Old Harney went into the water again, directly above her. It was even rougher in this channel, and the waves washed over him. He battled to the surface, raising an arm into view in a plea for help.

There was at least one good head up there. He saw the cork life-ring sail over the railing, trailing a light line. It hit the water just below him, and as it swept past him he caught it. They drew him in against the side while somebody thrust down a boat hook for him to grasp, and pulled him up. The packet had not slackened its speed.

Old Harney never paused to close their gaping mouths by answering their questions. He could make his way around this packet with his eyes shut, and he plunged straight for the boiler room.

He saw then the accuracy with which his mind had pictured it. Just as he stumbled down the companion to the boiler deck, young Trumley opened the firebox, preparing to pitch more wood.

"Stop it!" Old Harney roared. He was by young Trumley's side in three long steps, banging the door closed. The young sprout showed a very natural astonishment and objection, but the old man had no time for polite explanations. He pushed Trumley out of the way with a rough shove, kept him away with glowering eyes while he pulled down the fire, and opened the steam escape valve.

He was not aware that they were gradually losing headway until the old, familiar voice of the captain came rattling down the tin speaking tube.

"What's the matter with the steam, Trumley? For criminy sakes, you wanna pile us on the rocks?"

Young Trumley whirled around then, bellowing: "Have you gone crazy, Harney?"

"Harney?" The skipper's voice boomed out of the tube in bewilderment.

Old Harney was still at the firebox when the captain came pounding down the companion, a half hour later. The *Sophie* had tied up safely at her old berth, having finished the trip without the lethal cherry glow above the stack. Now the captain stalked across the deck, his eyes big in his head.

"How'n the devil did you get aboard, Harney?"

For the first time it dawned on Old Harney that the captain had not even seen what had happened at the little, rock island, so busy had he been with his bigwigs and his yelping down for more steam. Save for the alert passengers on the deck below, Old Harney would have been drowned and the *Sophie* blown to smithereens. Besides this, reaction was wearying him, his burnt-out elation at firing the *Sophie* again leaving an ash of irritation.

"Rid out on a sturgeon, you old goat!" he snapped. He checked his dampers, making sure everything was shipshape before leaving. He paid no attention whatsoever to the captain, letting the old knothead follow him clear up on the deck and to the head of the gangplank. There he turned for a parting shot. "I just now realized you was fool enough to think you could take her out on this excursion all by yourself, without a man what understood her to fire her!"

"But, Harney! I never figured you wanted to. I figured you were too danged old."

"Old!" snorted Harney, and stomped down the gangplank.

Even though it was almost summer, Old

Harney sneezed four times while he was fixing his breakfast the next morning, two double headers. He finished his breakfast, then with a shrug of resignation got the old washtub, and heated water to fill it.

He was seated with his pants legs rolled up, his feet in the water, and an old blanket over his shoulders when he saw the procession filing down the path, carefully skirting around the garden so as not to trample the young plants. Old Harney didn't even have time to get his feet out and his socks on before Sam Prescott was standing in the open door, Judge Hooker behind him, old Captain Cavender and half a dozen others in the rear.

Sam Prescott smiled. "Can we come in, Harney?"

"Looks like you're already in," the old man growled. He decided that, banker or not, he was going to give his old feet the hot soaking they deserved.

They all piled into the room, and Prescott continued to smile. "Harney, nobody realized what a fix the *Sophie* was in last night until Cap'n Cavender found some melted rivets under the boiler. Young Trumley admitted he was piling the wood in every which way. It's not his fault. He just never had any experience with an old-type piece of machinery. But, Lord . . . when I think of what could've happened . . . !"

"That's right," Old Harney grunted. "Don't blame the kid." He had expected that nobody would ever realize what had almost happened out there, and it would have suited him better if they had never found out. Now there was no sense in talking about it. He glared his accusation where it belonged, the captain.

"Well, the town's pretty grateful, Harney. There's the matter of your shack here. The land's sold, and there's no talking the terminal company into letting you stay here, for they need the space. But, well, Cap'n Cavender's got something to say to you."

The captain stepped forward then, looking sheepish and ill-at-ease. But in a minute Old Harney realized he was still the man he had been.

"You never read me off half good enough last night, Bill," he said. "All the years you fired for me, I never worried a mite about what went on down in the engine room. You plumb got me outta the habit of even thinking about it. I. . . ."

"Hell, there's no cause for such a fuss . . . nobody got hurt," Old Harney said, trying to dismiss the subject.

"Tell him what you've got to say, Cap'n,"

Prescott reminded.

"Well, Bill, they're taking the *Sophie*'s berth away from me on account o' them new elevators, too. So the town's deeding you a site for her, right there above the landing, in the center of town."

"Deeding me a site?"

"Yep. We want you to live aboard the *Sophie*, Bill, and take the proper care of her. There'll be a little salary with it. And you'll be right there at the end of Main Street."

Old Harney stood up in the tub, his face suddenly black with rage. "Be damned if I want any charity!"

The captain looked at him and grinned slowly. Then he came back with a stream of real he-man language, such as Old Harney respected and understood.

"Don't you go getting proud on me, you old turkey! It's a long way from charity. The town wants to show you it's grateful for what you done for its kids. You ain't got no right not to let 'em."

After a thoughtful moment, Old Harney nodded. That was true. And it would be even better than the old shack here, to live aboard the *Sophie*, showing visitors around, sitting on the shady deck of an afternoon, chinning right where he could watch all that went on. But he couldn't get up much steam about it right now. He thanked them, and hoped they would go.

They did, all except one, who hung back. That was Charley Bevers, the barber. He looked kind of sheepish, and, when the others had cleared out, he stepped forward, keeping his hands under his coattails behind him.

"The wife and little Myrtle was on the *Sophie* yesterday, Harney," he said. Then he swallowed hard and continued self-consciously. "I was up late last night fixing this." He brought his hands into the open.

Old Harney stared. It was a shaving mug. There was gilt on it, and he could scarcely believe his eyes as he looked at it. The fancy lettering spelled his name in bright shiny gold: **Bill Harney**.

"She's going right up on the top shelf . . . along with Cap'n Cavender's and Judge Hooker's," Charley said. "I'd be proud to have you come in whenever you can."

Old Harney settled back in his chair and wiggled his toes in the cooling water. He ticked off the days in his mind. One . . . two . . . hell, almost a week and a tough old turkey like him could certainly throw off the sniffles in that time.

"Thanks, Charley," he said, his voice trembling a little from emotion. "Reckon I'll be needing a shave all right, along about Saturday night."

Strangers in the Evening

Many things stirred in Marlow's mind as he watched the action at the upper end of the bottom. He stood on the ridge above his homestead, his rifle over his arm, after a short scout in pursuit of a deer that had appeared on the mountainside above his cabin. It had escaped him, and now his interest was wholly occupied by the scene below.

The rider whipped out of the brush, following the old game trail, and pulled down his horse in confusion. For a moment he sat there, staring down toward the cabin.

In the way of a man much alone, Marlow spoke aloud: "Running. It scared him to find a settler back here. I hope the jeebow keeps right on going."

The rider halted only for an instant, then came on slowly. Like he aimed to stop. Marlow scowled. He had seen him higher up on the ridge, riding fast then. This was far from the beaten trails to Jacksonville and the other gold camps. A man just wouldn't have any sensible reason for riding through this country. Or any good one. A few times Marlow had had passersby whose motives were just the opposite. Good or bad, he didn't like company. He didn't want to be bothered.

He started down the slope at an easy, swinging gait that still made time. He wasn't a hating man, but he had never had much liking for another, either. A man of thirty, self-raised so to speak, didn't have much feeling of fellowship left in him.

Marlow knew there were plenty of fine people in the world. He just hadn't run across many. He hadn't developed much interest in hunting them up. The kind he had known had engendered in him a strong desire to go it alone. That was the simplest and safest thing. Though he had neighbors, he hadn't invited visitors. He had a homestead, and he aimed to run it.

He crossed the bottom, displeased by this development. He had a fundamental philosophy, as a man who keeps to himself has time to work out. What a man got had to come from inside himself, from his heart and head, and it had to flow out through his own back and hands. Life had beaten that into Marlow beyond forgetting or even neglecting. And there were plenty of people ready to benefit by what he produced. A man with sense packed off finally to where he wasn't troubled.

Marlow found satisfaction out here in the mountains, a law and order in the wildness about him superior to what he had found among men. He could work with that regularity, study and understand it, plan and toil and make it yield what he wanted. A man could call that a religion, Marlow guessed, for it gratified a deep hunger in him — a hunger for self-sufficiency.

The oncoming rider had slowed his horse to a walk, and was moving thoughtfully along the open river bottom. Marlow reached his stump-filled yard and stood watching him. The man was armed, but that meant little in this back country. He would be hungry, and Marlow thought of the supper he had already started, a good one of elk roast, Irish potatoes, and biscuits, for he always ate well.

He recognized the feeling stirring in him as conscience, bidding him to offer hospitality. The stranger would be welcome to eat, but the pause would make it mandatory to put him up for the night. Marlow kept thinking of that first impression, the man's moment of confusion when he caught sight of the cabin after his fast ride along the ridge. Marlow didn't like that. He decided against any show of friendliness at all.

He went into the cabin, catching the supper's hot, rich smells at the door, and stood his rifle in a corner. Though he had made a sufficiency for himself here, it was not abundance. His root cellar held a winter's store of truck from his garden, and the cured hams and sides from a hog he had bought to raise and butcher. He had a span of oxen for his plow and wagon, a heifer that would calve in another month to give him milk and cheese and butter. He had a flintlock rifle and single-action revolver, and the rest lay in his own back, hands, and head.

Marlow came to the door when the stranger pulled up outside. The man was thin, much younger than Marlow had estimated, scarcely more than a kid. He looked at Marlow with open, level eyes, and the settler could sense no bad in them. Marlow pegged him at around twenty and wondered why he was riding the back trails and what had made him uncertain back there. The horse was unshod, sore-footed, played out.

"Howdy!" the boy said. Then, obviously trying not to, he turned a look back over his shoulder, along the trail.

Marlow didn't like that, and it set the decision in him. "You're out of your way, ain't you?"

The boy wet his lips and smiled. He was good-looking, and there was a merry cast to his features for a moment. "I'm Syl Vespers. Riding from Red Bluff to Jacksonville. Got smart and thought this was a short cut. It sure gave me a long, rough ride."

Something did, Marlow thought. Yet it took an honest man to offer his name, unless this Vespers was trying to be artful and disarming. Marlow decided to stand pat.

"They call me Marlow. Jacksonville's a long piece from here, but there's a settlement after Sterling. A man can follow the crick, even at night."

He was staring, suddenly. Three more horses broke out of the brush up the river, the way Vespers had come, and Marlow had not noticed them on the ridge top. They didn't hesitate. They crowded their horses. It looked as if they had almost caught what they were after, and Marlow remembered his own situation. He had no taste for four overnight guests — much less than for one.

He watched Vespers turn to stare in the same direction. It was less surprise than resignation that came over the kid's face. Vespers swung down but made no move to extract the rifle in his saddle boot. This eased Marlow. He didn't want a fracas in his own door yard.

Vespers stood by his horse, watching. Once he looked at Marlow, about to say something, then decided against it. Marlow didn't speak, for another man's business was not his. He looked at the horse. There wasn't anything left in it. Vespers knew that and accepted it. But he wasn't going to make a fight.

Marlow was tense, feeling a touch of human sympathy, which he had never lacked. In a dry voice, he said: "Friends of yours?"

"I don't know who the devil they are," Vespers said. "But I can tell you what. . . ." He broke it off. "Never mind."

The riders came on swiftly, Vespers and Marlow both watching them.

"Well, a man plays out his string," Vespers said softly.

Without knowing quite why, Marlow said: "Stand up to 'em, kid. Two's more than one. It'll make 'em think."

"Thanks," Vespers said.

Marlow regretted the impulse when he thought it over. He knew nothing about this situation, and taking a piece of it could only bring him trouble. A man's eyes and open manner weren't enough to make a stand on. Marlow had known disarming people before, who showed color finally, color a man didn't like. But he hadn't promised anything beyond lending his presence to a sort of bluff.

Life had taught Marlow to be detached. When a man wanted nothing more than the ability to do for himself completely, he found himself too busy to take on the cares of others. Marlow hated dependency, and he frowned on it in others. He wasn't selfish; he was all too aware of a quick response to real distress. But he knew too many who made their own troubles, then turned serenely to another for help. He had no idea as to why this Vespers was in trouble. But somewhere he had made a mistake, which made it his own fault and his strictly personal problem.

But even as he reminded himself of his beliefs, a feeling welled up in Marlow, and he knew he was going to help this youngster to whatever extent he could. It distressed him more than anything, for he suspected what the feeling was. He had been a long time alone out here. This strange attraction to Vespers and his plight disclosed a hunger for a man's own kind. If that still lived in him, Marlow thought, it revealed a crack in the self-sufficiency he had sought to build. Winter was just ahead, with its dark and depressing months. Did this mean that they would be as — well, yes, as lonely as last winter had been?

Marlow said: "Bring your rifle into the cabin, kid."

"It ain't your trouble, Marlow," Vespers said, and it gave Marlow the shocked sense of the boy's having read his mind. Vespers seemed on the point of refusing, then withdrew the weapon from the boot. His shoulders were square as he stepped into the cabin.

Marlow was calm enough to look to his cooking supper. He took the roast and bread out of the clay oven built against one side of his big fireplace.

Vespers watched him with hungry interest, indulging for a moment in forgetting his troubles. The boy took position against the far wall where he could face and cover the door. Marlow waited with only a mild curiosity about it all, not wanting to get too interested in another man's predicament.

Through the open window and beyond a break in the brush he saw the others drawing near. They had slowed their mounts, riding leisurely, and the settler suspected this was to conceal the urgency of their chase. Marlow didn't like this any better than he liked the manner in which Vespers had arrived.

Marlow stood in his doorway when the three rode up, aware that he made a forbidding figure with his long hair and worn buckskins, one arm stretched from sight indicating that it reached toward a rifle. The three stared at him, offered no greeting, obviously pondering why this backwoodsman had put their man behind him.

One swung down, a man with a rough, impatient movement, and stepped onto the porch. Marlow saw no symbols to indicate that they were lawmen. There were marks upon them, and a strong sense within himself suggested that they were quite the opposite, specimens of the lawless breed who ran the back trails of the Siskiyous and Klamaths.

The man said: "Howdy, neighbor. You got a friend of ours in there, though he might try to deny it right now. The kid got mad at us. Pouted off by himself. We want to patch it up again."

One of the mounted ones sniffed and said: "Something good's cooking in there, Sands. Let's eat."

Sands regarded Marlow, the expression in his eyes roughening. "We'll eat if our good friend here's got the decency to invite us. Maybe even if he ain't. Settler, how about putting us up for a night? While we make peace talk with the kid?"

Marlow said: "No room. And no spare grub. There's another homestead down two, three miles. It's a big cabin, and they like company. I don't."

He began to sense that the bluff wasn't going to work. These men were determined. Marlow guessed they were in the habit of having their own way.

"Joe, put the horses in the barn," Sands said. "The kid's, too. Fork 'em hay, and if there's any grain, they can stand it."

He regarded Marlow steadily, speaking over his shoulder, his eyes narrow and brittle. He wore a holstered revolver, and he seemed to challenge Marlow to beat its speed trying to catch up his rifle.

Sands and Vespers could see each other, Marlow knew. He also knew his own position made it impossible for the kid to try to use his weapon. Marlow hung for a moment in deep thought. He had assumed this, interposing himself before Vespers. The decision was up to him. Marlow sighed. He had done his best to run a bluff, but he didn't want a fracas built out of other men's quarrels wrecking his peace and his hard-won possessions.

He counseled himself. *Easy. You can feel your way through this. They won't ring you into it unless you stay goaty.*

A rider caught the bridles of the two riderless horses, the whole moving out of sight at the corner of the cabin. Marlow stepped away from the door and his rifle, thus giving his assent with only a small, outward show of distaste. Sands grinned, looking on into the obscurity of the interior.

"Kid, either put that gun with the settler's or make your play. You've seen my work. It's up to you to decide if yourn's better." He grinned. "And remember your big friend may get in the way of a piece of lead."

He was serene, supremely confident, his hand still apart from the grips of his gun. Marlow didn't like that little show a bit.

Marlow looked at Vespers. The boy's face was slack with resignation, but there was steadiness in his body when he walked over and put his rifle beside Marlow's. The settler realized there was a healthy fear there, but it was under control.

Marlow felt a touch of pity. Maybe Vespers was calling himself a fool for letting himself be overtaken at a place where he had someone else to consider. But it was too late now. Marlow saw Vespers accepting that, trying to think his way out. Just as Marlow meant to feel his way through the crisis. The more he studied Vespers, the more Marlow liked him. He thought he was beginning to understand.

It was Vesper's own folly. *A man plays out his string,* the lad had said. He had probably been in league with these hardcases and changed his mind. The back-country gentry wouldn't stand for such desertions, the settler knew, when dangerous knowledge could thus be carried away. It had its own way of putting a stop to such things, a gunshot delivered with the aim of finality.

Marlow reasoned that Vespers would have explained it and asked help if he hadn't had something to conceal. Marlow was glad of his own restraint, which probably had saved him from the deepest of folly. Still, he was sorry for the kid.

Sands waited on the porch until the others came back from the barn, and they took their time about it. They came up excitedly, one calling: "Hey, Sands. This mountain man's got himself a fine saddler. He's got a fat heifer down behind the barn. I sure hanker for some fresh beef. And he's got a dugout full of everything a man can think of to eat. You been worrying about where to provision. Well, we found the place. And we can pack it on his horse."

Sands scowled and came through the door, realizing that this open, callous statement might be enough to drive Marlow toward his gun. Sands got between the rifles and the two men inside. When his companions came onto the porch, he said: "Take these pieces and throw 'em into the river, Joe. This settler's got a six-shooter over there on the wall by his bunk. Get that, too."

One of the men obeyed, stepping wide of Marlow and Vespers when he came after the revolver. Vespers looked at Marlow with misery and apology in his eyes.

Marlow was sick at heart, cursing himself for not having ordered the kid on. It was too late now, and he was going to pay the price with his firearms, his horse and cow, and everything he had stored ahead for himself. He thought of the long while it had taken him to accumulate those things, and recklessness rose high in him.

He put it down as he had his other urges. A man prospered by working with things and not against them. That had become his religion. One that he had applied here in the wilderness to his advantage. He had believed in the principle, trusted it, and he still did. He would continue to feel his way.

Sands, reading this reaction, grinned at Marlow. "We've got nothing against you so far, settler. Just behave yourself and you'll be all right. We'll see. Meanwhile, let's eat." He looked at Vespers. "You just take it easy, kid. Tomorrow we ride on together. All friends again."

"You lay off Marlow," Vespers said, "and I'll give you no trouble. I brought this onto him, and he was only trying to be decent."

"What Marlow gets is up to him," Sands said. He was thoughtful a moment, then added: "And up to you, of course." His eyes carried a warning.

Marlow got the import. Sands was telling Vespers not to divulge the reason for all this, which would automatically turn Marlow into a dangerous and doomed man. Marlow had a tightness in his throat, a hope that Vespers wouldn't break and do so just to ring in help on his plight. So far he hadn't, but, if he had to endure this suspense until morning, he might. Marlow began to give that a thoughtful worry.

He ate with the intruders because he was hungry, and there was no point in disturbing routine. A meal prepared for one made poor pickings for five, and a man said

— "The hell with starving in the midst of all this plenty." — and went out to the root cellar. Marlow had never kept it locked. When the fellow returned, he carried a ham. The other man set a skillet onto the fireplace grate, while the first began to carve up the ham.

"Sands, do we butcher that heifer?" one asked. "It'd be cool by morning, and we could have it for breakfast. We could pack a quarter along."

Sands thought a moment, then shook his head. "Too much work. He's got plenty all ready to go."

Night came on, and Marlow saw that the hard ride across mountain country had put fatigue in his unwelcome guests. His hopes of discovering an opportunity to save his stores were shattered when finally Sands said: "Marlow, you and the kid can sleep solid tonight. One of us'll be awake to protect you. And we don't want any monkey business outta either one." He grinned. "One of us'll be using your bunk, settler, so you better find a soft spot on your floor."

Marlow slept very little. Time after time he shaped up a plan, only to have it fall apart. He regretted deeply now that he had not made his play while he had had something of a chance. He had let that pass advisedly, so he had to accept what lay ahead.

By the time the intruders began to stir at daylight, he had decided to stick to his plan and his principle and slide through with the least damage possible. A man had to work with wildness, whether in country or in humanity.

Sands's two companions sliced and fried the last of the ham for breakfast and used generously of Marlow's flour to make biscuits. Marlow watched the fruits of his hard labor disappear and pictured what inroads they would yet make when they departed. He was resigned to that. He had proved his self-sufficiency once and could again, charging this loss to the lesson learned.

Yet, when Syl Vespers roused and shoved to a groggy stand, Marlow had a new concern. The kid looked older by ten years. Marlow thought: *He might break and try to touch it off here where I'd have to help him.*

But Vespers didn't all through breakfast, and he didn't when the men brought up the horses, Vespers's and Marlow's with them. Marlow swallowed. They had located his pack saddle. It was under a heavy burden, things they had taken from his cellar. It looked as if they had cleaned it out.

When Syl Vespers walked out of the cabin and mounted his horse, Marlow felt something squeeze his heart painfully.

Vespers grinned at him, saying: "Thanks, fellow. Wish I'd never brought it to you. But like Sands says, they're friends of mine. So I reckon I'm of a feather. Hope what we took ain't cut into you bad enough to hurt."

"Shut up," Sands said, and swung onto his horse. His two men followed.

Marlow watched them ride out, going back into the mountains. They might take Vespers far into them before they shot him, or they might wait only until they were beyond earshot of the cabin. But Marlow knew that Vespers was doomed to die before many hours had passed. That had been only too plain on the faces of all of them. Marlow pondered it, and this was the only thing that disturbed him now, for he had dismissed his horse and his produce completely. He had liked Vespers, whatever his past and whatever his foolishness.

Marlow came to a decision without actually weighing the situation or his chances of doing anything about it. Yet they were better odds than they had been at any time in the past twelve hours, for Sands and his cronies believed they had left a truckling backwoods settler, impotent and resigned, behind them. And Marlow knew that Vespers's parting words had been designed to put a face on it bland enough to exempt his friend from any last moment spite or abuse. That was enough for Marlow, and he swung away from his cabin, his only weapon a hunting knife that he had slipped into his belt.

He knew every bit of the country around his cabin. By striking directly up the mountain, he could come onto the ridge trail that looped and probed the ravines. If he were fast enough, he might get there ahead of them. Beyond that, he did not plan, trusting to the spur of the moment. The only question was whether they would let Vespers live that long.

Marlow was thankful for his hard, lonely life here, for it had given him wind and stamina. He crossed the brushy bottom and struck swiftly up the hill, and he didn't slack pace until he was on the top. He knew he was ahead of the party, his only fear being for Vespers. He threw himself flat in the brush by the trail and lay there, catching his breath and letting his trembling fatigue subside. He allowed himself only a few minutes, then rose, and studied the terrain.

He selected a tree he could climb that hung above the game trail. He went to it and lifted himself up into the lower limbs, pressing flat at his selected point. There was a long wait, moments when his mouth stood dry above an aching throat. But he had heard no gunshot. They would have to follow the trail this far, whatever direction they meant to take afterward.

Marlow's hand held his knife when he dropped, yelling: "Fan out of here, kid!"

He landed limply behind Sands, as a great cat might descend upon a deer. But he didn't drive the knife, for he had a distaste for such killing. He took Sands out of the saddle, both landing in a hard crash on the earth. It threw consternation and confusion into the bolting, scattering party, as Marlow had wanted. Sands's horse wheeled off up the trail.

Marlow saw that Vespers had ignored his order to light out and, instead, had jumped his horse toward a man, reaching from the saddle for its rider. But Marlow had his hands full and lost track of the ruction. He put the point of his knife at Sands's throat, growling — "Keep still." — and reached for the man's still holstered gun.

He failed to get it. Another gun cracked behind him, the slug kicking up a pillar of dust by Marlow's head. In the same instant Sands jerked himself aside, rolling away from Marlow's knife. Marlow sailed after him.

Shoved up on an elbow, Sands got his gun free and fired blindly. It was a split second too soon, and the bullet sighed harmlessly past Marlow's ear. Then the settler's big hands closed on the man, jerking Sands to his feet. He batted him hard across the mouth with a force that made the man's eyes show white for a second. A gun fired again, and something hooked into Marlow's buckskins without touching flesh. The settler closed a hand on the gun in Sands's grip, arresting it, and took a look about him.

The man, Joe, had swung down and stood beyond a wheeling horse, using it for shelter while he tried to get in a shot at Marlow. Beyond, Vespers and the other man were in a brawl on the ground, slamming, choking, rolling.

Sands growled: "Why, you tricky son-of-a-bitch! Didn't figure you had a ounce of fight in you."

Marlow lunged into him, driving him down, and they rolled together, Marlow fighting to keep Sands's body between himself and Joe until he could get the gun he wanted. Sands slammed out, kicking and butting with his head, but Marlow held on.

In a moment he had the gun, and he

whipped it savagely across Sands's head —
two swipes, and the man lay still. Marlow
climbed to his feet, panting. Joe had swung
onto his horse again, not liking the look of
things. He flung a shot at the settler just as
Marlow fired, then Joe flopped out of the
saddle.

Vespers rose from a still figure on the
ground. He had his man's gun in his hand,
and his shirt was ripped off, his face
scratched and bleeding. He staggered
toward Marlow.

"Never was so surprised in my life. And I
never was so glad of anything, either."

"You all right?" Marlow asked.

"A lot all righter than I'd've been if you
hadn't made that play."

They gathered the guns and brought their
men together. Joe was dead, shot through
the head, but Sands and the other were only
beaten into insensibility.

Vespers swung onto the one horse he
could catch and rounded up the others.
Marlow wondered what the kid would do
now.

As if reading the question in the settler's
eyes, Vespers said: "Well, we better pack
'em down to your place, Marlow. Lock 'em
in that root cellar of yours, maybe. Reckon
you'll have to stand having 'em around long

enough for me to send the law out from Jacksonville."

"The law?" Marlow said, staring.

Vespers gave him a slow grin. "Did you figure I was on their side of it? Hardly. And if I'd've told you what it was, they'd've tried to kill you along with me. That was all they wanted, to shut me up."

"None of my business, even yet," Marlow said, but acknowledged he was curious.

Vespers was still grinning. "Took you for a man who liked it on his lonesome, but I got nothing to hide. It was one of them blunders a man can make and land plunk into boiling water. They held up a gold-dust runner over on the Yreka trail yesterday morning. They shot the poor devil down. The dust'll be there in Sands's saddlebags. It was just my luck to be coming down them switchbacks from the other direction. Maybe you seen my horse ain't got any shoes. Been down on my luck lately, and he was the best I could buy in Red Bluff to ride through."

Marlow was grinning back now, the first time he had ever been so warmly drawn to another man. "For a tight-lipped cuss, you can sure be long-winded."

"It was quite a little caper. I heard the shooting and was fool enough to fog up to see what it was. Johnny to the rescue, maybe. They must've meant to kill that poor runner from the start, for they weren't masked. I got a good look at them . . . too good. Hadn't given 'em time to finish the job and clear out. They started throwing lead, and something give me a itch to hit off up a ravine, fast as my horse could dust it. Kept it up all day, barely staying out of range. They sure didn't aim for anybody to stay alive who could identify 'em."

They threw the bandits across the horses and took them down to the cabin. Sands and the other man had roused by the time they were locked in the root cellar, but showed no spunk beyond a steady, bitter cursing.

Vespers swung onto his horse and said: "Glad you got your horse and stuff back. They got good guns, so you can take your pick to replace what they threw in the river, like I done. I'll tell the story to the deputy marshal down in the gold camp. Reckon by now he's looking for the men who murdered and robbed the runner. He'll take the thing off your hands, and . . . well, thanks, fellow."

Marlow was staring at him. He felt no particular relief at having recovered his property. In fact, he was conscious of a sense of loss, and it dawned on him that this was because Vespers was riding out. Deeper than that, he had a sense of satisfaction such as he had never found here in his wilderness storehouse. He knew suddenly what it came from, the fact that he had done a wholly unasked and unobliged thing for another.

Again Marlow made a fast decision. "Got any particular plans, Syl?"

"Well, I reckon I'll keep on hunting me a gold claim where a man can pan wages anyhow."

"Ever consider homesteading?"

"Guess I have. I come off a farm. Marlow, there's only about one man in a hundred out here strikes it big. Most of us're lucky to earn our bacon and beans."

Marlow was thinking fast, running entirely contrary to what he had always considered his grain. "Lot of good land open around here. Time yet to get a cabin up before winter. I got plenty of tools and grub for both till you could get going. Think it over. Then maybe you'll want to ride back out with the marshal."

"Want to?" Vespers' eyes widened, a broad smile breaking on his lean face. "Marlow, scared as I was, I admired what you've got here. If you don't mind having somebody horn in on you, I'll sure be back with that marshal."

Marlow watched him ride off, then looked about him with satisfaction, at his rough cabin and stumpy land and wild environs. A man with hands, back, and head could do a lot with it.

With a good friend and neighbor, he could have self-sufficiency.

Man Breaker

Dan Ketel got back to the house, finally, though he crawled every foot until he was near enough to yell for Lois. He blacked out then, the pain and portent from his dangling leg breaking through the willed repression he had needed in order to move at all. His last clear thought was of the burden he had put upon her, and, in view of her mounting heaviness, he hated that.

His first reflection, after an indeterminate time, was that she hadn't tried to move him to the house but had shaded his head with her apron. He was belly-down, his head turned, and he brushed the cover away. His wife wasn't there. He was in the gully below the day corral, where he had quit crawling. He didn't have to look at the jagged angle of his lower, left leg to remember what had put him here. He raised his head, thinking to call again, but he didn't.

He heard a horse moving up above. In a

moment Lois appeared at the top of the bank and looked down at him anxiously. She was in the saddle. Anger spilled in Dan. Maybe he needed to release the small but compounding frustrations of the past hours in which each movement had been a major agony and each surge of will a sure defeat.

"Get off that horse!" he yelled. "You've got no business in a saddle!"

She put the animal on down the slope, a good rider in spite of the fact that the pommel was hidden by her abdomen. Her face was drawn with worry.

She said: "I oughtn't to ride for the doctor, I guess. But I'll go to the Moss's and send one of them."

"No!" Dan thundered, in protest to everything that implied.

"Dan, what happened?"

"Horse rolled on me," Dan said. "On the talus, coming off the rim. Pinned me on the down side and went clean over. Broke my leg and some ribs, I guess."

He saw her face pull tighter. "Why, that's at least two miles."

"It's a million," Dan answered. He was starting to sweat, because there had been horror in the hours it had taken him to get here. And because it was plain, unbearably hot and had been for weeks, driving him distraught because of the short water for his cattle. He had been crowding his horse, as he had himself lately, but he didn't mention that. "If I hadn't been on a half-broke oreana, he might've come in so you'd have known. The critter must have hit for the brakes. Seen nothing of him afterwards."

Lois was swinging her horse about. "Dan, shade your face again. I'll send Moss for the doctor and fetch the other to help get you to the house. Now, you take it easy. Do you want a drink?" Her quick tenderness stood in her eyes.

"No," Dan said. He was terribly thirsty, but knew she would have to dismount to get water for him, then mount again. She had had a little trouble at the start, and the doctor had warned her to stay off horses. It had been hard on Lois.

Everything was hard on her out here, he guessed. He swallowed his protests at her going to Moss's, since it was the only way she could avoid the long ride to town, for she would never let his leg go with what care they could give it themselves. And beyond that was the herd and all the hard range work the long dry spell had required. She couldn't handle it, and he wouldn't let her, so it was Moss or his scrawny kid or nobody. Dan winced, in pain and in bitter distaste.

It didn't gravel her the way it did him, and this irritation bit at Dan. "We could do with neighbors," Lois had commented, when the nester family settled in. "I'd like another woman closer than twenty miles of me. Especially with a baby coming and things not quite right." Dan had admitted her need of that, though Lois had never seen the nester woman, who was the same stringy, hang-dog sort as her man.

Dan Ketel was a cattleman born and bred, and now standing against the first settlers coming in to gobble the open range under the Homestead Act. Moss had cut out a strip of Dan's water and a section of his best free grass. He had simply appeared without warning with a rickety wagon, a scraggly wife, and starved-looking boy in his teens. Since the crazy Homestead law a man could claim only a measly half section for himself and risk his herd to the whims of riffraff like that.

"Now, you take it slow," Dan said sharply to Lois. "You walk that horse, going and coming, and if there's any hurryin', let them plagued nesters do it."

Lois smiled at him now, her confidence restored by his steady temper. "Yes, Dan. I promise."

Pain rolled its spasm through his body as

he watched her ride away, and he knew he had a long wait here. A rider hurrying could make it in an hour, but he knew she would walk her horse as she had agreed — unless her anxiety got to crowding her. He put this worry from his mind. But he didn't know just what she would find over there, either.

Lois didn't realize that the last time they had met, Dan had told the nester to keep out of his path, and this had been no time to tell her. It was the bitter thing, and the sodbuster would probably laugh at her instead of obliging. Dan might have been a little rough, but he had heard about this new breed, land-hungry and hard-scrabble, coming in from the East.

"Understand you clodhoppers figure to make out on rustled beef," he had told Moss that day, down on the edge of the nester's claim. "Don't let me find any sign of that. Just to make sure, you keep them feet off my grass. That goes for your family, too."

Dan Ketel admired a real man, no matter what his calling. But he hated a weakling. Instead of bristling and giving it back, Moss had looked startled and apologetic.

"This is outcountry, Ketel. It's a long haul to anywhere. We'd ought to get along." Moss had his hands shoved under the bib of his faded overalls in the granger way, and he had shifted his weight on his long, skinny legs. Dan had pulled his horse around and ridden off. He was thinking of this in pain-racked rancor when he blacked out again.

The next time his senses cleared, he grew disturbed by something outside himself. The air was sticky still, more so than it had been so far in the drought. He didn't like that, nor the patch of discernible sky. A great, white cloud had rolled across it, though not yet in the shape of a thunder-head. But the weather and this congealed atmosphere were breeders of an electric storm, the one thing needed to bring utter devastation. Dan lay with an upward stare, thinking of Lois and her slow ride across broken country. Lightning frightened her, and she was on a skittish horse.

The thing that happened staggered Dan. There was a moment in which the atmo-sphere darkened, this mantle seeming to swirl in tiny dots. Then it began to pelt and bounce and roll about him. Hail, hard hail, from the size of a marble to that of an egg, pure ice rattling heavily into land-trapped heat. It could kill a steer or a man or a woman. He knew that it covered the whole range.

Dan Ketel began to swear in the soft, deadly way of a man brought at last to despair. His time sense was gone; he couldn't place Lois anywhere on her errand. Some instinct made him cover his head, and the beat on his back and hurt leg was nearly beyond bearing. He felt his shirt tearing, and some place back there he had lost his hat and never troubled to get it again. He laced his fingers and pulled his hands tight to the back of his head. It came to him slowly that he had to get to the barn or die.

Yet, his concern was for Lois as he crawled forward, and this deadened the pain somewhat and let him at long last gain the top of the gully. He had to stop there, panting and nearly gone, hearing the heavy, cricket-like racket on roofs and ground and his own skull. The pellets had bounced on the bank, leaving it fairly clear, but now there were two inches of balled ice beneath him, and he could feel blood trickle down either cheek from his scalp.

It had turned colder, a part of the high wind that was tossing moisture into the upper air to freeze now descending with the precipitation. He was quite a distance from the barn, and would have to round it to reach a door. *But how far is Lois from Moss's? Will she run her horse or be beaten to death where it catches her?* This frenzy started Dan crawling.

He couldn't move on the insane ice blanketing that had been the seared, parched range an hour earlier. He could do nothing but hunch his shoulders and try to cover his head and still his mind. He knew he was done for, and this caused him no feeling. His imagination could show only Lois, fleeing unheeded upon her horse or thrown flat somewhere, trying to protect her swollen body. Pain needled through his mantle of hopelessness.

He thought it was giddiness when he saw a rider loom out of the white-striped obscurity, across the ranch yard. It wasn't Lois, but the bent, high figure of a man whose clothing hung in tatters. It was Moss, and fear rose terribly in Dan Ketel.

"Where's my wife?" he roared.

Moss didn't answer, coming on. But he looked up, and under the flattened, old hat Dan saw a bruised, swollen, and bloody face. He had ridden through the pelting hail without pause, apparently. Moss staggered against his horse when he swung down above Dan. He pulled in a long breath before he spoke.

"Back yonder, Ketel. To my place, though her time's on her from the riding and the poundin'. She was in it a little while. Ketel, don't you worry. My woman knows about them things."

But Dan Ketel had let go.

The hail had stopped when he opened his eyes, and his first impression was of a blinding flash of light, then of rolling, sharp-close thunder. He was in the house and on the bed, and the scrawny nester must have carried him there. Moss wasn't in the room, and Dan couldn't hear anything but the pealing rolls of thunder. *He left his place in it. He rode here in it. To help me. . . .* Dan Ketel shook his head in amazement.

He called, but there was no answer. Anger boiled up in Dan then, for this hard-scrabbler had no right to make Dan Ketel so beholden. His woman had no right to be tending Lois in her hour. It was a shaming ingratitude that he recognized, but he couldn't help it.

Dan Ketel would have none of it. He shoved himself to a sitting position, finding then that his head had been bandaged, his leg splinted, and in his wrath he ignored the fiery spasms in his chest. He swung off the bed and got upright. By using the back of a chair to support him, he managed to hobble to the kitchen. Moss wasn't there or anywhere.

Dan got to the pantry, where he reached

135

for his bottle of rarely used whiskey. He took a long pull and felt the heat, then pulled again. It strengthened him and fanned his anger, and he began to roll and swing his way to the back porch.

It was a disturbing, unnatural scene. Black clouds had swept across the sky and were split momentarily by streaks of lightning. The thunder rolled down through what was unmixed heat and cold, and over all the land lay the melting blanket of hailstones to a depth of several inches, dissolving in standing water and rising mud. Dan Ketel swore at it savagely and went on into the yard, careless of his footing and of everything.

Moss's horse was gone. Maybe Moss had gone home or headed for town and the doctor. That would be rough going now, as the squatter's ride through the hailstorm had been. Yet, even as Dan stood there, he heard a horse, then saw the man come sloshing into view from the direction of his claim. Moss had an old blanket coat on now, and was hunched tiredly in the saddle.

"Ketel," Moss said, as he rode in, "your wife's had her young 'un, and she's doing well enough. I sent my kid for the doctor. They should be back tomorrow evening. They'll stop to my place and tend your woman, then come over here. So I reckon you'll have to put up with me till this thing is straightened out." For the first time the settler stared. "Ketel, what're you doing up and out?"

"Don't need you," Dan said, aware that it sounded short. "Get home and look after them. I'll get along. But thanks . . . for all you done."

Moss swung off his horse. "Ain't nothing over there any woman can't handle. Ketel, I ain't no cowhand, but I reckon this is raisin' Ned with your steers. What you want me to do, or try to?" He drop-reined the horse and strode across the porch. "But first I need a little coffee in my belly. It's cold an' hot and crazy as hell all over." He disappeared, and a moment later the lids on the stove were rattling.

Dan stumbled to the kitchen door, went in, and closed it behind him. Moss was whittling shavings for a fire. He had washed the blood from his face, but still looked as if he'd been worked over in a saloon ruckus. Yet there was repose in his features, and maybe it was the doggedness that had to be in the breed to let it survive.

Dan motioned to the whiskey bottle on the table. "Help yourself."

"Thanks," Moss said, beginning to pile

his shavings. "But a man in my line cain't afford a taste for it. Got to learn to goose hisself other ways. Where you folks keep your coffee?"

Bet he ain't been able to indulge a taste for that much, either, Dan thought, pointing to a shelf visible beyond the pantry door.

"You got a boy," Moss resumed. "That's what a man always wants the first time. We never had more than the one, ourselves. Good thing, maybe. Kids make good hands, but they got mouths, too. Depends on how a man gets along. Ketel, I ain't a 'puncher, but I can ride a horse and recognize a steer from close up. What needs tendin'?"

"It's coming night," Dan said gruffly. "Reckon what harm could be done's done already. If the hail didn't run 'em, the thunderstorm will."

"If they can ketch footing," Moss said, and grinned. "I'll get out and see what's brewin'."

Reaction came to Dan while he watched the nester drink coffee — first a weighting fatigue, and as his will let go, a resumption of the steady pain in his leg and chest. He nearly asked Moss to get him the whiskey, but something the man had said about its goosing qualities stopped him. He had refused coffee, but now Moss rose without

138

request and brought some. Dan emptied the cup, and had started to roll a cigarette when he caved forward onto the table.

"I'll get you to bed before I go," Moss said, and he came over.

"No!" Dan growled and stood up. Using the chair again, he got into the bedroom by himself, keeled onto the bed, and let go of it.

It was daylight when he wakened, brighter, a new day. He had been undressed and put in bed and carefully covered. The room was warm, there was racket in the kitchen, and he could smell coffee.

He was too sore and weak to try to get out of bed. He yelled, and in a moment Moss entered in his easy slouch. The squatter's battered face had a new quality now, that of deep weariness. Yet he grinned.

"Well, Ketel," Moss said, "things ain't so bad. Your herd was jumpy, but it hadn't spooked yet. Ice stopped 'em. Managed to get 'em into the bottom. Only found a few down. It won't hurt you much, I reckon."

Dan lifted his weight in the bed. "Moss, that'd take a man half the night."

"A cowhand," Moss agreed. "Took me a mite longer. Come by home, afterwards. They're doin' sprightly over there. Ketel, what you want me to fix for breakfast?"

"Anything you can find, and all you can eat. You've earned it." Though he had meant no harm, Dan was sorry he said that, for he saw the nester straighten. He made his stiffened cheeks grin at Moss. "Then crawl into the missus's spare bed, and sleep your head off. I won't need anything."

Moss brought his breakfast, and it was sparse flapjacks and coffee. He went out, and later Dan heard him go into the sitting room, and after that it was quiet. Moss had availed himself of the old, horsehair sofa in there. Dan Ketel lay staring at the ceiling.

Logically the situation was in hand, though it gave him no relief. He knew what it was that disturbed him, and at last he faced it. He had no inclination to impugn the nester's motives, but the happenings — astonishingly as Moss had met them — had given Moss an enormous advantage.

Dan Ketel was grateful, but he was also beholden, and Moss was still a squatter occupying what had been a parcel of Dan's best graze. Right or wrong, his wish to see the place vacated and restored to his own use had not lessened. The whole cow country felt as he did, and it wasn't in him to make his peace the way it stood.

The Moss boy came with the doctor in

late afternoon. After that, there was an hour of agony for Dan while the three men strained at his leg and got it set so the doctor could put the cast on. Dan refused whiskey, though Moss brought the bottle, and he refused the pills the doctor offered. A couple of times he caught the nester studying him with a strange interest. Then Moss took his boy and went out, probably to see what needed tending before night.

"These new people are a strange breed," the doctor said, bandaging Dan's chest. "Tough as they come. But it looks like this has finished Moss, so you'll get your grass back, Dan."

"Why?" Dan asked sharply.

"Didn't he tell you?"

"He's quite a spieler, but he never said anything about himself. What's wrong?"

"There wasn't a blade of hay or oats standing after that hailstorm. Nor a stalk of corn or a vine in his garden. In ten minutes Moss was cleaned out."

"I'll be blamed!" Dan breathed. "Knows it, too. He was home twice since then."

" 'Course, he knows it. Take a blind man not to."

The elation that stirred in Dan shamed him. The hailstorm had solved the situation for Dan Ketel, without his lifting a hand against Moss.

The doctor started his long, tired return to town after reassuring Dan that Lois and the baby would be all right. Dusk crept in, but Moss didn't return from his chores. Dan Ketel lay in the twilight, easing and tasting the satisfaction of deep trouble surmounted. He tried to figure a way to repay Moss. He had a little cash saved, but it wouldn't be fitting to offer it. He could let him have a couple of steers to beef.

He heard Moss return and move about the kitchen, making supper. When the nester came into the bedroom with food, Dan said: "Doc Faraday was telling me about your crop."

"Weren't a thing a man could do, Ketel."

"What do you figure on now?"

"To get in my fall plantin'."

"You mean you'll hang on?"

"Why, sure," Moss said in genuine surprise. "When's a better time than when you've got to? Ketel, I just come from there. Your wife sent word that she 'n' the boy are fine. You can take my word that they look it. But we had best plan. It'll be a while before she can tend a baby and you and herself, or even come home. You'll be laid up for weeks, and no-account all fall."

Dan sensed what Moss was leading up to, or thought he did. He said quickly: "I'll hire a man and a woman, too. There's roundup coming, and heavy work. I'll send out for a cowhand, maybe one with a wife. Thank you kindly, Moss. I'm beholden to you. If you'll run that errand, I won't need to trouble you again."

"No trouble at all," Moss said, and turned quiet. He went out in his padding slouch.

Dan was ashamed of himself, but he felt no relenting. Moss had been on the point of trying to make a job for himself and maybe for his gaunt, poker-faced woman — one that would let them winter and get on their feet again and stay put. Dan aimed to repay them any way he could, except that, and there wasn't a cowman in the country who wouldn't understand his feeling about this.

He was awake two hours the next morning without hearing Moss stir through the house. It was surprising, for the man had been carefully punctual in his nursing chores, thoughtful and handy as a woman in such things. Hungry for his breakfast, yet more curious about the nester, Dan sat up and gingerly swung his cast over the edge of the bed. It was easier than it had been before the fracture was tended, and he shoved to a rocky stand. Using a chair to help himself again, he made his way out.

The house was empty save for himself, and there had been no kitchen fire that morning. *Guess I run him off,* Dan thought, and the reflection troubled him. He hadn't aimed to hurt Moss's feelings or to show any sign of ingratitude, however irreconcilable they might be as neighbors.

Dan got a fire going and started breakfast, getting about so well he decided to make a real crutch and have done with idleness in bed. A sense of independence came to him, which was a tonic mixture in his long depression. Yet, he knew that at best he could only hobble about the homesite for a long while. When Moss or the boy showed up, he would send a letter to Pat Quarran on Bar S, asking for the loan of a man for a spell. He probably could tend Lois and the baby himself as soon as they could be brought home.

He ate his breakfast, smoked a cigarette over extra coffee, then hobbled slowly out to his small smithy to see about a crutch for himself. He halted in the yard halfway there. Maybe it was his new sense of freedom, or again the hearty breakfast digesting comfortably in his middle, but he thought suddenly: *I wonder what they've got to eat over there? No meat likely, and probably no coffee. Maybe nothing but what can be saved from the ruined garden. Lois couldn't send word they were going hungry. Not by a man like Moss. And I never once thought of that.*

Shame hit him then, a raw humiliation at the Dan Ketel who had delayed a lot of meals but never missed one entirely. And it wasn't the thought of Lois's going on short rations, but an insight he had never had before into human futility and despair. *And he never said anything. About what the hail had done to him, nothing at all. Maybe he hoped I'd neighbor, the way he done. But he never said anything at all.*

Dan went on to the shop. Within the hour he had a crutch made and padded well enough to do him. If there had been an extra horse up, he would have saddled and ridden over to Moss's without delay. He thought: *By damn, I'm a-goin' over there if I have to crawl like I did coming down from the rim. I'm going to tell them they'll winter and get along till a new crop comes.* He returned to the house to get his hat, then started out, hobbling slowly but steadily.

It was better than five miles, and by the time he was halfway he was exhausted, with his armpit rubbed raw from the clumsy crutch. But he had topped the rise, and far below he could see the saucer where Moss's claim lay, a quiet, homey spot, its devastation concealed at this distance. Dan paused to rest, and was still sitting when he saw a horseman appear far to the left, coming down from the distant timber.

He knew presently that it was Moss, and something bulky lay across the cantle behind the man. *He's had to rustle finally. Not on me, but Bar S from the direction he's riding.* Anger flared in Dan Ketel then, a spewing rage. It was not against the nester but himself. He shoved to his feet and started out at a tangent, aiming to intercept Moss before he got home with that shameful piece of meat.

Moss sighted him presently and made no effort to dodge, instead turning his horse and riding directly toward Dan Ketel. Dan knew for sure it was a cut of meat. A rifle lay across the nester's lap. His skinny body was held erect, his head back, and there was a surprised reserve in the man's face.

"Ketel, what the devil're you doing out here?" Moss demanded from the near distance.

Relief nearly dropped Dan Ketel in his tracks, for he saw that it was neither beef nor veal but a hind quarter of venison. Moss had been up in the timber to shoot his meat, a long-chance effort at this season, and Dan knew he must have been trying for it in his other unexplained absences. There was a look of satisfaction in the man's gaunt face now, though he made no mention of the matter.

"Got a hankerin' to see my wife and boy," Dan said, grinning. "There weren't any horses up."

"Never figured you'd be needin' one," Moss said, and he returned the grin. "Ketel, you're a hard man to down."

Dan didn't say anything, but he knew now he had changed his mind about this man quite a spell back without being able to admit it. He didn't give two hoots if he was a nester — Moss was all man. And a prideful one. Dan saw suddenly he wasn't going to be able to dispense largesse with an open hand.

Moss swung down. "Well, you can ride from here on."

Dan didn't object, for it was only a short distance for the man to walk, and he himself was played out. But it surprised him that he no longer minded being the weak one, taking help from a stranger, because the quiet understanding in Moss held no question of equality. They started on.

And now Dan Ketel could see the devastation wrought to this man's crop by the quarter hour of heavy hail. The big field where Moss had done his first planting was flattened, ravaged, laid waste. The tarpaper siding on his drab, little shack had been ripped to shreds. The garden was as if a herd of cattle had stampeded across it. Moss seemed to take no notice as they came upon these sights.

Moss's boy came out of the barn, and his hungry eyes went at once to the cut of meat. A scraggly dog barked and leaped at the venison until Moss cuffed it down. They went on to the shack door, where Moss bawled: "Missus Ketel, get a pretty smile on your face! Here's a man to see what you brought forth!"

Dan didn't mind letting Moss help him down from the saddle. The door came open, and Moss's wife stood there, tall and brown and faded, but not the woman Dan had remembered at all. She, too, looked at once to the meat, and Dan saw her eyes narrow for the merest instant.

He heard Lois call: "Dan, is it you? What on earth . . . ?"

He got up the crude step and hobbled into the shack. Lois was in the bed that stood across one end of the room, and he knew it was the Mosses'. Dan saw something beside her that she had moved into prominence.

"Aimed to get back in time to fix his breakfast," Moss said heartily. "Took me longer than I figured, and he got impatient and started over. Ma, git your skillet hot, and we'll eat."

Dan went to the bed, and there was no need for his wife and him to speak. Lois lay quietly, a happiness on her face all women show when their lives have been fulfilled, which is a little deeper when it has been hard and frightening. She pushed away the blanket the Moss woman must have dug up, and Dan Ketel saw his son. He grew aware then that the Mosses had quietly gone outside, and, awkward though it was, Dan went to his knees beside the bed.

"I'm grateful," he told his wife. "I'm truly grateful."

Her eyes rounded. "Why, Dan . . . it's nothing, really. I want another and another."

"To everybody," Dan said. "For everything. Lois, I want to help them, and I don't know how to. Moss is a proud man."

"Dan, don't try to help them. Just neighbor."

Dan said nothing about the big breakfast he had had, and ate venison and corn bread with the Mosses and Lois. He saw the contentment that it gave these people, the simple relief of danger shoved away and forgotten for a spell. He felt it, too, and in that hour knew the first real happiness of a lifetime.

It was easy when he said: "Moss, this sounds right nervy. Like your company, but my wife's got you beat. Seen you've got a wagon. Could we fetch 'em home, do you suppose, a-layin on straw in the bed? And could your missus come and tend her till she's up and around, with you and the boy tendin' my stock? Hate to ask it, but we're in a fix, and it would sure help."

He saw skepticism enter Moss's eyes, then go away. The nester glanced at his wife and read the veiled relief that Dan also saw.

Moss said: "Why, sure, Ketel. No trouble at all. Let's get at it."

Whistle on the River

Titus hated shadows. Winter or summer the deep purple patterns tilted from the rearing, green-stippled mountains and fell across the silvered width of the river. The Landing and all the broad flat behind it were darkened, subdued, with the yellow splash of the sun never reaching them. Frisking down the Columbia gorge, a continual east wind knifed cold into creature and object; it built great, glistening ice sheets on the rocky eminences to Washington and Oregon, and turned the earth of the cove into a brittle plain over which the wooden wagons rattled and clattered.

The only open expanse was directly above, escaloped patterns of sky where light burned or glowed or snuffed to near extinction, but a man could not walk always with uptilted head. Not even a man like Titus Evart, whom The Landing counted as its own.

Styles Evart was coming out of the machine shop, frowning, his slight figure bent as though billowed by the strong wind. Titus grinned to himself, thinking: *It's the same old story. He bristles like a bantam rooster, but the work doesn't get done. The* Jenny's *still on the ways . . . and a long way from built.*

His older brother was coming toward him. Styles Evart favored his mother's side of the line: the rather slight stature, the instinctive haughtiness, the deep-going sense of superiority that was forever translating itself into works and defeating its own aims. A grim amusement rose in Titus as he watched the nervous, short-stepped gait. This morning Styles had something special worrying him.

Styles grunted — "Come up to the office, Ty." — and never stopped.

Titus turned from the ways on which the *Jenny's* unfinished hulk lifted, the scent of oakum and calking cotton and heated tar tingling in his nostrils, the vibrant ringing from the machine shop beating his ears. The *Oriole*, which a little earlier had left mail and passengers at The Landing, sent a hoarse, muted whistle from some place on up the twisting gut of the gorge.

The small structure that was the office of

the boat yard and wooden landing stood in the middle of an open area, a frozen, gravel road running around it, along which sundry utility structures were strung. Styles shoved open the door. Inside, he removed his sheepskin greatcoat and knitted cap. In the doorway to the side room that was his private office he hesitated, turning back toward Titus with a stiff grin.

"The *Oriole* brought another letter from Curtis. He'll be up on the *Boniface* tomorrow. You know what that means."

"Yes. He's canceling the contract." Titus digested the news, not surprised at what had long been foreseen, but still a little shocked by its advent. "Well, you can see his point," he reflected. "We were to deliver the *Jenny* in October. Now it's November." The impulse was strong in him to add: *It's been the same with the last half dozen boats.* He resisted this, a delayed sympathy for Styles running through him. It wasn't Styles's fault. A man couldn't help the way he was born. If fault there was, it was Jonathan Evart's for dying, for getting himself killed by the very thing he had devoted much of his life to creating.

"What can we do about it, Ty?"

It wasn't often that Styles asked for advice, and now Titus grinned at him. "Let him warp his hull down to Portland. Tell him to take it and be damned! After all, there's the family pride."

Anger crawled slowly across Styles's thin, arch-nosed face. "You're glad to see it, aren't you?"

"Not exactly. But it's no surprise."

"You could've managed things better?"

"I've never said that!" Instantly Titus regretted the savageness he let creep into his voice. His own deep dissatisfaction had tricked him into taking a foul swipe at Styles. When Jonathan had been crushed by a toppling hull, six years before, Titus had still been in school in Portland. Styles had not asked to have the heavy responsibility of The Landing thrust upon his young shoulders. But he had done his unselfish, if inadequate, best to meet the obligation. Titus said quickly: "I'm sorry, Styles. I don't know what gets into me."

Styles gave him a long look and turned away, and Titus knew the mood. He would talk no more on the subject — this proud, twenty-six-year-old Styles Evart, with everything he had tried to do a failure around him — not with a brother four years his junior. Titus stood there a moment, trying to bring the right words to his tongue.

Through the front windows he could see

the boat yard with its three ways, all but one empty and fallen into disrepair. Above ran the timbered tramway with its giant blocks and massive lines. The big, steam donkey, intended for pulling steamboats onto the ways for repair, was there on skids, but it had been long since fire had warmed its boiler. Beyond was the dwindling pile of lumber, once the stockpile for repair work and new construction and now sparse and picked over because there was not money enough to keep it replenished. It was all stark evidence of dwindling prosperity, of approaching bankruptcy.

Against all this, Styles Evart had done his level best, and it had been insufficient. Yet, Titus could not articulate these things. They were the intangibles that tied his own hands like new hemp rope. They were the things he hated yet could not voice to Styles without showing that hatred more than he cared to.

He went outside. The racket in the machine shop drummed up again. The east wind whipped tiny knives into his cheeks.

The dead could not return, yet it seemed that his father was always here. Lesser men could not pace to the tracks he had left about The Landing, and this was not their fault. Jonathan Evart had been a giant, a huge man with a rolling chuckle, who had only to conceive an idea to see its incarnation.

Some sense of the titan within him must have guided Jonathan Evart when he chose this site on the river, twenty miles above the town of Vancouver at the confluence of the Columbia and the Willamette, a thirty-acre flat at the base of deep mountains rising on the Oregon shore. When Titus was still a baby, Jonathan had started his wood yard, supplying fuel to the steamboats plying the river and connecting the fresh-water, inland seaport of Portland with the mineral-rich, emerging empire east of the Cascade Mountains. He had prospered, and he had added ways for the construction and repair of the packets, and prospered more.

He had built a community that now crowded the flat, for his enterprises took the hands of many men, some to cut cordwood on the mountain, others, in summer, to haul it down to the yard and bank it out in unending ricks where the chipmunks barked. Still others were needed to load it onto the steamers, and many more to man the boat yard. Cut off from the world save for the passing steamers, this village of more than a hundred souls had been Jonathan's pride and joy, and over it he had reigned benign and supreme.

Titus passed now through the wood yard, an excitement that had been stirring in him since morning, and underlying all the rest, directing his steps toward the landing where the packets stopped to discharge and pick up passengers, mail and small freight, besides taking on fuel. The *Bluebell* would start downstream presently, and, though he knew that Ewen Barcliff would be on it, he wanted to witness the departure with his own eyes.

The wooden landing joined the village on the east. The *Bluebell*, downward bound, had stopped there for wood, and Titus observed that he had guessed its leaving time closely. He saw Ewen Barcliff standing at the rail, but his gaze flicked quickly away from the man, turning to the slight figure it sought on the wharf.

Huldah Dalquist waved to Barcliff, who was her father, turned quickly and started for the far end of the dock, and Titus knew she had not noticed him. He hurried after her, overtaking her on the long slant leading down to the road connecting with the main street of the village.

Titus grinned and said: "I thought maybe you'd go with Ewen."

She looked at him quickly. "Why, no. I

157

had nothing to go down about."

A pulse was crashing in Titus's ears, partly of fear and partly of expectancy. *What if she suspected that he had plotted to send her father away overnight? Plotted to break the fence Ewen Barcliff had unintentionally built about his daughter simply with his presence? Plotted to give them a chance, at last, to see each other and clarify the thing between them?* He said: "Then you're not afraid to be alone?"

Huldah laughed. "Here at The Landing? A place even the sunlight can't reach."

"You hate it, too, don't you?"

"Why . . . do you?"

"Yes."

After a long moment she said: "That's funny from a man who's being married tomorrow. You intend to live here, don't you?"

"Yes. I can't get away."

"Why are you telling it to me, Titus? Does Leonora know how you feel?"

"I don't suppose so. We've never talked about it." He looked at her askance, seeing her so tall and slender, so charged with something he could not understand, yet so gravely calm. He had to see her. He had to know what was there before tomorrow.

"You should have told her." They had

come onto the main street of the village. Huldah stopped in front of the store and post office. "I've got a few things to buy. If I don't see you again before the wedding, I wish you happiness, Titus. Leonora's a prize for any man."

He wheeled toward her, looking down into her deep, brown eyes. "It's a long time until tomorrow."

Gravely, studiously, she regarded him, then turned quickly away and went into the store.

A guilty feeling came over Titus as he took a devious course back to the boat yard. It hadn't been quite what he expected when he had maneuvered to get Ewen Barcliff, who was the machine-shop foreman, sent to Portland to see about the castings for the *Jenny*'s wheel journals. Yet, he was certain that the deep chord forever struck in him by Huldah's presence, by the very thought of her, had its counterpart in her. Before tomorrow he had to know what it meant.

Striding along the frozen road, the decaying village all around him, Titus smiled without amusement. The Evarts owned every foot of ground and every structure on this small, flat chip at the base of the mountain, and the drain of it was what was ruining them. Despite their bluff and

159

pretense, everybody knew that. Unable to admit the difficulties in which it had caught itself, the family could not retrench by slashing the big payroll by lopping off this expense and that. Styles had a genius for losing business rather than attracting it. The Landing must rock on, proudly and stubbornly as it always had, until its final ruin.

Ruin was not far away now, and ruin would mean freedom, Titus reminded himself. Freedom from the purple shadows that so strangely could swell his heart with fear. Insistent in him again was the knowledge that he could save the yard if he could have the chance, if he could bring himself to rebel against Styles and Lambda Evart, his mother. For he was of Jonathan's flesh and blood and kind. He could make things move. He could start things humming again with daring, vision, and profit.

But even if he had the heart to take control away from Styles, would he want to save the yard? Its failure would mean that he could escape. Then, in time, he himself could pull the cord that ripped the hoarse scream of a packet through the deep chasms of the gorge, rather than merely hear it with deep, sick longing. Then there would be no question of gratitude to Styles, of family loyalty and pride, of a dead man's rights.

He had not wanted to return to The Landing after his two years of advanced schooling in Portland. Even in his boyhood its shadows had frightened him, giving him a gnawing hunger for light. He had planned, after school was finished, to defy Jonathan and go on the river. Then Jonathan had died, putting them all in the trap.

His boot heels thumping on the hard earth, Titus considered the unbreakable intangibles that bound him here. First there was Styles's deep need of his help in the task Styles had not elected for himself, even if Styles would not let him have any of the management. Behind that was the iron will of Lambda, to whom there was no alternative but the carrying out of Jonathan's will. Mortising it all was Leonora, beautiful and fragile and remote, whom he loved. Daughter of Luther Rockey, the yard superintendent and one of Jonathan's first employees, she, in turn, loved The Landing where she had been born. She would not consider leaving it, or having him away from her and off on the river.

In spite of Huldah Dalquist, tomorrow's marriage was urgent. Titus wanted it as quickly as possible. Leonora would save him, give him peace in his trap. He had to find this, for his savage urge, his bitter amusement at the plight of The Landing could not be entertained by an honorable man. He knew that, however much he might desire it, he could not make his way to the light in that fashion. The Landing could be saved, and he would have to do it. Duty and Leonora would give him contentment in it if only he could find escape from the haunting image of Huldah Dalquist. Huldah was the keystone to the entire problem, and he thought he knew how to destroy her. Then tomorrow he and Leonora could be married. The day after tomorrow he could be happy here.

The whole trouble at The Landing was mismanagement; in a dozen ways he saw how this was true. Styles lacked Jonathan's driving force and easy dominance over others. There was a faint arrogance in him that aroused resentment, a bewildered but stiff-necked stubbornness. If only Styles would not try to hide his helplessness behind bland persistence. The sly little that Titus, in his capacity of glorified clerk, could do toward achieving discipline and order, efficiency and economy, morale and good will, Styles countermanded imperiously with some move of his own. Styles could not accept his failure, and would not, and Lambda stood solidly behind him in everything. And always circumstances had prevented Titus from simply rebelling and clearing out. So, having to stay, he had to make it as painless as possible. He thought he knew the way.

The flames crackling in the big fireplace brought cheer into the large Evart sitting room. For days the larger, more pretentious parlor had been given over to the wedding. Now the rehearsal was over, with the bridesmaids, the best man, the stripling attendants gone. Lambda Evart and Leonora were still in there, engrossed in the small touches so unnoticeable to a man and so important to a woman. Styles was strumming on the big grand piano in the music room, with the Reverend Thomas, up from Portland to perform the ceremony, in a deep chair beside him, listening.

Titus was sprawled before the fire, alone in the sitting room, thinking of Leonora, of how bright-eyed and excited she had been, how beautiful and precious. When he had watched her, earlier, a pride of possession had come to him, and it lingered yet. He had always known her, and he had always loved her, but he was rushing her into this marriage, seeking stability for himself.

It was on this rising note of relish, his gaze deep in the cherry embers of the fire, that the fear struck him again, that nameless, baseless sense of apprehension that came so frequently of late. It started sweat in his pores, and it shortened his breath and put a panic desire for movement in him. It came always when he was watching fire, seeing the red-hot tongues wrap about the fuel, consuming it. Now his hands tensed on the arms of his chair, and he sat upright, willing the fear away.

Styles's music splattered in his ears, and for a long moment he listened to it minutely, squeezing all else from his thought. Relaxation came slowly, letting his tall body bend back against the contours of the chair.

After tomorrow! he thought. *After tomorrow!* His desire for peace became a tremendous thing, his desire to surrender and receive the quieting stroke. A man could stand only so much of bitterness.

Styles was in his music, escaped into it, and for an interval, as he thought of it, a sense of deep sympathy came to Titus. In that moment he saw Styles objectively for the first time, the shy, slight male replica of Lambda, alien to Jonathan but obedient to the last breath. Whatever had been Styles's secret dreams, he had never asserted them. Like Titus, he had gone through the village school, then had gone out to Portland for two finishing years. Then he had returned to The Landing to understudy Jonathan. What had he put down? What had Lambda herself put down in the three decades she had lived here, with only an occasional trip outside, in a web a man now dead had woven so tightly about them all?

Abruptly Titus thought: *We've never gone at it right. Always we've sensed the rivalry in each other. Styles knows I criticize him in my mind, hold him responsible for the fix we're in. That makes him stubborn, makes him meddle and ruin everything I do to try and get the yard running right. Tonight . . . no, in the morning . . . I'll tell him. That we can talk things over and work together. That we can pull out. It'd please Lambda. And Leonora.*

He thought with strange interest of the sympathy between Leonora and Styles. Always she defended him, quickly and fiercely. "It's not his fault he wasn't ready when he had to take the full responsibility for things, Titus. He kept you on in school, didn't he? He was only doing what your father did to him, when he made you come back to the yard. He knew it was what your father wanted. Sometimes your . . . your smug superiority infuriates me, Titus."

The last of the fear was gone, and a peace of sorts came to him. The sonorous clock on the mantel told him it was after ten. Leonora would be wanting to go home soon, and he would walk her down the hill. He would tell her on the way how right everything was going to be. He had to make it right. What man could not change, he had to accept, and to remain sane he had to accept it without rancor.

The hoarse cry of a steamboat whistle came through the night. Titus rose quickly and crossed to the big bay window that overlooked the river. The Evart house was perched on a small ledge above the village, and now he could see the scattered lights. There was the merest trace of a moon, enough that he could make out the dark, hulking silhouettes of the yard and the looming mountains on the Washington side. Then the packet drifted across his range of vision, almost indistinguishable save for the pinpoints of light at its ports and windows.

Excitement crawled in him. Yonder was mystery, color, stimulation, and warmth, the strange, gay, moving life that the steamers knew. The boat had whistled for nothing more than a cheery salute to the sleeping landing, and acknowledgment of the works of Jonathan, and now it passed on behind a distant screen of willows.

Sighing, Titus turned toward the parlor, halting in the big archway to watch his mother and Leonora rearranging the bower of artificial flowers for the tenth time. Leonora had not noticed him, and in the unguarded moment her lips were parted, her face alight with eagerness, like a child's. Again warmth stole through him. Here, too, was beauty and mystery. His own. Then she saw him and turned, smiling.

"I was ready to call you, Titus. I'd better be getting home."

Her small hand in the bend of his arm, his long pace shortened to match hers, they went down the winding, frozen road. Yet, Titus found that he could not explain how he meant to settle things between himself and Styles, how he meant to find peace. And only once did she speak.

"It's going to be beautiful, Titus."

"Life?"

"Well, that, too. But the wedding, I mean."

He was conscious of disappointment, aware briefly of the essential evasiveness of her. He had never yet caught her and pinned her down to an exact man-and-woman understanding. The marriage meant the beautiful wedding and the lovely gifts and her coming to live in the big Evart house with its two servants. But that, he told himself, was the childish charm of her. He wanted to keep her so, a fragile, lovely child, enchanted and filled by the passing moment.

He did not go in, but kissed her at the front stoop, shyly, aware of the mechanicalness with which she met the gesture. Then he cut off toward the boat yard and walked aimlessly past it before he picked a devious route toward the house of Ewen Barcliff.

Huldah answered his slow rap almost instantly, giving him the impression that she had been expecting him. Yet she looked at him closely, saying: "Titus! Why?"

Without waiting for an invitation he stepped quickly inside. They regarded each other for a studious moment. Then, with a slight laugh, Titus said: "Didn't you guess I would come?"

"I was . . . afraid of it, yes. Titus, you mustn't."

He pushed past her and found a chair and seated himself elaborately. She wore a different frock from the one she had worn that afternoon, which meant that she must have fixed herself up a little. Excitement leaped in him. She had expected him, and now was only shy. She took a chair across the room from him, sat straight and tense in it.

"Your trick in sending Father down to see about those forgings was pretty obvious," she said.

He laughed again, but he was no longer quite so sure of himself. From the start he had at once felt a deep understanding of Huldah Dalquist and had been as deeply baffled by her. She and her father had been at The Landing only since spring. Fleetingly he remembered his first glimpse of her, in the early summer. He had been fishing, down below the point, and, looking up absently, he knew that he had not been observed, and he had stood watching her, the eternal river breeze pressing her skirt tightly against her slim legs, and a deep excitement had kindled in him. Then he had seen that she held a red rose in her hand. She had stood for a moment, looking out over the river; then, leaning forward, she had dropped the flower into the water and in deep absorption watched it float away. As she had turned away, she had seen him, but before he could move or call she had hurried up the bank and from sight.

He had put the story together by himself from what he heard later. She had been married for a year to a young packet officer, Herb Dalquist, who had died when the *Idaho Falls* had blown up, three years before, just above Vancouver. Herb Dalquist's body had never been found, with only the image of him left within her, as the image of her had, in that moment, impressed itself indelibly in Titus Evart's thoughts. The rose had been a message to Herb Dalquist, and what it had contained made a gnawing curiosity in Titus's mind.

They had met on frequent occasions since, at church and local parties. She had never mentioned the incident. Yet she had been aware of him, intensely aware of him, as he had been of her. Titus had sensed that, sensed the fire that was in her, too, knowing that he could direct it toward himself if he chose. And now he confessed to the many little ways in which he had tried to do this.

He said: "You don't want me to go, Huldah."

"What I want and what I have to do are different things. I know why you came, Titus, and I'm not flattered. You came to cheapen me. You thought if you could turn me into trash you could forget. In your way, you came to kill me."

It staggered him, the directness with which she went to the very core of the impulse that had moved him. Stubbornly, brutally, he said: "But I've got to forget you."

Huldah's laugh was low. "How simple men make everything."

"Simple? No. It's a hell of a way from being simple."

"Did it occur to you, even, what will happen if somebody saw you come here?"

"I was careful of that. Nobody saw me. And nobody will see me go."

She smiled bitterly. "Then I'm perfectly safe, of course. See! You're succeeding in what you set out to do. You've turned me into trash in spite of me. You've made your mind accept the fact that I'm a woman you can visit this way. A merry . . . widow."

He crossed to her, lifted her to her feet, and drew her to him. She resisted for only a moment, then suddenly let him take her lips. Finally she said: "If I thought I could make you free, Titus, I would. But it wouldn't be this way. You've succeeded with your murder. So go while you are as free as you are."

Enervation came to him with something of a shock, and he admitted what he had known from the start — that she was sincere. Obliquely he thought of the rose and the river, and savagely he said: "You were right. I was trying to destroy you to free myself. I had to see what was between us, and I've done neither of us any good. I'm sorry." And turning, he plunged from the room.

The sting of guilt and defeat were pronounced as he strode back up the hill toward the Evart house, which was now dark save for a lone light in what would be the music room. Titus's lips twisted bitterly, his passing sympathy for his brother destroyed. He was caught, caught, caught, and a part of his fury turned against Huldah, who had refused him escape, who had refused to reveal her mystery and make him free.

Leonora. Fleshless, immature spirit whom tomorrow he would marry. The rose, red as fire. He found that he was trembling, the old fear crawling in him again. There was no escape, no door, no light. Only the purple shadows of the mountains, forever beating into his nerves.

Halfway up the hill he halted and turned, letting his gaze sweep over the benighted village to dwell on the boat yard and the wood yard next to it. Fire. That was the obsession that had been in him, fire secretly set in the dry bark that would leap and growl and grow until The Landing was destroyed.

This was what he had feared — that he would do it. No one would know, and he would be free, beyond the grasp of family loyalty and responsibility. He shook his head as though the idea could thus be dislodged and hurled from him, and started on up the hill toward the house.

He was nearly up the stairs when Styles's crisp voice said — "Ty!" — and, turning, he saw his brother standing in the big archway below. Titus hesitated, then went back down, following Styles across the darkened sitting room to the music wing, where a pendant lamp burned low. Styles gestured toward a chair, himself taking the piano bench.

"I've made up my mind, Ty. You can save the yard. That's something I've always known and hated. You have all the gifts of Jonathan, but I've deliberately kept you from demonstrating them. You'll never have to learn what it is to face a responsibility you want to meet, only to find yourself not up to it. You're lucky, kid, and it's all yours. I'm getting out."

Titus whirled, shock and unreasoning anger spurting through him. "Mine! You're not shoving it onto my shoulders, now that you're finally up against it. I want no more of The Landing. For all of me, it can rot."

Styles smiled, fleetly and bitterly. "Angry talk, kid. You and I have always been caught in the trap of a dead man's works. I've played out my part. Now I'm at an end, and I'm free. Yours is beginning. Since you won't fail, you'll never be free. And maybe I'm not so poorly off, after all. Your ability will bind you. My weakness lets me out of it."

"But what do you mean to do?"

"I don't know yet."

Rebellion was crowding Titus close to recklessness. "Look here! I've got something to say about this. I hate the place. I'm getting out, myself."

"Leonora would never let you. She was born here, and she loves it."

"Leonora'll do what I say."

For the first time anger clouded Styles's eyes. "You're not making her unhappy, Ty. That I won't stand."

In sudden suspicion Titus rasped: "Are you in love with her?"

"I don't know. It was always you and she. Schoolmates, and then sweethearts. I've never even answered my own question about that. And now we'd better go to bed, kid. There's a wedding tomorrow, you know. Yours."

"Damn it, Styles, this is your mess. I tell

you, I'm clearing out."

"No."

The voice was Lambda Evart's, coming through the doorway. She entered the room in a faded silk wrapper, her faded eyes stern in the lamplight, her faded hair pillow-tossed. "I listened. I'll have no more of this talk, Titus."

Titus faced her. "I've reached the point where I don't give a damn about family pride. I don't give a damn if my father's work lives or dies. I don't give a damn about Styles's feelings. What right has a dead man to force me into something I hate?"

Lambda Evart took a seat, and in the lamplight her face looked strained and very old. "Because you are of his name and his blood. His responsibility becomes yours."

"Why?" Titus demanded. "Jonathan made his choice. He did what he wanted to do. What right did he have to plan the same thing for me? And Styles?"

"Because when a man creates something, he is responsible for it. The village was founded on your father's idea. After that, it became objective and no longer belonged to him alone. The village is people, people other than ourselves. There's a certain amount of coming and going, but most of them have been here for many years.

They've planned their lives around The Landing. Some of the younger ones, like Leonora, were born here. Unless we Evarts keep it going, their lives will be seriously disrupted. We put life here, and we have to sustain it. That is the relation between a man and his works. They've believed in us, and they've built on that belief. That's why Jonathan planned to have his work cared for after he was gone. That's why I've held his sons to it, cruel as it has seemed at times. I'll have no more of this talk. Do you understand, Styles?"

"Yes, Mother. I guess I always have."

"And you, Titus?"

"Yes, Mother." The tone was without conviction.

She turned in the doorway. "Good night," she said and was gone.

The red rose, red as fire. Titus waited until Styles had gone up to bed, and, when he left the music room, he turned, not toward the stairs, but toward the front door. Standing on the verandah, he heard the distant, reëchoing hail of a river boat. Resolution abruptly filled him.

What Lambda Evart had said was only the articulation of the things that had held him here, things he had felt without voicing, without clearly understanding. But things forged of the hardest steel. And yet what Lambda had said did not lessen the injustice. Jonathan should have known that one generation had no rights over the next.

The icy road beat solidly under his feet. Titus thought: *Styles himself claimed Jonathan is in me. And what Jonathan made, Jonathan could destroy. There can be no question of honor and duty to something that doesn't exist.*

All around him lay the sleeping village. Titus made his way carefully down a back road, skulked along a rick-skirted lane of the wood yard. He had the exact spot in mind, the little shack the wood handlers used when they came in out of the weather to get warm. The fire was kept banked with coal.

The shack was not locked, and he stepped into the dark warmth, his gaze going instantly to the low, glowing red of the draft. He knew without seeing that there was kindling in the big coal bin in the corner. Shavings. A neat little wigwam of sticks. A match.

He was quite calm. He made the preparations, dragged a match alive, thrust it quickly against the kindling so that the light of it would not glow too long in the windows. He stepped outside, pulling the door shut gently. His mind was bright with a sort of detached interest. This was the ideal spot. Wood was piled closely around the shack, most of it cut since early summer, dry and tinder-barked, and there was trash. It was near the ways with their heavy spillings of grease and pitch and resin. The wind was right, the fire equipment scattered, the water lines frozen. He had only to be in bed before the fire was discovered.

He skulked up the hill, went silently into the house. From his room he could see a faint pink glow in the yard. He stared in exultation. The works of Jonathan were finished. The dead man's trap was destroyed.

A whistle sounded on the river.

It was only the screaming of a steamboat, somewhere in the twistings of the great gorge, echoing and reëchoing through the dark, looming mountains.

"No! No! No . . . no!"

The elation went out of him like a bursting bubble, and in its place was sudden terror. He bounded from the room and raced down the stairs and into the outer darkness. He stumbled through the wood yard with his lungs bursting in his chest.

He was too late. Flames had burst through the roof of the little shack. Now the lack of means of fighting them was a horror to him. Cupping hands to his lips, he screamed: "Fire! Fire!"

It quickly grew incoherent. The village was long trained in sleeping with one ear set for the sound of whistles in the night, for the particular signal that meant a packet was putting in for wood. All Titus knew was that by the time he had found a pail, filled it with river water at the foot of the ways, and raced back up the long slope, other figures were hurtling through the light from the dancing flames that now completely enveloped the wood handlers' shack and were eating into the trash pile behind, toward the wood ricks. Running, shouting figures. Titus now had only a numb emptiness where his mind had been. A bucket brigade was formed. Fire leaped over two wood ricks, now, and they were logs burning in a giant fireplace.

"The whole landing'll go, sure as you're a foot high!" somebody gulped. "The wind's set for it!"

"And the very day young Titus was going to get married! What a shame!"

Then the figure of Styles loomed before him. "Get some men, Ty! We've got to move the wood away from the fire! That way, we can hem it in!"

The calmness in Styles's voice soothed him. Titus whirled, bellowing: "Onto the wood piles west of the fire! We've got to clear a ring around it!"

He was obeyed with energy. On all sides of the spreading flames the wood ricks began to dwindle, as men, women, and children picked up stick after stick and raced away. A half dozen men with wet gunny sacks stood solidly between the fire and the boat ways. Abruptly Titus realized that a conflagration had been prevented. Weakness hit him, his legs trembled, and he thought he would fall.

These people, half clad and disdaining the freezing wind, were fighting for The Landing. Here was what Lambda Evart had meant. *Styles*, he thought. *I've got to tell him that I set it.*

He moved around the burning area, hunting Styles. For the first time he saw Leonora. She was on her knees in the road, with others standing near, and something was stretched on the frozen earth. Titus swerved forward and looked down.

"Styles, Styles," Leonora was saying over and over again. "Styles."

"He's all right," a man told Titus. "He was working on the leeward side in all that heat and smoke. He wouldn't come out till we carried him."

Titus turned quickly away.

★ ★ ★

It was mid-morning when Titus, with a wrapped package under his arm, headed across the flat toward the river. There, squatting on the bank, he unwrapped the package.

It was a miniature steamboat. Titus squinted at it, hefting it, moving it from side to side. Then he placed it on the water. A little push, and it nosed out into the current. He watched it grow small in the distance, disappear at last in the hollows of the rippling surface. He straightened, turning, and saw the girl standing on the bank above him.

Huldah Dalquist came slowly down to him. "I saw you coming this way, Titus. I . . . I've worried about you. I followed you."

"I'm glad you did."

"What was it, Titus?"

"A model I made when I was a kid. I used to pretend I was its skipper. It's launched, at last. It's on the river."

"Are you sorry?"

"No. Glad."

"Then I want to tell you about the other time, when you saw me here. It was more than a sentimental gesture, Titus. It was farewell to things that couldn't be. It was facing the future. That's all a person can do."

Titus looked at her. "You heard the wedding's off, or you wouldn't have come here."

"Yes."

"Leonora told me, this morning. She didn't realize it was Styles until last night."

"They're suited to each other."

"And Huldah . . . I torched the wood yard, last night. I tried to destroy it."

"You never will, again."

"No. And now I want to forget it. And, Huldah. . . ."

"Yes?"

"I'm glad I couldn't murder you. I'm glad you're whole . . . and here."

She laughed. "It's cold. Let's go."

The *Boniface* came in at noon. It brought Jared Curtis, manager of the big Cascade Line, for whom the *Jenny* was building. That he had come in anger was apparent the moment he stepped into the office. Coolly, Styles beat Curtis to the jump.

"You've come to cancel the contract, and I wouldn't blame you. I admit that things were pretty bad, but we've reorganized. I was only acting as a sort of regent, Curtis, until my brother was ready to take control. He did so, this morning, and he's already made some changes. Maybe you noticed there is activity around here."

"I did." Curtis's eyes appraised Titus. "Always said the boy's the spitting image of Jonathan. You know, your father built the Cascade Line its first boat, did our repair work. That's why we worried along with you. I came to tell you the deal's off. But now . . . how soon can you have her finished?"

"A week," Titus said. "But don't credit me with being Jonathan. I guess he split himself between the two of us. Styles and I are running The Landing together."

Curtis got up. "Well, split or whole, the river needs men like Jonathan was. Always has. Put The Landing on its feet again, and there'll be business."

Through the window Styles watched the portly figure moving down toward the ways. "That was easy," he breathed. "A whale of a lot easier than I ever thought it would be."

Titus smiled. "Not so easy, I guess. Jonathan put a lifetime into getting that kind of an answer out of Curtis." His gaze strayed beyond to the Washington side and the tips of the mountains, glowing in the cold, winter sun.

Stagecoach Pass

The rider brought his horse along the drifted edge of the stage road, halting as he came abreast the Concord's high box. Stolid and preoccupied in the pelting, snow-laden wind, the driver had given him only half an eye until then. He swore in surprise and pulled down the three spans of straining horses. The big Sacramento-Roseburg stage settled to a clogged stop on the unbroken road.

"Dave," he said, "what are you doing down here in this weather?"

There was nothing above the mountain notch but a depth of black sky filled with the snow. Powdery mists moved along the high timbered walls of the cañon, torn and driven by the wind. Now and then the depressed evergreens spilled their burden in an abrupt, silent crash.

The rider was young. His cheeks were blue and stiffened as he stared up at the man on the box.

"Sam, you've got to get home. It's Ellen. She fell down the stairs, and had her baby. She wants you, and the doc says you ought to be there. It's bad."

The driver swore again — softly, because of the two women within the stage. He was a blocky figure, bundled, his big Jehu's hat flattened about ears and cheeks and held there by a knitted scarf.

"Dave, I'll be lucky to get this rig across the Umpquas before it bogs down." Sam Inset shrugged his head upward at the threatening sky. "It's only starting."

Dave Judd nodded. He was Ellen's older brother, and concern for her had flogged him the seventy miles from Looking Glass Valley. He kept staring up at his brother-in-law, his chilled face held in a grim set.

"This horse'll get you there before the road chokes up. If he plays out, you can swap for another. Ellen had a hard tumble, and it hurt her bad. She wants you, Sam . . . she needs you. I can put your stage through. You gotta go."

"Yeah, I ought to. I sure wish I could."

The man above was disturbed, and worry flooded his level, gray eyes. Sam Inset was the best man on this swing line of the Overland. If the three adult passengers had felt concerned about the brewing storm, the knowledge that he was on the box would have comforted them. He simply inspired confidence when you looked at him. And seeing him, nobody would doubt his love for the girl he had married a year before, who had gone back to the valley to visit her folks before the expected child tied her down. Dave could always feel Sam's kindly concern just by being near him.

The coach door swung open. A fat, female face, ringed with curls and under a poke-bonnet, was thrust out above ample shoulders and bosom. The woman stared at Dave, then lifted a querulous voice:

"Driver, what're we waiting for? We ain't got time for roadside gassing." The woman frowned as she listened for Sam's reply, which did not come. With a look of grim satisfaction she banged the door shut again.

Dave looked up at Sam, desperation swelling in him. He was dog-tired, for he had been in the saddle since the small hours of the morning, bucking the freezing wind — remembering a young mother's frightened calls for her husband, her frantic fear that the threatened blizzard would pin Sam down short of the Roseburg terminal. Dave was twenty, and his sister was two years younger.

He understood the struggle putting its signs on Sam's rugged face. His responsibility was to his passengers, no matter what. The high climb to Stagecoach Pass, the steep decline, Cow Creek Cañon, Cañon Creek Cañon — all lay ahead. Unconsciously Dave spread a thick-gloved palm and watched three, fat snowflakes land upon it. Sam would never get the stage clear through. He'd be lucky to reach the next station at Six Bit Ranch.

Sam Inset twisted the lines about the brake pedal and swung down. He stared at Dave an instant, then walked back to the stagecoach door. Dave dismounted and walked over there, hoping he could say something to help explain this thing to the passengers. The heavy woman who had objected to the stop sat beside an equally fat boy. On the forward seat was an old man who looked sick and half asleep, and who even now was paying no attention. Beside him sat a girl, as pretty as Ellen, and about her age.

Sam looked at them thoughtfully. "Just heard my wife's bad off . . . a six months' baby. If the snow gets much deeper, there's a chance we won't get past the next station. This here's Dave Judd, her brother. A mighty good driver. If you're willing, he'll get you as far as I could. And I'll try to get home."

The fat woman listened with rounding eyes and opening mouth. "Risk our lives to a kid that don't look dry behind the ears? Driver, are you out of your head?"

Sam shrugged, and his voice was like a sigh. "All right, ma'am. Just thought I'd ask."

The girl had listened with interest, and she said quickly: "Oh, please go." She stared at the fat woman a long moment, less critically than thoughtfully. "Who could want you to do otherwise?"

The woman opened her mouth and closed it without speaking. Then she shrugged in reluctant consent.

Sam looked at the old man, who still had not roused from his stupor. The girl said: "I'll speak for my father. He'd say for you to go."

"Thanks." Sam looked gratefully at both women and swung around.

He took Dave ahead to get out of earshot of the coach. "You'll be lucky to get to Six Bit Ranch, kid. But you got to do it. I have no right to do this, even for Ellen. But I got to do it, too. Don't care if they fire me. It's my passengers. I'm responsible for them. *You got to do as good as I would . . . or better.*"

Dave nodded.

"I'll get 'em through, Sam . . . I swear I will. You go on. I'll get 'em through in spite of everything."

Sam stared at him again, then turned toward the horse. The wind was filling the cañon now with an ever-insistent whine. Sam swung up and was gone, simply dissolving into the curtain ahead. Dave climbed to the box, his thoughts momentarily upon his brother-in-law. Six Bit Ranch was only six or seven miles ahead, though beyond the high mountain pass. Sam had seventy miles to go, and he'd keep going as long as he could, or stop and freeze where he was halted.

It was colder on the box, but Dave was used to that, riding against it as he had been doing for many hours. He unwrapped the lines, laced them through his fingers, and started the stage. Fatigue racked him, and he realized he was hungry, for he had eaten nothing since the night before. But he had a job ahead. He understood that. Though he had grown up around horses and knew their ways, he had never handled anything like three spans hooked to a big stagecoach — with passengers depending on him, and with the blizzard he had raced since leaving home still pitted against him. *"You got to do*

189

as good as I would, or better," Sam had said, and Dave fully understood the size of that order.

He tried to relax but couldn't, and he gave the horses and road ahead a steady stare. The California-Oregon road climbed on into the Umpquas. The spans were hock-deep in the snow, which kept up an unremitting fall. The animals were sharp-shod and kept their pace, though it was cautious and plodding. An hour passed, and then another; and from landmarks he could recognize through the thick and gloomy downfall, he knew they were nearing the mountain divide.

He felt better when they topped the rise, followed the ridge for a time, then started down. The weight would be off the horses; they could travel faster, and the snow was not yet threateningly deep. He had a wish to share his rising spirits with the girl in the stage. He had liked the way she had encouraged Sam to go. But the fat woman with the oversize young one — Dave scowled.

He heard the growling rumble long before he saw anything. The cold flooding his body deepened, and he was suddenly on his numbed feet staring down the long grade. There were high mountain rises above them again. But he could see only a short stretch of the road and the vanishing tracks of Sam's hurried horse. The big Concord was rolling easily now, slackening the traces.

Then he saw it — an enormous débris of snow studded with young evergreens. It lay deeply across the road, baleful, beyond the soft curtain of falling snow. It angled hard against the bald mountainside, which was scooped along the stretch whence it had come. The slide ran on below, disappearing into the cañon. But it had found a base down there and come to rest — piled high as his head across the road.

He pulled down the horses two lengths from the place, physical illness holding him motionless for a long moment. Then he fought down the stupor, shook off the fear. Securing the lines, he swung to the ground and walked forward. He hadn't needed to. It was real and not a figment of his over-wrought imagination, which he had actually hoped for a moment that it was.

You got to do as good as I would, or better. . . . Dave held to those words, fighting down the panic in him. The air was colder at this height, with a cutting drive. The snowfall was heavier, the carpet on the ground much deeper. The next stage station was probably only four or five miles ahead now, but it might as well be a thousand.

"What are we stopped for, driver?"

Dave hauled around to see that the fat woman had again opened the door and thrust out her head. The question had probably come on its own impetus, for she had recognized the obstruction, and horror had painted itself grotesquely on her heavy face. He walked back, but the woman had banged the door shut as if she, too, had hoped she could make it all unreal that way.

He was thinking furiously. He knew he would find shovel, axe, and other tools in the boot. But it would take unending hours to clear a way through that snowbank large enough to drive the outfit through.

The door opened again, and the girl got out. Beyond her, as she descended, Dave saw the fear-stupefied face of the fat woman. The little boy had been leavened by her emotion and was whimpering. The girl shut the door and walked to Dave.

"We . . . we won't be able to get to the station, will we?" There was worry in her voice, but it was controlled, as were the features of her striking face.

For some reason Dave felt the impulse to confide all to her, knowing she would understand and might even be as helpful as she had been before.

"Unless we try to walk," he said. "That'd

be risky. We'd have to climb up the mountain and around the slide, and it'd be deeper up there. We'd still have four, five miles to follow the road. Your dad . . . he looked kind of sick."

"He is," the girl said. "He's worn out. We were nineteen days on the Overland to Sacramento . . . three days more here. I . . . I'm afraid he couldn't stand an ordeal like trying to walk out."

Dave nodded, for he had sensed that at the start. He might help the fat woman and her boy wallow through, but this girl would never leave her father. He tried to make light of it and said: "I sure appreciated your coaxing Sam to go, miss."

She smiled slightly. "It was you, mostly. You looked so desperate. I hope he makes it and your sister will be all right." She was thoughtful a moment. "You came from the north. Do you know where Looking Glass Valley is?"

"Why, yes. I live there."

"Do you know the Gills?"

"I sure do. They're our next neighbors."

"Well!" the girl said. "Edith Gill's my sister. We're going out to live with them. I'm Amy McDowell."

"Well, now," Dave said, and for some reason he felt better. "Then you'll be next

193

neighbors, too."

Amy McDowell let a slight worry show. "If we get there. We'll freeze to death if we have to stay here too long, won't we?"

"Not if I can help it," Dave said, turning quickly to hide his face.

He swung into action, his mind settled, a plan roughly shaped. He opened the boot, removed some of the luggage, and took out shovel and axe. He hoped to discover a piece of tarp, and relief filled him when he did. Then he drove the stagecoach as close to the slide as the triple spans would permit. It was when he started to unhook the horses that the fat woman finally created the crisis he expected.

This time she descended heavily from the coach and stumped toward him.

"You aim to dig in and try and wait it out?"

"I aim to keep you warm as I can while I try to dig through."

The sunken eyes rounded, outrage climbing above the fear. "You couldn't dig through that drift in a month of Sundays. Why can't you notch a trail we could follow across the top on foot?"

"There's no telling what that slide's resting on, down in the cañon, ma'am. It could move again any minute."

"Better risk that than freezing to death."

Dave turned toward her. "The old gentleman's sick, ma'am. He couldn't make it."

The woman sucked in her lower lip and nibbled on it. She kept looking at Dave. "In a case like this it's your duty to save those as can be saved, ain't it? Me and the boy could walk it." She smiled, with a fawning touch to it. "With your help, that is."

"Ma'am, that'd still be a gamble. The best chance for everybody is right here."

Anger came then, and the puffed jaw shoved out. "Then help us across the slide, and me and the boy'll go on by ourselves."

"I can't let you, ma'am." Dave stiffened, and stared straight into her eyes. "You'd lose your head before you'd gone a mile. You just ain't got the stuff it'd take to get you through by yourself. And I won't desert anybody, no matter what."

The woman swung heavily, paused in long thought, then climbed back into the Concord.

Dave unhitched the horses and moved them around behind the stagecoach. Working the front wheels and straining with all his strength, he got the big vehicle as close as he could to the slide, angling it on the road until it stood across the wind. Then he bunched the animals on the upwind side so that, with mountainside, slide, and stage-coach, they formed a crude and windy box.

He took the tarpaulin and climbed to the deck of the Concord. Its panels were thin, and he draped the canvas on the windward side, the air current slatting it hard against the body. He secured the upper edge, then swung to the ground.

The axe was sharp, for drivers on this swing line often had downfall to clear from the road. He took it, with the shovel, and climbed gingerly onto the slide. The pelting snow with its vapors formed a curtain so thick he could not trace its course far down into the cañon. But the slide seemed stabilized, and he trusted himself to it and began to dig out one of the small evergreen saplings it had carried down.

In half an hour he had a fire started in the windbreak, with four saplings crosshatched upon it. The needles flared up, the brisking blaze throwing its heat onto the near side of the Concord. If he could keep this side hot enough, it would help warm them inside.

When the fire was going good, he got the foot-warmer out of the Concord. It was a large, oval tube that, in cold weather, was refilled with heated sand at each station. He placed the warmer beside the fire, close enough to heat quickly. The rough enclosure blunted the force of the freezing wind, and the mountain updraft carried the smoke away. He removed his gloves and warmed his hands as if he were washing them in the heat.

A childish voice rose in a wail: "Ma, I'm hungry."

Dave frowned, waiting for the fat woman's answer, but she kept quiet. He put the warmer back inside. Then he took the axe and began to work his patient way up the mountainside. Time after time he wallowed down again, dragging heavy limbs from the lowskirted evergreens. He built the fire a little bigger, and, when he put his hand on the outside panels of the Concord, he found them hot.

He opened the door and asked, "Warm enough?"

Amy McDowell smiled at him. "Why, we're quite comfortable."

The little boy scowled at Dave. "I'm hungry."

"If you want to chew on a snowball," Dave said, "I'll bring you one." He shut the door roughly.

He kept bringing in fuel until dusk began to thicken the obscurity of the storm. The signaled night lent a deep melancholy to the high mountain scene. Dave began to grow aware of a persistent dizziness within himself. He was exhausted, chilled too deeply to be warmed by his moments at the fire, and he needed food. From time to time he would take snow into his mouth and let it melt. Despite the numbness of his face, hands, and feet, a fever seemed starting in him. But his hardest work lay ahead.

When he was assured of fuel enough to last through the hours of night, he took the shovel. Ever since they had halted, he had no intention of trying to clear the road. But a ramp might be notched to the top of the slide, tramped and packed as he worked at it. And then it could extend across what he now knew to be a distance of two hundred feet. Then down again. A man might accomplish that — if he could hold out.

He swung into the rhythm of shoveling, and kept at it until the torturing cold drove him down to the fire. Soon it was full dark, the steadily continuing snowfall detectable only in the firelight and the soft impact on his face. He got his ramp built, and by that time it was tramped enough to give a possible footing to the horses. He began to extend the notch across the slide.

The boy started to wail, steadily, his complaint raveling into the low moan of the wind. As Dave descended the ramp, he felt himself sway for a moment. He opened the coach door with a rough jerk, but at that moment Amy McDowell spoke up.

"Ma'am, he gets his feeling from you. If you'd try to feel hopeful. . . ."

"He's hungry," the fat woman snapped, "and so am I. He's scared, and so am I. If we ever get out of this, I'll see that driver's fired."

"Ma'am," Amy McDowell said, and her voice was sharp, "the regular driver could no more have prevented the snowslide than this one. He could have done no more toward taking care of us. For your boy's sake, you ought to keep up your courage."

"He deserted us!" the woman screeched. "To die in the blizzard while he saved his own skin!"

"Lady . . . ," Dave began — then closed the door sharply before he said too much. But a numbing, new fear had climbed into him. She was going to make trouble, even if he succeeded in bringing them through. It would cost Sam his job. Disgracing him. *You've got to do as good as I would, or better. . . .*

Daylight found him on the far side and digging a careful descent. All night he had tramped back and forth to refreshen the fire, halting to warm himself only when he was too numb to go on. In some dimmed part of his mind he understood that he was wretchedly sick. It was a fact he didn't dare to face. And in all the long night there had been only one bright spot, when Amy McDowell emerged and insisted on relieving him at the shovel. He had refused, but the offer had strengthened him.

The downfall seemed a little less in the dawn, but maybe that was only the effect of the growing light. But Dave knew a good four inches had been added to the blanket already on the road. The horses might pull it, but there would be slow, hard going all the way down the mountain. There might be other drifts, as bad or worse than this, before they reached the little Cow Creek valley.

But the big, untested thing was still at this site. He couldn't see the bottom of the slide even yet. Was it stable enough to hold the weight and jar of the heavy vehicle and horses, even if they could cross without bogging hopelessly? It needed only to start moving again to sweep the whole outfit into the murky depths of the cañon.

He didn't dare pause to think about it. Returning to the stage, he began to lead the chilled horses forward and to hook up. Inevitably, the Concord door burst open.

"Driver!" the fat woman called shrilly. "You ain't going to drive us over that?"

"No ma'am," Dave said. "You're going to walk while I drive over light."

"What if it sweeps you down? How'd we get on?"

"Ma'am, you can worry about that. If it sweeps me down, I'll have my own hands full, and I won't be around to see the rumpus you'll raise when I get you through."

When he had hitched up, he helped the passengers out. The old man was still dull-eyed, sunken within himself, obviously played out. But if he had made a complaint yet, Dave hadn't heard it. Amy McDowell gave him a brief smile, and he saw that the hope in her eyes, which had never died, was bright now. She had trusted him. The fat woman stalked to the fire with her son, and appropriated the space on the warmest, downwind side.

"Luck!" whispered Amy McDowell as she passed close to Dave.

He didn't mount the box. Holding the reins, he stood on the upper side of the stage by the front wheel. The vehicle had been so close that by the time he was hitched the leaders stood upon the slide, the swing span on the ramp, and the wheelers at the bottom. He spoke gently, casually, to the animals. Numbed, they were eager for motion. They tightened the trace chains, and lifted the Concord out of its small drift.

They sank to their knees but kept their footing. The stagecoach plowed deep, but slowly moved to the top of the ramp. The drag lightened there, and the outfit crept out onto the slide, barely contained by the notch Dave had dug with so much labor. His heart was slamming; he held his breath, and the old dizziness haunted him every step across. Yet nothing moved but stage, horses, and himself. He let the outfit roll down the far ramp; then in spite of himself he buckled and fell into the untramped snow on that side.

He was up instantly and looked back to see the fat woman coming energetically across the slide, dragging her boy. Dave went back to help old man McDowell up the climb and across the top, Amy supporting her father on the other side.

Dave couldn't hold himself in, and he said: "Ma'am, you've had a real worry with your sick dad, and you never peeped."

She smiled across at him. "Don't call me ma'am, Dave. Not if we're going to be next neighbors. Will we get down now?"

"I can't tell you a thing beyond the stretch

I can see, which ain't much," Dave said. Then he added: "Amy."

He got his passengers inside, gathered his tools from careful habit, and put them in the boot. He felt better when he mounted to the box, and knew it was because of the girl he had found in the storm. But he was sick, though he still couldn't admit it fully. He started the spans on their wallowing way through the heavy snow, hardly daring to watch ahead for fear of what he might see.

It gave him only an edgy relief when he realized that distance was slipping behind. Then, when the road came abruptly onto the valley floor, exultation beyond repressing swept up in him, and he let out a yell. The flats presented even deeper drifts, but a half hour later he saw the muggy outlines of the stage station.

A man came onto the long-roofed porch, waving his arms in excitement. Dave brought the stage to a halt there, and for a moment thought he was going to pitch from the box. He managed to swing down, hearing the station keeper jabber: "Never been so glad to see anybody. Inset said to watch for you. Nearly rid out to meet you, but the missus said I'd only freeze afore I got there."

Dave knew he had to hold on a few seconds longer. The station man might remember, but the others wouldn't know. He supported himself limply on the front wheel, gasping: "Feet . . . hands . . . frost-bitten, I reckon . . . mustn't go in where it's warm . . . mustn't . . . rub snow. . . ." Then he slumped and fell into the soft carpet under his feet.

He wasn't surprised to learn he had slept the clock around. He found himself alone in the bedroom of this settler's cabin that doubled as a stage way station. His first thoughts were not of his passengers, who were safe now, but of Sam Inset. A wish that was close to a prayer filled his being. Sam must have got through. It had to be that way. And Ellen — she and her new baby had to be all right.

He saw his clothes over a chair, and they had been dried carefully. He stared at his hands and worked his fingers. He slid a hand under the covers and felt of his feet. They were tender but unbandaged. He had come through all right. Then he realized how enormously hungry he was. He got his clothes on, but the boots were too much. He padded down the stairway in his stocking feet, his whole body sore and aching.

The stairs came into the cabin's big living

room at one side of the huge fireplace. There was a crackling fire, and the room's warmth wrapped about him. He saw Amy and the fat woman and little boy seated about the room, and looking at him with varied expressions. The old man, he supposed, was resting up in bed somewhere, too.

The fat woman was scowling at him, but Amy smiled and said: "You look fine, Dave. Did you notice it's stopped snowing? Hasn't since yesterday afternoon."

"That's fine," Dave said. "Then we'll get on . . . if I can get boots on my feet. But first somebody's got to scare me up something to eat."

"You can ride as a passenger from here on, and without any boots if need be," Amy said. "The company sent a man out from Roseburg to help you. Your brother-in-law asked them to, after he'd seen your sister. So there's word . . . she's better. Having him there did that for her, I know."

Dave closed his eyes for a moment, then opened them. There was still the fat woman and the complaint she was going to make against Sam. The company knew of the defection by now. If a passenger raised hob, they could not treat it lightly. Then the station woman came in, and he went out to the lean-to kitchen to eat.

The relief driver and station keeper came in together from the barn. The company man had made a long, hard ride from the division point after the snow stopped the day before. Just because it was good to hear, Dave made him restate the fact that he had seen Sam, that Sam had said Ellen and the premature baby were better. Then he followed the other men into the big main room.

The company man looked at the women and said: "Well, we can roll again whenever you're ready, and nobody the worse for wear."

"Nobody the worse . . . !" the fat woman gasped.

Amy's voice cut her off. She had drawn the little boy to her and lifted him onto her lap. She smiled up at the company man. "You should have seen this brave little fellow. He was just awfully hungry, but after I told him how brave he was, there wasn't a whimper out of him."

The company man glanced skeptically at the boy. "He looks like a jim-dandy."

The boy stared back, then began to grin. "Gee whiz, it was fun!" he announced.

Amy sent a friendly look toward the fat woman, who was still scowling a trifle. "His mother's lucky to have him, and I'll bet she's proud. Think what the neighbors will say about the frightful experience we all shared together."

The fat woman began to smile.

They were almost ready to leave when Dave got a chance to speak to Amy alone. He gulped: "That was sure fine, and it surprised even her the way you turned her feelings right side out. I sure appreciate it, and so'll Sam."

Amy dismissed it. "We're going to be next neighbors. That means people who live close to each other. We're going to, aren't we?"

Dave pulled in a long breath. "I sure hope so," he said.

Renegade River

I
"Rough-And-Tumble Warning"

The late October sun laid little warmth on the rocky flat carved on the south shore of the Columbia. Its pallidness was a reminder of risk more than a source of warmth and comfort. For weeks there had been talk among the wagons that winter had now reached this high desert, just east of the last mountains already capped by snow. Beyond, on the Willamette, it was said, it would keep warm and secure much longer.

They had only to reach the valley, but there were these mountains stretching two thousand miles across the plains. Rarely less than a mile high, they had but one passage, which was the gorge of the Columbia. The emigrants had come this far on wheels grinding deeper the ruts of the Oregon

Trail. Ahead was water, churning wildly, and the emigrants were deeply uneasy while they waited for passage on one of the boats working the river.

Sam Emerick was neither worried nor deeply sympathetic. He had joined a group of wagons at the headwaters of the Snake, having tired of the dwindling beaver catch in the Rockies. Dropping south to the Oregon Trail from a rendezvous in Pierre's Hole, he had since heard much unfounded talk about the natural wealth and ease of the Willamette Valley. He had been there once with others in a daring and hopeless attempt to invade the broad, rich fur territory held by Hudson's Bay Company. The idea behind these wagons, now scattered from the rapids the voyageurs had called the Dalles to the rise of the gorge itself, was false, spread by overly enthused explorers writing of their journeys, magnified by dreamers, and the quickly hopeful ones. The truth was: no land upon the earth offered a man free and effortless sustenance.

From his camp Emerick could see the Lenox wagon. The girl was inexpertly peeling potatoes they had bought for a high price in trade goods from local Indians well versed in the art of extortion. On his previous trip, Emerick recalled, his group had been forced to pay the Wahclellahs dearly for portage beyond the impassable mid-gorge cascades, which had been mainly a tribute for being left unharried. The girl's brother was talking with a hard-eyed man dressed half in buckskin and half in cloth, who would be one of the boatmen exploiting this pitiful little army.

Emerick knocked the dottle from his pipe, rose, and strolled that way. He was long, loosely jointed, and again he felt the hint of winter in the air. Still less than thirty, his lean, brown face had the agelessness of hard experience. He stopped near the girl, smiling. "Your brother looks like he's making a bargain. I'd advise against that boatman, ma'am. I don't like the looks of him."

There was quick anger in the eyes that lifted to his. "I've told you before, Sam Emerick, that when we want your services, we'll hire them."

Emerick's face held its easy grin. "And I tell you again, they're not for hire, miss. I'm giving them to you. And you'd better tell Miles to send that buzzard packing, or I will."

Celia Lenox rose to her full height, the tin basin of potatoes still in her hands. Emerick couldn't resist studying those hands. Religiously worn gloves had kept sun and honest work from affecting them. Celia noted his half-amused scrutiny and stamped her foot.

"Why do you persist in treating us like babes in the woods?"

"Because you are, ma'am. Maybe you'll find it out slowly, or maybe it'll come in a rush. Miles Lenox has advertised his money too well, trying to buy an easy way into this country. I've heard him hinting that you're bringing a fortune with you, that he's going to be a big gun in the valley. Sweat's the real coin out here, and you and your brother are poor in it. Yet, there are those who would like to take your money away from you."

Emerick went on to where Miles Lenox stood talking to the boatman. Young Lenox was little more than twenty, a well-built, good-looking lad but showing the effects of much time spent indoors. As Emerick came up, he heard Lenox saying: "That's satisfactory, Minot. We'll leave all but a few things and start down with you in the morning."

Minot was a big man, unshaven, with a broken nose. He turned an unfriendly stare at Emerick.

Calmly, Emerick said: "He's wrong about that, Minot. I'm running this party. We won't be needing your boat."

Miles Lenox swung around, his eyes clouding. "Will you mind your own business, Emerick?"

Something came into Minot's eyes, then, suspicion and a crafty scrutiny of whatever he held in his mind. He grunted: "So this lad's been bothering you. Mebbe he needs a lesson." He turned suddenly, throwing a fast punch at Emerick.

The trapper stepped back. The blow didn't even come close. For a fraction of time, there seemed to be neither motion nor resentment in him. Then he came in with a savageness that drove the burly boatman backward. Minot covered his face with fists and elbows, yet a tremendous stamina was in him, and, balancing himself, he surged back.

People ran from the wagons, forming the inevitable ring. Emerick's fur cap came off, releasing a cascade of yellow hair. He still seemed loose as water as he side-stepped Minot's rush, hooking a short blow to the man's temple. Minot stumbled forward, weaving. He went to his knees, and, as he lifted himself, he brought a knife from between his shoulder blades. He stepped a quarter circle before Emerick, studying him. He held the knife's handle against his heaving chest, blade pointed. He made an unexpected motion, tossing the knife, catching it by the tip, back-swinging, and hurling it.

Emerick had sensed the trick and stepped aside. He feinted at Minot's belly, then drove in overhand. Minot tottered, already groggy. Then suddenly he collapsed on the ground.

A boy had picked up the knife, and Emerick took it, and broke its blade. The crowd scattered, and Emerick grinned at Miles Lenox.

"I hope that showed you something. A knife's a sneak tool. He's probably picked up the talk that the Lenoxes are wealthy. You'd be foolish to put yourself in his hands through a fifty-mile gorge."

"It shows me that you're meddling!" Miles Lenox bunched his muscles, slowly relaxing as he remembered how poorly Minot had fared.

"Dave Woffin's starting his cattle down in the morning," Emerick said. "His brother and son're taking the family down on a raft. He's willing to have you along with your horses and mine. Fix yourself a light kit, enough to last until we meet in the gorge in a few days. I've got the raft finished. In the morning, your sister and I'll start down with your wagon and equipment."

"I'll be damned if you will! What do we care about the equipment? We're going down before snow flies, which will be any day. We can buy a new outfit in the valley."

"Who from?" Emerick asked softly. His arm swept an arc against the hills rising back of the flat. "Yonder's a score of wagons and stoves and bedsteads the emigrants abandoned here. They're down in the valley now, hunting a new outfit. They won't get it until the ships can bring it around the Horn. They'll have to winter the best they can." He kicked Minot's prone body. "When this animal comes to, tell him to get to hell away from here or I'll make a better job of it."

Back at his own camp, closer to the water's edge, Emerick poured coffee from the blackened pot and drank slowly. He again fired his pipe and went down to the water. For a week he had been working on the raft that bobbed there in the water. It was shaped of twelve logs, eighteen inches through, forty feet long, bound by cross logs and lashed with ropes. It was only one of many under construction from the timber at hand, one of scores that, this season and previously, had dared the great gorge and its rapids.

Emerick looked at the Columbia and for

the first time felt doubtful. Not in his ability to penetrate to the valley but as to his responsibility. It would be far easier to take his saddler and two pack ponies over the cattle trail, and be done with the willful and foolish Lenoxes. Yet there was no abandoning them at this point. He had committed himself — though they did not know it and would gladly be rid of him — the night back there on the trail when Garret Lenox, their father, had died.

The raft was ready to leave. Emerick swept the stretch with thoughtful eyes. Mass disaster could easily strike here. Trains crossing the plains arrived, by necessity, in late fall. Here on the high desert, winter often descended quickly, hovering close upon the arrival of the travelers at the Columbia, ground weary from the long march.

The last mountains were always discounted until men viewed them for the first time. They were not mountains that could be crossed at will. They could not be crossed anywhere except by cattle and pack animals or through the river gorge. Many abandoned all equipment, made frantic by the imminence of winter, and took the trail. Others braved the river and rafted their equipment down.

Now that there had been several migrations, a cut-throat business had risen on the Columbia, practiced by men who had themselves passed dangerously down a season or so before. The fur companies' *bateaux* and fur barges had plied the river for years under the sure hands of the voyageurs. Now enterprising settlers from the valley came up with boats of their own, when the first columns of the season reached the river. They demanded terrific fees for taking down the settlers, often without equipment. They found many, crowded by desperation, willing to meet their terms. Of this class were the Lenoxes. Of the preyers was Minot. Emerick spat into the river and told himself that he would gladly have washed his hands of it but for Garret Lenox.

The man had been dying even when he started West, fired by that sad hope so many held that in the fabulous Oregon country they would surely find health. Lenox had been a man of means enough to have spoiled his children, yet a man to whom experience had given some wisdom. Emerick had felt a liking for Lenox, and they had frequently talked away long evenings.

When he had felt quite sure of himself, Garret Lenox had said: "I won't make it,

Emerick. I've known it for weeks. Will you keep an eye on these youngsters of mine? They're headstrong and pampered, but underneath they're sound. I turned everything I owned into gold, and it's in that cowhide trunk in our wagon. I trust a man with your eyes, Emerick. My children are mighty independent, so don't ever let them know I talked to you about it. But watch out for them, will you? Miles is the most impulsive, but Celia's got a temper."

II

"Downward Bound"

Rain came with the dawn, cold and sweeping, hard driven by the gorge's eternal wind. The feel of it ran nervously through the vast wagon camp, and rafts that were not quite ready shoved off in reckless haste. Emerick crawled out from his buffalo robe in the first dawn, sniffed the air, going at once to rouse the Lenoxes.

"I'll have breakfast with you this morning, then we'll break camp."

Eyes puffed with sleep, Celia Lenox looked very young as she peered at him from under the wagon flap. Miles had slept on the ground, beneath the wagon bed, and he turned in his blankets and stared up at Emerick. The trapper filled the day's first pipe, unhurried and friendly. They saw the unwonted activity in the camp, that had previously had little to do but wait, and were not insensitive to the pushing urgency in it this morning. It was get away day.

"We've got to go," Celia said. "I guess we'd better give in to you. Get dressed and start a fire, Miles."

Emerick tried for a breakfast fire that burned soggily in the driving rain. He abandoned it quickly, calling: "We'll eat anything cold you've got in your grub box, Celia." He was amused to note that Miles Lenox had slept in a night shirt, while most men out here removed nothing beyond boots and hat at night. He saw the worry in Miles's eyes as the lad watched the uneasy stir all about. Celia dropped from the wagon, excited now that movement was at hand.

They ate from the grub box, then quickly broke camp. They drove the wagon to the water's edge, where the raft was tied, and there unhitched again. Emerick took Miles and the Lenoxes' fine, though gaunted, team to where Dave Woffin was forming his six oxen for the long drive over the cattle trail.

Woffin looked at Miles with some distaste, grunting: "We're set to go."

Emerick brought up his saddler and pack animals, which carried his own possessions. He looked at Miles closely. "Just keep up with Woffin, and let him be boss. The trail's bad and climbs across the top of cliffs that're two thousand feet high. There'll be snow up there. The trail drops to the river again about half through the gorge. There's a ferry there to take the animals across to the north bank, where the way's better on down to the portage. If we miss you at the ferry, go on to the portage. We'll need your team to pull the wagon across. It's about five miles long and a hellish road."

Miles nodded stiffly. Emerick went back to the wagon at the edge of the water where the girl waited. She watched his approach with a guarded look to her eyes, as though doubt lingered about her placing herself and the family fortune in his hands. He saw her shrug slightly and knew that, while she would never like him as a man, she had resigned herself to what lay ahead.

Emerick removed the wheels from the wagon and placed them flat upon the raft. Next he begged help to pry and wrestle the running gear to lay upon the wheels, securely lashed to the raft. The loose items — the trunk of gold coin among them — were stowed here and there and fastened down. Thus laden, the raft sank deeply, and with Celia's and Emerick's own weight it seemed on the point of submerging.

Excitement beat in Emerick as he cast off, crying lightly — "On to Oregon!" — and it pleased him that the girl smiled at the cry. She was seated on a box in the bow, and he saw that her expression was carefully painted over an underlying anxiety.

The river formed a great horseshoe here at the Dalles, first bending south and north as it swept between the gorge promontories. The raft steered easily, but rough water lay ahead. He settled to the sweep. Boats passed them, downward bound and heavily loaded, and he wondered about Minot.

It was much colder out on the river, the wind building a chop that washed across the raft. The girl lifted her feet, at Emerick's suggestion, to rest them on a cross log. She stared closely at the river and twice she glanced about in uncertainty. It stopped raining presently. All the boats were ahead of them now, the rafts likewise lost from view, and loneliness spread over the water.

The chop worsening as early afternoon passed, Emerick steered shoreward, hugging to the bank. Within the gorge proper it was difficult to judge time, for shadows thickened, and the earth dragged tediously by. Often they would glimpse another raft — at times two — ahead or behind. Again in the closer twists there would be only themselves, sharing the savagery of the river and the silent indifference of the cliffs.

Emerick hoped to make the passage to the cascades portage in six or eight days, but there was no telling. A stern vigilance was required of him each minute. The land fell away on the north bank. It became a matter of picking water that offered the least danger, here of hugging a quiet, inshore reach, there of going ashore at some rapids to lead the raft along by ropes.

In the late afternoon Emerick let the raft sweep behind an off-shore rock, misjudging the speed of the current until he felt its quickening effect at the stern. Water washed over the raft and climbed to his ankles. There was the sense of their being entirely without support in a river half a mile wide. Celia screamed and in that second Emerick was on his feet. They were in quieter water before he realized he had been laughing.

He looked at the girl. "Are you all right?"

Celia swung on the box, her cheeks white. "Sam Emerick, I hate you!"

The skin across Emerick's cheeks grew tight. "That's not a revelation, ma'am. Did you get wet?"

She refused to answer, turning to face down the gorge again.

Deepening shadows warned Emerick

night was at hand. He planned to keep traveling until they found a camp a raft ahead had made, where Celia would welcome the presence of others for the stormy night. Yet they came upon none, and he began to realize that the raft close ahead was traveling dangerously late in the day. He headed toward the north shore.

"We'll keep traveling until we find somebody else!" Celia warned sharply.

"We'll make a camp and flag the raft behind." Emerick nudged the shore, and, when the girl made no move to snub in, he let the sweep go, picked up the rope, and leaped to the bank. He took a turn on a boulder and let the raft's stern swing downstream, where it readily idled.

After a moment the girl rose and let him help her ashore. He said: "We'll get a fire going, first. That'll draw the next bunch in. Plenty of room here, and enough scrap wood. I'd guess we've come six miles. Better than forty to go."

He collected downfall from the rough, high bank, whittled shavings, and got them a fire. Celia came to the fire, holding out small hands, and Emerick saw she was shaking from cold. He whistled lightly as he unpacked gear and brought the equipment to the fire.

"Why can't we go faster?" Celia asked.

"We've got to get there right side up."

Emerick had supper ready by the time full night fell, and still their camp had brought no one in from the river. At last he got his hand gun and gave it to Celia. "Now relax and eat."

It was going to be a miserable camp, Emerick knew, but he climbed high on the slope and brought back boughs from the evergreens, allowing them to steam by the fire until they were dried out. He made the girl's bed in a spot sheltered from the wind by boulders, giving her his buffalo robe. At last he said: "Turn in. I'll smoke a while."

He sat facing the river. The sky held only a trace of light, seeping through clouds like flossed wool. The breeze stiffened, and Emerick smelled rain. He heard the sound of Celia's retiring, and, remembering the gun to which she had clung, he grinned without mirth. Disapproval of the gulf between them was mounting in him. He was a mountain man, geared to the conditions in this country. Perhaps that was why she hated him, but she could have let the feeling be without fear of him. He wanted nothing from soft and petulant women; he wanted only to reach the valley and be rid of his obligation.

On this shore the cattle trail would be across from them and high above. There would be snow up there. He thought of Miles Lenox and felt a moment's sympathy for Dave Woffin. Drowsiness hit him, and at last he got his bedroll, threw on more wood, and bedded down by the fire.

Rain came again before dawn, slanting on a freezing wind. Emerick climbed out of his damp blankets and went to Celia's rocky shelter. She did not stir. He arranged the buffalo robe to cover her entirely and used his hand axe to make a trench at the head of the bed. Satisfied that she would keep dry, he threw more fuel on the fire and sat by it, his own unprotected bedding now soaked.

By daybreak Emerick knew they would be unable to resume their journey immediately, for the broad expanse of the river was a wicked chop for which the clumsy raft was no match. He heard the girl stirring as morning came on, and presently she emerged from behind the boulders. She did not look at him, only stared at the rough river.

"So that's what we'll have for today."

"We'll have to stay here until it's settled a little, ma'am."

She started to say something, but thought better of it. Emerick handed her a cup of coffee and a slab of bread. "Too wet to cook anything but soup, and we lack the bone for that."

The girl said: "You enjoy showing off what a hardy character you are, don't you?"

Morning wore away, the sputtering fire doing little to comfort them. Loneliness pressed in until even Emerick felt its depressing effect. He harbored a certain sympathy for the girl, but her stubborn refusal to talk, except for rare, barbed shots, kept a clamp on his tongue. At ten the rain stopped, but the wind held.

It was the girl who first saw the boat that appeared below at noon, coming slowly upstream. She jumped up in excitement, waving her arms frantically.

"Better wait till you see who it is," Emerick growled.

"I don't care who it is! I want to get away from here!"

She kept waving and calling, and finally the craft slanted across. It was small, with only two oarsmen. The man forward wore a plainsman's hat. Emerick could not see the second clearly for a few minutes. Then he turned, catching up a rifle.

III

"Camp No. 2"

When the small craft was a hundred yards off shore, Emerick sang out: "Stand off, Minot! Keep on rowing!"

The rowing ceased, the boat drifting westward on the current. Minot's face showed the battering it had taken, and he stared at Emerick with hard eyes. "So you're holding Miss Lenox a prisoner!"

Celia said to Emerick: "Let them come in!"

He turned to stare at his gun in her fist. Her eyes were steady, triumphant. "I'm going down the river, Emerick! Let them come in!"

"You fool!" Emerick breathed.

"Lower your rifle!" Raising her voice, she called: "Come on! He's holding me forcibly! I want to get away!"

Minot dug an oar then, willing to take his chances in the strange deadlock. After a moment, Emerick lowered the rifle, shrug-

227

ging. The boat nosed the bank above the bobbing raft, but the two men did not leave it.

"If you've got any valuables, miss, you'd better bring 'em!" the man with Minot called. "Don't trust 'em to that gent!"

Emerick saw uncertainty stir in Celia's eyes. "Well, Abe Rust," she said, "I thought you were anxious to get me down to the valley and pick your claim. Do you just enjoy riding the river in weather like this?"

Rust looked startled, and the trapper remembered having seen him with the emigrant train. "Minot offered me good wages to help on his boat. He's going to help me pick a claim when the season's over. So there's no rush." Rust laughed nervously.

Minot scowled. "Bring anything you want to keep, ma'am, and we'll turn back down from here. Glad to help you. They'll string Emerick up if he dares come down to the valley after I tell 'em about this!"

At last the girl swung her gun from Emerick to the boat. "It seems to me you're both too anxious about my valuables. I'll take my chances with Emerick. Shove off!"

Rust let loose with a string of profanity. Minot made no move to stop him, staring first at the girl, then at Emerick. Presently they swung the boat about and resumed their slow progress upstream.

Emerick grinned at Celia. "You changed your mind fast, ma'am."

She shrugged, not meeting his eyes. "I guess you were right on that issue. That man Rust decided me. He was a bad actor on the crossing. Miles was fool enough to talk big to him, until I made him shut up. I thought then that Rust showed more interest than was necessary in our exact plans."

"Then he's the one who tipped off Minot, and they threw in together on it. They mean to have your money, ma'am. We'll be fighting them all the way down."

"It's my fault for letting them find us. I'm sorry."

Emerick turned to study the river. "We've got to change camp, and it looks as calm out there as it's likely to get today. We'll start again."

It was bad on the river. They covered only three miles in what they had left of daylight. Emerick made camp on the south shore that night, picking a spot below a promontory, where they were sheltered considerably from the driving wind. Yet it was as miserable as the preceding night had been. Celia showed a marked nervousness as darkness pressed into the gorge.

"Those men, Emerick?" she asked. "Do you think they'll try to jump us again?"

"They'll have to locate us again, first. They're fooling around some place upriver."

Fatigue was telling on Emerick. His bedding was still soaked, and even the girl's was damp. He dozed by the fire, sheltered somewhat among the rocks. Morning came without their being disturbed.

"Better weather," Emerick said when the girl wakened. "At the risk of your slapping me, may I cry . . . on to Oregon?"

Celia smiled. "I'm too cold and tired to slap you, Sam Emerick."

He was partly pleased that she was relenting toward him, now that it had been clearly demonstrated that he had been right about this gorge passage from the start. They made good progress, camping at night where a river flowed northward into the Columbia. It had stopped raining, and they cooked a hot meal, and afterward Emerick was cheerful.

"Tomorrow, if we don't hit trouble, we ought to reach the ferry. That's where we'll meet Miles and Woffin, if they haven't beat us and gone on. Which I doubt. The weather's been even worse up there on the cow trail."

Minot and Rust were never out of Emerick's mind. He knew they would keep trying until they had what they wanted. They were only waiting for the advantage.

It was mid-morning when Celia called: "There's somebody trying to wave us down! It's a woman!"

A skirted figure stood on the south shore, waving frantically. A raft bobbed in the current before her, heavily loaded. Emerick shoved the sweep over and made in. A middle-aged woman had waded a little way into the water in her desperation.

"My man's down sick!" Her words tumbled over one another. "Our raft swamped two days ago, and he nigh killed himself making shore and saving our stuff. That night he got sick. I can't handle the raft alone. Yesterday a boat came up. I know they saw us, but they wouldn't stop."

Emerick's gaze met Celia's. "Rust and Minot."

She nodded. "Can we take these people with us, Emerick?"

He shook his head. "He'd be worse off than he is here. We'll have to get the ferryman to come after him. The other boats'll be working again, now that the storm's over, but we can't be sure they won't be like Minot." He turned to the woman. "We'll go right on, ma'am. A boat'll handle better and travel a lot faster than a raft. It's your man's best chance."

They made good distance that day, yet darkness caught them short of the ferry. So they went on to the point where the crude boat carried the cattle of the emigrants across the Columbia. The trail swung down the valley of a side river, near their camp of the night before, then west again to the base of an impassable mountain of basalt that loomed hard above the water. The north shore broke less precipitously back, beyond here, affording a trail on down to the portage.

Emerick tied up above the landing and climbed to the cabin above where lamplight shone through the oiled, undressed deerskins used as windows. Barstow, the ferry man, was a strapping fellow. A younger edition of himself sat at the table, eating. Emerick explained about the sick man. "I wish you'd try to get him through. I understand there's a doctor at Fort Vancouver."

Barstow nodded. "There is, but I'd have to wait till morning."

"Well . . . if that's the best you can do. A cattle party was to leave word if they passed here. Woffin and Lenox. You ferry them?"

"Nope." Barstow scratched a whiskery jaw. "Lots of folks get sick coming down the gorge. Getting so the buzzards hang around it."

"It's a tough one."

"Shucks, there'll be towns strung along it, some day. Make camp by the boat, if you want to, mister. Can't offer anybody hospitality, for it's all we can do to keep supplies on hand for ourselves. Your friends might've had real trouble in the mountains. It was wild up there during the storm, I guess."

Next morning Emerick watched the Barstows start upriver after the sick man, the crude boat plying slowly against the current. Emerick began to fret about Miles and Woffin, recalling the lad's physical condition and willful ways. The desire was in him to scout the cattle trail, but somebody would have to watch the raft and the Lenoxes' trunk.

At ten o'clock, Celia said: "Emerick, something's happened to them."

At last Emerick said: "Would you stay here alone while I scout back a ways?"

"I'd rather do that than keep worrying."

Emerick took the trail, moving fast. At the end of an hour he was working up the side valley by which the cattle route dropped from the heights. He struck snow presently, and it showed no marks of recent travel. At noon he topped a sharp rise and across a flat saw a slowly moving party. It was breaking trail through the fresh snow. Emerick could detect only one man. He slogged forward.

"What happened to Lenox?" he called.

Woffin, leading a train of oxen and horses strung together, jerked a thumb over his shoulder. Emerick closed the gap between them.

Woffin managed a sour grin. "He's just played out," he called. "I bundled him up good and tied him on your horse. Has he been a damned saddled sore! Seen anything of my family?"

"The ferryman didn't know, but they must've gone on down."

Lenox was lashed in Emerick's saddle, keeled forward onto the animal's neck, blankets about him. He was not unconscious and, hearing the talk, lifted himself, staring at the other two with dull eyes.

Emerick grinned at him. "Shucks, boy. Get you down to camp and warmed up good, and you'll be all right."

They reached the ferry in late afternoon. The ferryman had returned with the sick man and his wife and had gone down to the portage. Celia showed grave concern for her brother, but Miles perked up under the heat of the campfire and considerable boiling coffee. The girl turned to Emerick. He could see pride in her eyes.

"Minot was here again, with Rust and two others. I kept them from landing at pistol point. They went on down."

Emerick stared at her. "Four men? Then he's picked up a couple of hardcases to help. And if they went down, it means they'll be laying in wait for us."

IV

"Last Haul"

It took two days to ferry the animals to the north shore. The river was a mile across, Emerick guessed. He and Woffin helped with the rowing, while the Lenoxes remained at the south landing to watch their possessions.

Once the six oxen and three horses were on the far shore, Dave Woffin looked at Miles Lenox. "You better go down on the raft, boy. I've got enough on my hands with these critters."

Miles said: "I'll hold up my end from here on. I'm going with you."

Woffin did not protest, and there was friendliness in his eyes. Privately he had told Emerick that Lenox had made a real fight of it in the heights, but his strength had failed him, and, though he had carped and tried to act a proud part beyond his abilities, he had shown sand. The way was easier ahead, and the animal train was soon out of sight.

Emerick crossed again with the ferry boat, and by noon they were on the river once more. A few boats passed them, going up for more settlers, while one overhauled them, coming down with a full load. "Tomorrow night the portage," Emerick told Celia.

They camped that night where the gorge walls slanted low on either shore, and a threatening rain held off. Yet Emerick woke next morning to find a heavy frost upon the shadowed reaches and the ground frozen hard. It set a new uneasiness in him, for they were days yet from the valley. They ate a hurried breakfast and swung out into the current.

Late that afternoon they reached the upper landing at the cascades. The raft of Dave Woffin's family was waiting there, and Woffin had just got in with the animals, and the presence of so many people in high spirits pleased Emerick. He saw Celia run to Mrs. Woffin.

The wagon road over the portage was five miles long, climbing better than four hundred feet in that distance. It had been ground to a river of mud by the wagons that had passed here. Emerick saw that, although it had frozen the night before, during the day it had thawed, until the mud was slippery as gumbo now. Men worked late that night, unloading the wagons, replacing wheels, and reloading the equipment.

"We better go through together," Woffin told Emerick. "You can rope your horse onto the Lenox wagon, and, if they stick, I can help you. My six bulls've got a lot of ginger in 'em."

The last haul started at daybreak. Emerick allowed the Woffin outfit a good start so that they would not be piling on each other. Woffin's wagon rocked and skidded, so that the women and children climbed out, wading thereafter through cold mud that came nearly to their knees.

Miles drove the Lenox wagon. Celia remained behind to walk with Emerick. It was tough going, the wagon wheels striking rocks buried in the mud and canting over, the hind wheels skidding. By noon Emerick saw they were holding Woffin up.

"You go on," he told Woffin. "We're coming all right, but slow. Go ahead and get your camp built and your kids warmed up again." Woffin's wagon slowly pulled away.

An hour after that the Lenox wagon climbed across a knoll and started down the curving road beyond. The draft horses, assisted by Emerick's lighter animals, drew the wagon along easily. Emerick was between the wagon and the bank when he heard the grinding of the metal tires. The wagon's front wheels swiveled hard, the tongue sweeping toward the bank. The near horse was knocked from its feet, rolling over the tongue and piling against the other animal in a tangle of harness and threshing legs.

The hind wheels went about, and the wagon tottered uncertainly. Emerick swore softly, helpless as it went over with a crash, the two lifted wheels turning idly, streaming mud. The other animals were not thrown, yet they reared and piled in fear. Miles Lenox crawled out of the wreckage and over the wagon side.

Emerick waded the jelly-like mud, probing the road bottom with his feet. He found the rock, and it was too large, and his eyes narrowed in wonder that it should be here.

"Woffin couldn't help hitting this. He'd have left someone behind to warn us."

"It wasn't there when Woffin passed, Emerick," said a voice from the top of the brushy bank. "We just rolled it in there. Drop that rifle and step on it, so it sinks."

A belt gun in his hand, Minot stood at the top of the bank, Rust beside him with a rifle. Two other armed men slid down the bank, ahead and behind, wading toward the wagon.

"Drop it, Emerick!" Minot warned again.

Emerick let the rifle slip from his hand and saw it sink into the gumbo. Minot slid down the bank, Rust following.

"You're dropping your pretext," Emerick said savagely. "You're making it open armed robbery. You threatened to get me hanged. Do you know what this will do for you, if you try to stay in the valley?"

Minot shrugged. "I know, and we ain't staying. They're ships running down the coast, Emerick. I hear there's plenty pretty *señoritas* in California. This fool kid bragged he was going to start the biggest store in the valley. That takes a lot of money, so we figure it'll be worth it. Just don't make any trouble, Emerick. Rust, paw through that mess of junk and see if you can find where they been keeping it."

Rust plodded around the wagon and began to examine the littered boxes and bundles. Minot remained close to the bank, his gun on Emerick. The two new members of his group spread out on either side.

In a moment Rust called from beyond the wagon: "Cripes, there's more damned stuff here! Make that kid talk, Minot! Can't tell when another boatload might get in and the passengers come footing along."

Miles Lenox let out a sound that struck Emerick dismally as a whimper. Minot looked at the lad with brightening interest, then strode toward him, the liquid mud banking ahead of his legs. He slapped Miles hard across the face.

"Where is it?"

Miles Lenox straightened suddenly. Miles's hand struck away Minot's gun, a fist shooting out to smash the man's bearded mouth. Minot tried to step back — and he fell. Lenox landed on top of him, and they rolled in the mud.

Emerick took his long chance meanwhile, ploughing toward the man who stood a dozen paces down grade from him. The man fired too fast and, with no time to reload, clubbed the gun. Emerick dodged a swing of the gun, drove under it, and knocked the man down.

The gunman slid from under him, heaving out of the muck and throwing the gun. It glanced off Emerick's jaw, the jar going through the trapper's head. Emerick hit him again, reaching for his throat and holding on, remembering the two armed men remaining and not giving them a chance for a shot. He choked until this man lay still, then clambered up.

Celia Lenox held Emerick's belt gun on Rust and the other man, who had not suspected that she had it. Yet she was in a ticklish position, for, though she had made them drop their guns, they were widely separated and, one by one, moving up on her. Emerick saw the whiteness of her cheeks and knew she could not force herself to kill. The men saw this reluctance and kept moving in.

Lenox came out of the mud. He saw his sister's danger and ploughed forward. Minot's remaining pair rushed Celia then, and at last she fired. The man on her right went down as Rust hit her with his shoulder, knocking her sprawling. Miles and Emerick bore in.

It was over quickly. Rust had little taste for making a lone fight. Celia's victim climbed up, cursing, holding his right shoulder. The weapons they fished from the road bottom were too choked with mud to be used again. Minot and the man Emerick had choked were dead, and they bound the other pair with ropes.

It was a tough job getting the harness untangled and the wagon righted and the scattered load in its proper place again. Yet, they climbed the crest in late afternoon and, halfway down, met Dave Woffin coming up with two spans of oxen to see what had held them up. He hooked on, and at the end of another two hours they were at the Woffins' camp at the lower end of the portage.

Emerick went down to the river to wash, and, before he had reached the water, he saw that Celia was following him. He waited. The girl clutched his shirt and pulled him around to face her.

"Before I clean up, I want to know if I look enough like a pioneer woman to suit you," she said fiercely.

Emerick slowly began to laugh. She was covered with mud from feet to head, and he saw that she wore it proudly. He lifted one of her hands, the small hands that once had been so carefully gloved, and saw that they were red and raw. The smile left his face, and he looked at her carefully, softness coming at last into his eyes.

"I was wrong, Celia. A woman has a right to be lovely. You'll be lovely again."

She nodded. "I mean to be, Sam Emerick. We're safe now, aren't we?"

"I reckon, ma'am. It's an easy boat ride from here on to the valley. There'll be boatmen up tomorrow after business. You'd better go ahead, ma'am. Miles and I'll bring the raft through the rapids and your things on down. He's all right, too, ma'am."

Celia stamped her foot. "When will you stop calling me *ma'am?*"

"You're a rich woman, Celia. Miles will start his business and prosper. I expect to get me a little claim . . . farm a little, trap a little. There's no grand future in it, but it's all I want."

Her eyes came up to meet his. "Sam, you told me real wealth was in work and courage and stamina. I'm rich only if you think I have enough of that. Let Miles have the money for his business. I'll stay with the raft. I'd like to take my chances with you."

Emerick saw that she meant it, and all his restraint broke. He lifted her hands and started to speak, but she came into his arms, and words became unnecessary.

East Ain't West

When the cow horn sounded over on Crockett's east bank, Clem was canted back in a chair, half asleep and idly pondering what old Doc Garrick had told him that afternoon. It was dark on the river, though pleasantly warm, and, as he opened his eyes, Clem saw the lights of the other half of town in mild annoyance. The whole town and countryside seemed to know that the doctor had warned him against overexertion and to have organized against him.

The horn sounded again, and, with a deep sigh, Clem rose and tramped across the landing float onto the little ferry scow. The quiet waters of the Sandy rippled as he put up the guard chain, cast off, lowered his hind leeboard, and drifted out into the stream, the trolley squeaking as it rolled on the overhead cable. It would have to be oiled, in time — another infraction of the rest cure Doc Garrick had ordered for Clem.

His foot holding down the leeboard handle, Clem thought about it again. Doc Garrick had practiced half a lifetime in the town of Crockett, which straddled the Sandy, and was trusted, respected, and well loved. To Mrs. Garrick the sawbones would sometimes confide the real secret of his success. "When I can't find anything wrong with 'em, I give 'em what they think they need."

Clem Shays had naturally never overheard one of these confidences. All he knew was that he had been feeling anything but perky the past couple of months. Finally he had gone up to see the doc. After a lot of business with funny-looking doodads, the doc had said: "Reckon you're just run down, Clem. Take it easy for a while. Eat what you like and all you like and get all the rest you can."

Clem had left the doctor's office knowing that the doc had hit the nail on the head and that he was already on the road to recovery. The eating part he could handle, with his bachelor's privilege of cooking what he liked, the way he liked it, then eating it all by himself. But the resting, which appealed to him even more, was something else again. In the ferry business a man was on call night and day. True, hours often passed without it being necessary for him to stir away from his chair on the shady side of his shack by the landing. But you couldn't tell. It was this uncertainty that frazzled a man.

As the ferry scow nosed toward the east bank, Clem saw half a dozen figures huddled on the darkened landing slip, blotting out the lantern over there. At ten cents a head for foot passengers, this disturbance would at least be profitable. Clem snugged in, and the passengers hurried aboard.

"Make it snappy, Clem, for Pete's sake," a voice exclaimed.

Clem's annoyance mounted. He did not hurry as he performed his chores, then changed leeboards, canted the scow, and started back. He had a strange idea that his passengers were making a noticeable effort to keep their faces turned away from him, and they were all forward, as far away from him as possible. Less worried about his health, Clem would have chuckled about this.

The river was the dividing line between Crockett's better and worse selves. A wave of reform, a couple of years before, had driven the honkatonks to the east side. Behind Clem, at this moment, gambling, drinking, and hell raising were in full stride, while in front of him a shining example of civic propriety was already abed and dreaming. This segregation was a compromise for the time being, with the reform force in west Crockett already marshaling to continue its clean-up drive. East Crockett gave Clem a lot of night business, though this was only a fraction of his patronage, for through the iniquitous part of town ran the main wagon road to the Little Mano country and its prosperous cattle raising and agriculture.

Amused by this party of skulkers, Clem let the leeboard spring up, paced forward, and was at the chain when the double-ended scow nosed in, thus preventing their jumping ashore ahead of him.

"It's a mighty fine evening, Mayor," he remarked with a grin.

There was a sound that was like a snarl. Mayor Gabe Gilroy waited until the others had scurried up the bank. He was a big man, and he stabbed Clem in the chest with a stiffened forefinger.

He said, his voice harsh: "Was there any talk about this, it wouldn't surprise me none if Roscoe Froebel didn't make it a personal matter." He held out a bill.

Clem carried the bill to the lantern on the landing, and, when he saw that it was ten dollars, he handed it back. "You owe me fifty cents."

The mayor took back the bribe money and counted out some silver. "Don't let that ornery honest streak of yours get you into trouble, Shays," he warned, and clomped up the bank.

Clem tied up and returned to his chair, worried suddenly. He didn't understand it all, but he was beginning to realize he should not have played that prank. Gabe Gilroy had got himself elected on the reform ticket. There were those who said that he was exacting tribute from east Crockett, and there were others who answered that he was also indulging in its pleasures on secretive occasion.

That had been a prize coop of turkeys on the ferry, just now. Not only the mayor, but a couple of aldermen and the postmaster, the barber, and the hardware man. This was new business for Clem for, while the young bucks openly crossed back and forth on the ferry, there was a place half a mile up the river called Married Man's Crossing where the more discreet ones removed their shoes and waded. Clem had always thought that the mayor was wetting his feet in this wise, if what they were saying about him was true. The six men must have gone over that way, for Clem had seen neither hide nor hair of them until just now. Why they had resorted to the ferry to return he did not know.

What really worried Clem was Gilroy's reference to Roscoe Froebel. Froebel ran things in east Crockett and was a bad actor, a very poor man to cross. The mayor had meant to imply that, if this got out, Froebel would be apt to investigate the leak. Clem Shays had no hankering for such an investigation. Once in a while, in these parts, a man was found with a slug in him and a record of having talked or acted out of turn, which had been one of the reasons behind the demand for reform.

Resting, under these circumstances, might prove a mite difficult, Clem realized, and he decided to go to bed. A gaunt, tall man just short of middle age, he tramped down to the landing and rechecked the mooring lines. He went into the shack, shucked off his clothes, and crawled into bed.

He was asleep instantly and in a matter of minutes found himself at a shady, little pool that only he knew about up the Little Trunko. There was a dark shadow in its crystal waters; then he saw a whopper of a cutthroat trout, nibbling toward the surface. In glee he prepared to cast. Suddenly a woodpecker, over on a jackpine, set up the loudest racket Clem had ever heard, and the trout disappeared in a swirl of milky water.

Clem realized presently that somebody was knocking on his door. Grumbling, he crawled out of bed and went in his underwear to open it. A voice said: "Howdy, Clem. Let me in, quick."

Clem let his visitor in and closed the door before he struck a match to light the lamp. It was Marshal Kelsay, the town law-enforcing agency, and he looked riled. A stocky man with immense shoulders, Cocklebur Kelsay had been elected on the reform ticket also, and he was one of the town officials who had meant every campaign promise he had made. When the marshal set his mind to anything, he never took it off until the business was finished.

"Did you cross Gabe Gilroy and Tink Deward and that bunch?" Kelsay demanded bluntly.

Clem stared, unable to keep his alarm out of his face. "Why, I crossed some people, but it was awful dark, Cocklebur."

The marshal waved an impatient hand. "Clem, you did. I knowed they was over there, and I set a trap for 'em at Married Man's Crossing, but they got onto it, somehow. That's the only place they could get across without risking drowning, and the mayor ain't one to do that. So they had to take the ferry and depend on scaring you into keeping your trap shut." Cocklebur Kelsay's eyes were hard and accusing as he stared at Clem.

The ferry master shifted uneasily. "Now, Cocklebur, you know how I am about mooning off. A lot of people go across, and sometimes I couldn't tell you who they was half a hour later."

"Are you, or are you not, willing to testify that you brought the mayor and his party back over from east Crockett?"

"Why, even if I could, what good would it do?" Clem temporized.

Kelsay snorted. "It'd get them crooked politicians fired and help me really get this town cleaned up, that's what! Look, Clem, you're probably the only man in this town whose testimony'd be enough in itself. Folks know you for a strictly honest man, especially after what happened between you and Myrtle. You sure got a chance to do the decent element a service."

Clem was thinking hard on it. Though a bachelor himself, he would like to see Crockett a nice place for families, well enough. But he kept thinking of Roscoe Froebel. If he did what Kelsay wanted,

Crockett might have complete law and order, but it sure enough would also have a new ferry operator. Clem shook his head.

"Cocklebur, a man can't raise a stink like that on the basis of what he seen in the dark. I just don't feel positive on the subject."

After a frowning moment, the marshal shrugged. He started to speak, then pulled his lips tight and left.

Clem climbed back into bed with a sigh. He sure wasn't resting any. Not only was he halfway in dutch with east Crockett, but if Marshal Kelsay voiced what he suspected in west Crockett, Clem would be in dutch there, too. Drowsing, Clem knew he would sure hate to have Myrtle Cass, a leader of the reform, hear that he had passed up a chance to do the cause some good because he was scared.

What the marshal had said about Clem's unsupported testimony being entirely believed was true enough. The "ornery streak of honesty" Gabe Gilroy had referred to that night was what had parted Clem and Myrtle five years ago. Clem had had to be honest at a place where even Myrtle hoped he wouldn't be. Clem Shays himself had once visited a honkatonk.

His motives had been above reproach. Ham Goodyear, with whom he had once ridden up in the Little Mano country, had come to town. They hadn't seen each other in quite a while, and Ham liked to wet his whistle while he was jowling, so they had gone to this place. Clem hadn't thought anything about it. But even then Myrtle Cass had been building up the reform movement, and somebody with money invested on the other side of the fence had remembered that Clem and Myrtle were keeping company. A rumor had got started that quickly reached Myrtle.

All Myrtle asked was that Clem deny the rumor, knowing that his reputation would persuade the town. But Clem had admitted it doggedly. And being situated as she was, Myrtle had had no option but to send him packing. They had remained parted, ever since, and Clem's reputation for honesty had been even more solidly established.

Clem awakened the next morning to an excited world. As he fixed breakfast, Cliff Glass, a town loafer, came hurrying down the riverbank. As Cliff sometimes timed his arrivals to coincide with meals, Clem frowned at him. But Glass was unabashed.

"It's sure gonna raise hob with your business, ain't it, Clem?"

Clem stared at him. "What is?"

"Why, ain't you heard? East Crockett's seceded! They've closed their borders to us. There won't be no more traffic 'twixt here and there." Glass poured himself a mug of coffee and sat down at the table. "Smart move, if you ask me. If they set up their own town, Cockelbur Kelsay won't be their marshal any more. He'll have to stop nipping at their heels."

Clem ladled batter onto the flapjack griddle. At first, this seemed like a wholly welcome development to him. It would give him a chance to get in his rest cure. Yet, reflection showed him the error in this logic. It wasn't east Crockett he was thinking about, but the Little Mano country. If folks up there had to use the Cripple Ford ferry, two miles up, they might find out it was about as close that way and keep up the habit.

He got rid of Glass presently and spent a couple of hours resting. Then a lad arrived at the landing with a note for him. Clem recognized the penmanship instantly as the work of Myrtle Cass and, opening the note, read:

Clem,
The hour has struck for the forces of decency to arise! There will be a

town meeting at eleven to meet this crisis, and I want you there. Please, Clem.

"She wants me to bring back the answer," the boy said.

Clem ruminated. It was the first time in five years that Myrtle had made an effort to communicate with him. He found that his blood was coursing at a speed that Doc Garrick might consider dangerous. He nodded. "Tell her I'll come, boy."

He toted water into the shack and heated it, then bathed, and dressed in his best suit. This took longer than he had anticipated, so he had to rush up the long, dusty street to the town hall. It was crowded, and the militant spirit of the occasion was reflected in a rooster fight transpiring in front. Clem pushed inside and found a seat.

Mayor Gabe Gilroy was in charge, and he talked first, shaking his shaggy, silver mane and declaring that a town divided against itself could not stand. When he had finished to a thunderous applause, Myrtle Cass took the rostrum.

Clem shifted uneasily as Myrtle's glance licked over him hungrily while she elaborated the benefits of a loving wife and laughing children and a happy home.

"This action in east Crockett is a nefarious thing!" she proclaimed. "It is not a question of whether east Crockett is to set up its own government. It's a question of it having been engineered by Roscoe Froebel, whose character everybody knows." There was applause. "It's the decent element . . . that exists even over there . . . I'm thinking about. It has a right to a wholesome atmosphere. And west Crockett has a right not to have a festering sore so close upon its environs."

Clem nodded, thinking that Myrtle made a mighty pretty figure up there, talking so earnestly. Then she threw her bomb. She pointed an accusing finger.

"Clem Shays, did you, or did you not, haul Mayor Gabe Gilroy and a party of two-faced, local bigwigs home from east Crockett last night?"

Clem turned into a fountain of cold sweat. In that instant he saw why Marshal Cocklebur Kelsay had given up so easily the night before. He had decided to employ a far stronger force and so had gone to Myrtle.

Gabe Gilroy was looking anything but easy. He took his astonished gaze from Myrtle and shifted it to Clem, and, looking at him, Clem saw danger crowding the mayor's eyes. Clem dropped his glance to the floor and squirmed. Then he climbed tiredly to his feet.

"How did word about east Crockett seceding get over here?" He addressed the rostrum. "I ain't had a fare on the ferry since last night."

"Why, the mayor announced it," Myrtle said in triumph. "How did you know, Mayor Gilroy?"

His honor's cheeks had turned red as a sun-ripened tomato. He, too, climbed to his feet. He, too, tried to confuse the issue. "What is this?" he demanded.

"I been going to ask the council to close Married Man's Crossing," Clem said mildly. "I'm a public enterprise, and it harms my business. I sure got a kick coming when they start to transact official business that way." His only chance to escape having to tell the truth, he realized, was to force the mayor himself to admit having been over there the night before.

"You were in on the deal, Gabe Gilroy!" Myrtle Cass cried from the rostrum. "You were tied in with Roscoe Froebel before you even ran for election. You knew that sooner or later you'd have to support Marshal Kelsay in clamping down over there, so you and Froebel cooked up this secession so you can continue to draw your graft."

Clem wished she would shut up, for he saw that the mayor had turned into a dangerous man. Then Gilroy seemed to decide to stand on the threat he had made Clem Shays.

"A lot of mud-slinging talk I won't even dignify by denying," he said, and sat down.

Myrtle's inexorable voice cracked like doom. "Clem Shays, did you, or did you not, haul him home last night?"

"I did," Clem said weakly.

He left the hubbub of the city hall, not caring what happened next. Back down at the idle ferry, he got into old clothes again. Through the window he saw that they had erected a barricade on the east Crockett side. They sure didn't mean to have any more truck with their mother town. And Clem Shays would certainly be in for a dose of rest if he wasn't already in for something a lot worse.

Clem was not surprised when, shortly after noon, the cow horn blew over there. He went outside, looked across, and saw Roscoe Froebel himself standing on the far landing. Clem understood it. Froebel was summoning him to an accounting. Somebody over here had got the word over there. The horn blew again.

Much as he hated to respond, Clem knew that he could never tuck his tail between his legs. He tramped wearily to the ferry scow and started it into motion. His nerves tightened with every foot the ferry covered. The ferry came ashore with a gentle bump. Clem tied up and strode doggedly across the landing.

Froebel was a thin man with a black mustache and deadly, black eyes. His cold scrutiny sent a chill through Clem.

"Come up to the place, Shays. You and me've got a little business."

Clem did not think out what he did next. He pitched himself at Froebel before the man had a chance to claw out the gun Clem knew rested in a shoulder holster. He hit Froebel's chest with his shoulder and landed in the dust with him, driving in blows to the man's head that doubtless would have alarmed Doc Garrick.

Then, carrying Froebel's limp body onto the ferry, Clem shoved off again. In midstream the man roused and started yelling bloody murder. Men appeared on the east Crockett bank, and there would have been shooting had not their employer been in the midst of the target. Clem had Froebel's gun, and he laid its barrel efficiently across the town boss' head, and there was temporary silence.

On the west bank Clem rushed to the cow horn and blew it repeatedly. It was the tocsin he knew would arouse the jumpy town. He had an idea that east Crockett would presently decide to come across the river.

They began to gather, over there, scattering along the bank. The stream here was some four hundred feet wide, too far for a rock to be thrown accurately, but not too far for a slug of lead to get in reasonably dangerous work. Clem dragged the east side overlord into the shack and locked the door from the outside.

A gun exploded over there, and lead slammed into the wall above Clem's head. He galloped around behind the shack. Racket told him that west Crockett was on its way. An inferno opened up presently on both banks.

"Onward, the forces of decency!" Myrtle Cass's voice rang out. "This is the showdown!"

Clem was ready to acknowledge that it was that, indeed. They weren't firing at his shack, any more, for fear of hitting Froebel. Hunkered behind the shack, Clem had a feeling of utter helplessness. All the good gun hands in town were across the water, on

Froebel's payroll. Now that the west side had hurled the challenge, they might very well decide to come over here on a general clean-up campaign of their own.

Myrtle Cass wriggled down the bank toward Clem, a happy light shining in her eyes. She said: "Clem, I was so proud of you, back there."

Clem gulped and concentrated on the battle.

The river was a fortunate factor in it, keeping the two contingents reasonably well separated. Clem still had Froebel's gun, yet bloodshed was not to his taste. He scratched his head, stared at Myrtle, then had his idea.

"Where's Gilroy?"

"Locked up, pending recall and trial for malfeasance . . . and, I hope, hanging."

"Send somebody up to bring him down here."

Myrtle nodded and slithered away, having been deeply impressed again by her erstwhile suitor.

Clem studied the river. A skiff bobbed on the near side of the ferry, and a man could probably make his way to it in reasonable safety. He had decided that this could not go on if he was to get anything even resembling a good rest. Gilroy and Froebel were the main disturbing elements. If placed in the skiff without oars and started down river, they would wind up miles below town. Gilroy, at least, would not come back, and, realizing he no longer had a placid cow to milk, Roscoe Froebel might also elect calmer pastures.

Myrtle came back presently with two men who dragged a loudly protesting Gabe Gilroy between them.

The mayor screamed: "Just turn me loose and I'll get, blast you!"

Myrtle replied calmly: "Not until we see what'd run out if you got a hole in your hide, Your Honor."

Events got out of hand at this juncture. The firing from across the river doubled in intensity, and, peering around a corner with utmost caution, Clem saw that a number of men had climbed onto the buildings over there and were shooting from upstairs windows. What he realized next made him gape. They were not shooting across the river. They were lining their sights on the Froebel contingent, forted among the boulders on the river bank.

"The decent element," Myrtle breathed. "East Crockett has decided to purge itself."

That seemed to be the case. Quickly realizing that they were caught between two fires, Froebel's gunmen, one by one, began to rise and race for the water. They hit it like scurrying lizards, went under, and emerged only for a gulp of fresh air before they went under again. Within five minutes a largely submarine procession was moving downstream. The firing died, except for an exuberant blast now and then at an itinerant cloud overhead.

With elaborate satisfaction, Clem and Myrtle loaded Gilroy and Froebel into the skiff. West and east Crockett united in speeding their journey with bullets agitating the water in their turn.

It was apparent that the two sides of Crockett would now stay united in all civic matters. Somebody yelled for the ferry, and for hours Clem Shays drudged as he took contingent after contingent back and forth. He was worn out by the time elation had died down enough that he could again cant back a chair in the shade of his shack. He had barely pulled his hat over his eyes and closed them when the sound of footfalls, progressing down the bank, made him groan.

It was Myrtle. "Clem, I just had to tell you the news," she burst out. "They're running you for mayor. All by yourself. You're in, sure as shooting." There was a deep satisfaction in her face, as if, perhaps, she already saw herself running the town. In a moment she confirmed Clem's suspicion. "Why don't you come around to my place tonight, and we'll talk about your campaign?" she asked demurely. Clem knew then that he'd never catch up with the rest the doctor had ordered.

The Road to Jericho

The wheel was fixed, and none too soon. Lot Trask saw that his wife had walked ahead and was shading her eyes against the glaring distance where the ruts of Apple-gate's Cut-off vanished. She was wondering about Jim. But Lot was not in a mind to wait, he thought, tossing his drawing knife into the chest. A dished wheel had put them a day behind the emigrant train.

For himself, he would as soon finish the crossing apart from the big and noisy company, but a wagon needed protection on this trail. It was Indian country, on the stretch from Mary's River to the California mountains, waterless, grassless, empty, and lonely as the moon itself.

Rowena came back, to vanish on the shaded side of the wagon, where she had been playing some game with the children. Lot knew she was eager to catch up with the other wagons. Loneliness settled on her

266

sooner than with most. Her twin brother, Jim Quayle, was off with his gun, and, since Lot Trask had been born with a button on his lip, she had only the young ones for company.

He knocked the props from under the axle tree and lifted the tool chest into the wagon with an easy swing. The movement brought Rowena on, dark and tall and smooth-walking. Her slim body gave no hint of motherhood of a boy and girl of school age, an age that worried her, for they'd not likely find a school where they would settle on the Oregon frontier.

"When I fetch the cattle, we'll go," Lot said, trying to cheer her.

Her eyes gave him trouble when she looked at him. "Hadn't we better wait for Jim?"

"We'll likely meet him ahead. Or he can catch us. Hope he raised meat. We could sure use it, and water and grass. And we could use the other wagons, too, I reckon." He grinned at her. "We'll need to hump to catch 'em. Stir Tom and Molly, and get into the seat. I'll yoke up." It nearly ran him out of breath to talk so much.

Rowena shook her head, still detached. "Riding's too hot, and it's too rough. We'll walk on."

"Better not," Lot said. He could see for miles across the baking alkali, but there was an obscuring rise ahead. Rowena disappeared around the wagon, and he knew she didn't like to move on before Jim came back. Womb mates, they were as one person split into man and woman, but not apart.

Lot went out to the cattle pickets. The four draft steers were underwatered and worse fed. Their gauntness raked him, but water was ahead on the Black Rock stretch. He'd done risky things to take his oxen apart from the train's big herd and let them browse, such as was possible where little grew but scattered sage, and where little lived beyond lizards that took flight and fled from under each rock. The "little besides" was what concerned all who made this crossing: the embittered Digger Indians some folly had settled in this area who showed the savagery of their nature in their poisoned arrows. *Let them get in close among the rocks* — Lot shook the thought from his mind.

He saw that Rowena had hustled the children, and they were picking up the few things left out from last night's camp. Once or twice she flung a look far out, in concern for Jim, and this settled Lot. He wondered about twins, and if the manner of their birth made it so they could never live apart and unto themselves. It seemed true of this pair. Yet, she gave him all a man could ask, and had never shown a moment's crossness. He was satisfied.

Lot's world turned about his wife and children. About them revolved the many things needed to care for them properly. If a man did it right — and Lot Trask wasn't built to do anything he tackled otherwise — it left him little time for talk and dallying. But he wasn't given to brooding, and he put this also from his mind, and took in the sore-footed animals.

Nearing the wagon he heard a whoop, and young Tom's voice rang out. "Yonder comes Uncle Jim! Over the hill!"

Lot turned. Jim's horse had topped the rise and was coming along the trail ahead. Nothing crossed his saddle to indicate that he had shot any meat.

The oxen were under yoke by the time Jim rode in. He went past Lot with a nod and grin, then his eyes found Rowena, and he smiled. He winked at Tom and more elaborately at Molly, which made the little girl giggle. The horse showed sweat, Lot noted, and had been ridden hard. Jim looked easy, but there was something subtly wrong in his face.

Jim swung down, a solid weight on the sand, and walked to the water barrel strapped to the wagon. He filled the dipper and drank with distaste, for the water was warm and brackish. His faded shirt stuck darkly to a sweating, hard-muscled back. His long, lean face built sharp-pulled lines about his eyes.

Rowena came over and was like a morning glory opening to the sun. "If you're hungry, Jim, I can get to the grub box easy." The cheer was there, so easily restored by Jim.

"Never mind," Jim said, a little sharply. Then he grinned. "Too hot to be hungry. Rode miles and seen desert, but not a blamed thing to shoot at."

"You look too hot, or tired, or too something."

"Too hot. And I ain't been anything else since we crossed the Missouri." Jim unsnapped the bucket hanging under the wagon, dipped a splash of the precious water into it, and let the horse draw it up. Some place yonder Jim had ridden the horse too hard for the heat, though Jim was as fussy about livestock as Lot.

"Jim, something's wrong." Rowena looked relentlessly at her brother's face.

"Not if that clung-tongued scarecrow you

married's got the wheel fixed. Unless you mean there's nothing right about this plagued country he dragged us into." For once the grin that always came with Jim's chiding was a little thin.

Lot had nothing to return. He never did. He never even bothered to return Jim's half-hearted grin, for dourness was part of his nature. He couldn't climb the barrier of his lifeless tongue, so all he could do was get at things. He did now, finishing his chore and picking up the ox goad.

"We best get going," he said, and clucked to the cattle.

"Indians," Rowena said, persisting at Jim.

"Girl," Jim said, "there's thousands in these parts, and no doubt of it. But I ain't seen so much as a moccasin track. You and the kids pad on ahead of the dust, while I let Lot talk my leg off."

She was uncertain, but she turned away, gathering the children and moving forward out of the pall of alkali that marked each wagon's progress across the desert. Jim led his horse, his boots hitting hard on the sand beside Lot. He lowered his voice.

"Lot, I stumbled onto a sickenin' mess a long ways west of here. She was right. It was Digger work, with all the fancy touches to tie a knot in a man's stomach."

Lot never missed a stride, but his eyes narrowed for an instant. "The wagon train?"

"No. You mind that horseback party that rode past yesterday, headin' for the California mines? That's as far as they got. Four of 'em dead, but one's still alive. Some scab rock along there. Diggers hid 'em in it with the packs they didn't steal, so the train wouldn't notice when it come past. Then they took the horses and cleared out, I reckon. I hope so."

The oxen were laboring up the rise, their straining necks already showing sweat. Lot nearly called Rowena back before they disappeared beyond, the space ahead dark and baneful now, even in the late afternoon sun. He desisted, not wanting her distressed or worried, knowing she'd been no happier this side of the big river than Jim.

"How'd you stumble onto it?" he asked.

"The man that's alive crawled back up the trail. Arrow through his belly. Hardly more than a kid."

"He conscious?"

Jim shook his head. "And he may be dead by the time we get there. Lord, I hope that, too."

Night came on before they reached the place, a starlight filled with vague things too shapeless not to worry over. Lot was drawn tight, and he had his rifle across his shoulder. It was the first scab rock to run close, a likely place for an ambush, yet it would be folly to try to pull in a blind circle around it. He had made his family crawl into the wagon long since, and hoped they'd fallen asleep in spite of the wagon's continual jar.

"Say when, Jim," Lot said.

"Just a piece ahead." Then, after long moments: "Here. Over there. Looks like a log. Reckon he's finished." Jim's voice indicated relief.

They walked over, Lot with his long legs nearly past control. The shape lay on the sand, forlorn, unmoving. Lot dropped to his knees, his battered plainsman hat shoved back. The figure was face down, and the feathered arrow shaft angled from its side at the back. Lot knew even as he grasped the wrist that there was a faint pulse in it.

His face must have shown something, for Jim groaned. "He's still alive. It must have happened around noon yesterday. He's got a poison arrow in him. He's bled. He's laid all that time in the sun. And he's still alive."

Lot was thinking swifty, feeling the aura of this place and all that lay ahead of them. The man wasn't scalped, but only because the Diggers had been rushed to get away before the big wagon train came along. Maybe this one arrow hadn't been poisoned as heavily as they figured, or the man's clothes had rubbed enough off. The fellow did look young, and maybe nothing vital was hit inside.

"See if you can fetch the medicine kit without wakening Rowena," Lot said, his tone brusque.

"What'll we do with him, Lot? The wagon'd kill him if we take him along. We can't stay here. He's as good as done for, but we can't bury him alive. Or . . . or leave him like this."

"We'll do what we can," Lot said.

"Lot, it's two to one we've been spotted, one wagon a long ways behind the train."

"Fetch the kit," Lot answered.

He rolled the man farther onto his side. He cut the arrow shaft and pulled it out. He was praying that the man would die from this rough mercy. But as long as a bit of life remained, they had to cherish it. He was a deft man who had to talk with his hands, and over the years this had given him experience in crude medicine and surgery.

Rowena came out of the wagon, the first sign she had been awakened. She looked at the hurt man, then squatted across from Lot and for a long while was silent. Jim brought the lantern and presently, at a word from Lot, unyoked the oxen to let them rest. The star-flung sky hung above them in impersonal tranquillity.

Then Jim said to his sister: "You might as well know the whole of it. There's dead men yonder against the rocks. I'm going in to see if the Diggers left any water."

Quickly Lot said: "First, rustle a fire. You can heat water, Rowena, and scare up some cloth. We'll try to make him comfortable, whether he knows the difference or not."

Jim was gone a long while, and returned bearing dead sage and *chamiza* clumps. He vanished again, and Lot knew he had gone into the outcrop, anxious not only to scare up a few canteens of water, but to make certain nothing else lurked in there. Rowena crossed to the fire and busied herself. Again and again Lot picked up the young miner's wrist, to drop it in drawn impatience.

With Rowena's help they bound the wounds, after washing them with soap and hot water. It needed effort to take these restorative measures, to do anything that might strengthen the pulse in the slightest and bind them here the longer. Yet, Lot went through the steps, patient and careful, and outwardly it was without pause. With slow movements he got their brandy from the kit. He lifted the boy's head, poured, and saw a reflex swallow. He waited then, for it was out of his hands.

Jim came back and said: "Well, no water. Which means the Diggers are supplied, and could be hanging close even yet."

Lot looked up at him. "We only got your horse. Nothing to draw 'em. This can't last long. Then, if we crowd it, we might catch the wagon train at their next camp."

"Might," Jim said, and walked off. He got his horse and rode out. Lot didn't try to stop him, knowing Jim would ride a circle about them, scouting, and with the desert traveler's hope of finding unexpected water.

Lot searched the miner for identification. He found nothing revealing, though there was a worn picture of a girl. She didn't look like him, and was likely his wife or sweetheart. Lot didn't show it to Rowena, but put it back to be buried with the boy when they reached that point. He grew aware that dawn was washing the stars from the untroubled sky.

He said to Rowena — "Best make our breakfast." — and watched her stir from a slump by the fire. In that moment he saw her strangeness in this stark place, and thought: *I dragged her out here. Now I've pinned her down in this.* He wanted to say something, but there were no words. He got busy, bringing what they needed from the wagon. Then it was that he saw their patient lift a hand ever so slightly and let it drop.

Lot walked to him, and again he forced brandy down the swollen throat. Rowena, at the campfire, hadn't observed it. He thought how odd it was that they waited for death to release them, and that death would not come. Then he thought of the life that had kept up its flicker through the long hours before they reached here, and this steadied him.

Presently Rowena whirled, and her voice was released despair. "Why doesn't Jim come back? What's keeping him?"

"Now, Rowena," Lot said, his voice held quiet, "Jim's always showed inclination to stray off and poke around. Could be he's seen sign of water, or has raised game. He's armed, and we've heard no shooting."

"Or he got into trouble before he knew it."

"Best get on with breakfast. He'll be back and . . . it'll be over, and then we can go on."

He had a corroding despair of his own, its weight increased by a mounting guilt. He had known without ever facing it how much she and Jim had hated to tear up roots, to leave the known and secure for this ineffable and unending jeopardy, to give up friends and family for this isolation, whose only apparent reward was increased hardship. He had pressed it, because he was a man suited to such things, and without complaint they had come.

He thought: *Soon as Jim comes, we best put the boy in the wagon and go. The sooner he dies, the more mercy to him.* In the next breath he knew that they couldn't, and ever again escape wonder as to how it might have been.

He didn't want to move the boy at all if he could help, so, as the sun rose to throw its bright, beginning heat upon them, he yoked the oxen patiently and moved the wagon between. It roused the children, who descended from the wagon to have their morning boisterousness doused instantly by what they discerned.

"Who is he?" Tommy asked, and Molly merely stared with frowning, pained eyes.

"A boy who aimed to strike it rich in California," Lot answered, "then go home and marry his sweetheart."

"Was it Injuns? Will they jump us?"

"It was, and they won't," Lot said.

Rowena gave the children their sparse, simple breakfast, and Lot drank coffee. Afterward, he rationed a few swallows each for the oxen from the dwindling water in the barrel. Again he knew a moment of distress that he could give them nothing to eat beyond the desert's scant browse.

His wife walked over to him and said in a lowered voice: "Lot, something's happened to Jim."

"We'll wait a bit before we worry."

"Wait, wait. Travel, travel. And never worry." She went back, her shoulders held stiffly.

Lot judged it was eight o'clock when he made up his mind. Jim had been gone eight or ten hours, which was unaccountable. He went to Rowena.

"Reckon you'll have to tend the young 'uns. And the miner. I'll poke around a bit and see what I can see."

She pulled straight, wanting him to go, yet caught by something. "How can you go after him without a horse?"

"I'll pick up his tracks and mosey out a piece, and maybe it'll give us some inkling." He caught up his rifle, which he had kept against a wagon wheel.

Rowena dropped her gaze, and her hands clenched at her sides. "Lot, I can't stay alone in this place with those men there in the rocks, and the other. . . ."

"Diggers're the only danger, and here's the pistol," Lot said. "You'll be all right."

In a moment she said: "Yes, I can do it, Lot. Go on."

He put a little water into a canteen, then slung on powder horn and bullet pouch. He made a light motion of farewell, not wanting to disturb her further, and started out. He walked straight toward the scab rock, dreading it, but he had gained an idea of what Jim might have done. He entered the rock with a puckered feeling the length of his spine.

It was all that Jim had described, worse when a man laid eyes on it. Lot kept his gaze off the men, running it briefly over the rifled, scattered horse packs. Then he went on, and came out behind the outcrop.

It was not hard to discover the tracks of what must have been a dozen horses, the Indian ponies and those of the miners. They cut a straight and hurried line out from the ambush, and Lot had gone only a short distance when he discovered another set. These were to the right of the flight, those of a slow-moving horse whose rider was following carefully through the moonlight.

Lot had no idea why Jim had done this thing, but knew that he had. Pausing a moment, Lot squinted his eyes against the sun-glared distance that nothing broke but the far dip of an empty sky. In that moment he had his own rebellion. He had worked through a day on the wagon wheel, driven through half the night, and spent the rest tending the hurt boy. It was day again, more hot and hopeless than he had ever dreamed a day could be. He shook his shoulders roughly and went on.

It was three hours before the desert ahead showed any change. Then Lot wasn't sure what he saw. It took a long while to decide that it was dust lifting from a pinpoint on the flat, desert floor. There was no making out what caused it, at best, and now his punished eyes had taken to jumping in and out of focus. It encouraged and worried him together, and he managed to hurry a little.

The speck disappeared, and he knew it hadn't been anything. He went on, his gait a little lurching, with anxiety beginning to crowd into his mind. He still followed the plain trail of fast-driven horses, and here and there he picked up special tracks he was certain were those of Jim's mount. Yet why the man had ridden this way, and so far, was a complete mystery, and Lot began to fear he lacked the strength to keep going until he had found Jim — or to get back to the wagon.

Then, at last, he distinguished the horse with the empty saddle in the far distance, and he knew presently that it was Jim's horse. It was plodding toward Lot in a tired and patient gait. Lot hurried to meet it.

The animal showed sweat marks, more than this slow shuffle across the sand would raise. Lot caught the horse and swung into the saddle, having trouble balancing himself until he got settled. He swung it about and started back along its route, the rifle balanced across the saddle before him. Something had lifted dust, and not very far beyond. This horse had traveled fast.

He found Jim lying face down on the scuffed trail. Something knotted up in Lot as he lowered himself drunkenly from the saddle. There wasn't a mark on Jim, and yet he lay unconscious. Lot turned him onto his side, staring down, then bent in alarm above him. Jim was breathing in a snoring breath, and again and again his whole body moved convulsively. His skin was dry, intensely hot, and, when Lot pried up an eyelid, he found the pupil contracted.

He knew what it was, having seen it in the train after they entered the desert. Sunstroke. It was deadly unless immediately relieved by shade and cold baths and lots of drinking water. Lot's knees nearly buckled, and for a moment dizziness ran through him. He bent and got Jim up across the saddle. He lashed him there, took the reins, and started.

The sun was hard and hot on his back when he saw the scab rock he had so long been watching for. He skirted the rocks, not wanting to encounter their grisly enclosure. He came upon the emigrant trail, and a moment later saw young Tom bounding out from the wagon toward him.

Lot managed to steady himself, never having liked to show weakness before the young ones. "Boy, don't run thataway in the heat," he called as Tom panted toward him, then, as the boy came up, he added: "How's your mother?"

"All right," Tom gasped. "The miner, he died. What's wrong with Uncle Jim?"

Lot swayed a moment. All this, and it had done no good whatsoever! It had been a hard trial, a useless one, and now Jim was in mortal peril. He didn't answer Tom, but hurried himself, and saw Rowena running toward them as they drew near the wagon.

"Heat got him, coming back," Lot managed to tell her. "Fell off his horse. Poked way off downcountry, and I reckon it was to make sure the Diggers'd cleared out. Get water, girl, while I put him in the shade and get the clothes off him. We'll do what we can."

"Jim! Jim!"

Lot got Jim Quayle off his horse and stretched on the quilt Rowena hastily threw down on the shaded side of the big wagon. He fell to work at once, pulling Jim's clothes off, calling: "Fetch water, Rowena . . . a pailful."

"Lot . . . Lot . . . there's scarcely that much left!"

"Fetch it."

"But Lot, what'll we do then? The children . . . you . . . ?"

"Bring water."

He kept soaking cloths until he had Jim covered with them. He tried again and again to get him to drink, but Jim had slipped too far into unconsciousness. He tried brandy, but it only ran out the edge of Jim's mouth, and by now his body was alarmingly hot to the touch. The thirsty cloths kept sopping their scant water.

"If you can stand to stay alone again," Lot said, "and keep tending him, I'll light out for the next springs. Supposed to be a couple days' travel from our last camp, and we've come half that. Another fifteen miles, maybe . . . a day's travel with the wagon. If his horse can stand it, I could cut it to half that and be back this time tomorrow with what I can fetch."

Rowena straightened on the other side of Jim's inert figure. Her face was blank, and her mouth hanging open. "Lot, you couldn't stand it. You've already had too much."

"Takes water, and we need more for ourselves to get the wagon on." Lot managed to get to his feet and hold there without swaying. He knew Jim's horse was played out, that there was scarcely a chance he could ride it through and back with the extra burden of what water he could bring in containers. Yet he turned toward the horse.

Rowena caught his arm. "Lot, I won't let you. It'd finish you."

"We'll need more water for Jim. He's your brother."

"And you're my husband. No, Lot. We'll do what we can for him. And then wait."

There was authority in her voice, and something Lot had never dreamed could be there, a concern for him as great or greater than her fear for Jim. He looked at her in pure wonder.

"But Jim . . . ?"

"Lot, I learned something in the hours you were gone. That miner roused a little at the end. Enough to clasp my hand. I know it eased him through, and how I know that, I *don't* know. I was horribly ashamed of myself, for all last night I hated him for holding us here. Now you go and rest, and we'll trust."

The afternoon was mercilessly hot, without end, and by sundown their last drop of water was gone. Jim Quayle still lay inertly, but his breathing was steadier, stronger, and Lot thought the fever had dropped. In the coolness of the night he seemed to pick up, and now Lot Trask got his shovel and went into the rock cluster once more. He worked long hours putting away the remains of the miners who had perished here. Then he came back to the wagon with a strange sense of repose in him.

To his surprise, as he came up, Jim's weak voice said: "Don't anything ever stop you, Lot? When I felt myself fallin' off my horse, I expected to open my eyes in the hereafter. Who but Lot Trask'd walk out that far, worryin' about me?"

Lot straightened above him, scowling thunderously. "You plagued idiot, what in thunderation were you after?"

"Trying to make sure we weren't going to

get jumped. Then I turned sick coming in. Tried to hurry the horse, and that was a mistake. Fell out o' the saddle. Lot, damn your ornery hide . . . I appreciate it!"

Lot turned away hastily. He had taken only the short rest Rowena had forced upon him the day before, but he felt strong and steady. And warm inside. He wasn't worried. By daylight, likely, Jim could stand to ride in the wagon far as the springs, where they could camp until he was on his feet. After what they had put behind, they surely could get that far without water.

Yet he wanted to say something to Rowena, to tell her how much it meant to find he was as much to her as her twin. He wanted to say how sorry he was he had blinded himself with his own dreams, and forced her and Jim to come to this country. It was too late to turn back. Ahead lay more isolation and hardship, the kind of thing a woman like Rowena wasn't suited to. He wanted to put these things into words, but words had always refused to work for him. So he got busy, checking over the wagon, making sure the repaired wheel was holding up.

Rowena slipped across to him. "Lot, there's nothing that won't keep till you've slept a while."

"Rowena, I. . . . Plague it, I wish I hadn't brought you into such a lonely country."

She smiled, and her face was easier than it had ever been on the crossing. "Lot Trask, it's good for a person to be to himself once in a while. It gives him a chance to find out things about himself. And about others. It doesn't seem so lonely now I know I've got a husband who talks to me."

"You know I was born with a buttoned lip."

"Maybe. But there's no button on your hands, nor your shoulders. And it took me long enough to learn how to listen."

Know Your Headings

It began the day Cap Zangwill was killed, yet, thinking about it later, Lew began to believe that it really started the day his brother, Ollie, was born. Ollie must have got the idea while they were bringing Cap down the river, his giant's frame stilled there on the bunk in his cabin on the texas, the mark above his right eye showing what had stilled it.

Maybe Ollie got the idea in that moment when, at the wheel of the steamboat, *Swallow*, he heard the blast in the engine room when the cylinder head blew out, with steam and pieces of metal flying. Whichever it was, he had been ready to act by the time they were tied up in Portland and someone had gone to take Cap ashore for the last time.

Out of the Cascades and downriver, the *Swallow* had been misbehaving, and Cap had gone below to consult with Joe Tranto, the engineer. Joe had been knocked out cold in the explosion, for they both had been there by the cross-compound engines. Aside from Cap, the only damage had been this and a short scare to the passengers, and after emergency repairs Ollie had brought the packet home on one engine. He must have been recognizing his opportunity and planning his steps with every turn of the big stern wheel.

Coming down through the dull November afternoon, Lew had kept to the purser's office, glad of his duties. Upbound, the packet was always loaded with gold stampeders heading for eastern Oregon and Idaho, and they expected the purser, in addition to the packet's regular clerical chores, to advise them at length on the best place for a man to try his luck, on his outfit, and all the legal aspects of locating and filing a claim and growing rich from it.

Coming down, the situation was different only in detail. Some of them were bound only for Portland, and they wanted to know where a man could have a good time. Others meant to coast on down to San Francisco, and there were endless questions about the big ships in the seaboard trade. This day they all wanted to know about the explosion and Cap and Joe Tranto, mainly.

Lew was glad of this preoccupation, for he had liked the captain tremendously. Lew Vail, who was twenty-two, had been on the river less than two years. Because his brother, Ollie, was second mate and had stood in well with the captain and the line, and because Lew was the one of the Vail brothers who had had the benefits of extensive schooling, he had started as an officer, here in the purser's office. A big lad of slow gait and quiet, pleasant tongue, he filled his blue uniform splendidly, and his sober face, under the boat cap, was handsome.

When they had tied up in Portland, and the passengers were discharged, and cargo operations were under way, Ollie came into the purser's office. Ollie was much slighter than Lew, and he had pulled gravity onto his lean, weathered face, but beneath it burned something with the intensity of a high fever.

"We'll be tied up tomorrow while we make repairs."

Lew knew what he was thinking. The day after that they would be on the run again, for, heavy as the traffic was, the company could not spare one of its biggest packets for an hour longer than it had to, and Pete Wilmot, the first mate, would likely be in permanent command.

Ollie was thinking about Pete Wilmot's weakness and not of the fact that Pete's elevation to the captaincy would make himself the first mate instead of the second, and this preoccupation was what had fired him beneath the soberness demanded by the occasion.

"Yeah," Lew said. "I'd like to go to Cap's funeral. He was tough, but he was all right."

"They'll want to keep the old girl in service." Ollie Vail was not even thinking about the funeral. He was thinking about the river and the coming promotions, and he was on fire with this.

Lew felt a moment's understanding. He shared Ollie's love of the river. Ollie had worked his way up from a deckhand and, while doing so, had made it possible for Lew to have schooling he himself had never had. "The higher you can start, the higher you can go," Ollie had always maintained. "It sure wouldn't hurt to have a Vail in the shore-side set-up." Ollie's every waking moment was given over to the problem of advancement.

Lew knew that he would never cease to be grateful to Ollie for the sacrifices that had made it possible for him to go to school. This made it impossible for him to tell Ollie that he just wanted to be on the river, like

Ollie and Pete Wilmot and Cap, that he wasn't particularly interested in the shoreside structure and desk routine. This made it out of the question to tell Ollie to be glad that he and Pete were stepping up a rung together even if he couldn't be very sorry about Cap, and not to get any sly ideas.

At this point he had only sensed what Ollie was about. Later, in Pete Wilmot's cabin where he liked to go in his idle hours, Lew saw how accurate he had been. Pete was stretched out on his bunk with his boots off, scratching one foot with the toes of the other, and he waved Lew into a chair. Before they got to talking, the door opened. Ollie came in, and he had a bottle of whiskey in his hand.

Ollie said: "I think we ought to have a drink to the captain. We were his officers."

Pete sat up in the bunk. Lew saw him lick his lips and felt a moment's sickness pass through him. He saw then what Ollie was up to, clearly and to its logical end, and he would have stopped it there but for all the things that lay between himself and Ollie.

Pete said: "Get some glasses, pup."

Lew got them. They were water tumblers. Ollie poured them half full and handed them around. As he took his, Lew noticed that his long fingers were trembling, and there was a tightness around Ollie's narrowed eyes.

Ollie said: "Good sailing, skipper!"

Because this was exactly the way to drink to Cap, Lew felt a warmth that was almost like tears in his eyes. He took his gaze away from the hungriness in Pete Wilmot's face and sipped his own drink. He did not like raw whiskey and lacked the courage to dilute it with water, so he sucked it between his lips in a thin trickle.

Ollie put down his empty glass and left, and he did not take the bottle of whiskey, which was hardly touched. In this moment's clarity, Lew knew that Pete Wilmot saw the trap, too. Pete was eyeing the whiskey with a strangeness in his face. For an instant Lew decided that when he left he would take it, with a laugh, saying that Ollie was too tight-fisted to have forgotten it if he hadn't been upset about Cap. Then he knew that he could not do this, for it would be too obvious. It would say to Pete: *Everybody knows you can't be trusted with it, Pete. Just like Ollie knows it. Just like he wants to get you started on one of your benders so you'll be filthy drunk when they decide who's going to take Cap's place. So they'll promote him over your head.*

Lew knew that Pete wanted him to go

now, so he left, hating what this thing had become. Pete had been sober for weeks on end, and now he wanted to be alone with that bottle. He wouldn't come out of his cabin until it was gone and he had slept it partly off. Then he would go ashore and wander uptown, then come back with maybe four or five quarts of whiskey, shut himself in his cabin, and not show up for four or five days. That was the way Pete Wilmot drank, with deadly seriousness, alone and trying to destroy whatever it was in him that brought on the black mood.

Anger rising, Lew went to Ollie's cabin. "I'm surprised you're not already ashore having more stripes sewed on your sleeves."

Ollie grinned. "I know it when I've got a chance to cut a corner, kid." He seemed to feel no embarrassment, no need to justify himself. Nobody had ever tried to help Ollie Vail, he would sometimes say. Plenty had tried to knife him. He had learned to punch when he saw an opening and to hell with the man it hit.

Lew knew that there was some basis for this. Competition for officerships and command was keen on the river. A lot of men won promotions who had not earned them through merit. He tried to think of how it had been when Ollie was a mere roustabout, with little promise of doing better for himself. He tried to remember how unselfishly Ollie had kept him in school. Ollie didn't care much for good times, but he did care about money in the bank. He could have had a lot more of it except for his kid brother.

Lew didn't say anything more. Ollie was doing the smart thing, according to his own lights. After all, maybe Pete Wilmot deserved it.

Everybody liked Pete Wilmot for just this irresponsibility. With more self-control, he would have been a master long ago. Back in his own cabin and sitting glumly on the bunk, Lew thought about it. Pete was one of those men whose natural skill and adeptness made everyone overlook his faults. He was ten years older than Ollie, and he had been promoted in spite of himself, simply because, when sober, he was a damned good river man and because he religiously respected the company rules against drinking on duty. Since nobody ever saw him drunk, his periodic lapses were overlooked. Aboard and ashore.

Cap had liked Pete and had done much to protect him. They had been good friends. This is why it put a feeling close to nausea in Lew's stomach to think that Ollie had picked a moment when grief would be in Pete to pose his temptation.

As with everyone who is popular, there were stories about Pete Wilmot. A tall, gaunt man, slow moving and soft speaking, quietly humorous and always thoughtful, he captured the interest of everybody, and people talked of him frequently in a way that could scarcely be called scandal-mongering.

Yet, the only first-hand information Lew had about the man was that Pete's wife had left him a year before, and that there had been a little girl. This, though, was not the cause of Pete Wilmot's drinking but one of the consequences. Before then, Pete had gone on his benders at home. Lew had felt a secret sympathy for Mrs. Wilmot. She had not wanted the little girl to grow up watching those things. There must have been much pleading before she decided it was hopeless.

Lew had never seen Mrs. Wilmot, but he knew something that Pete would not like for him to know. Once, when Pete kept to his cabin unusually long, Lew had gone there. Pete had been asleep on the bunk, and the cabin had reeked with unwholesome fumes, and Lew had turned to leave again when he halted, staring.

There was a small locker fastened to the bulkhead at the foot of Pete's bunk, as in all the cabins, for storing personal gear. Now the small, hinged door was open, and Lew saw there was a picture fastened to the back. A pretty woman with blonde hair, and with a little girl beside her who was the image of her mother. Both looked a little self-conscious and proud.

Pete Wilmot had kept this picture on the back of the locker door, so that it could be shut from sight whenever anybody else was in his cabin, so that it could be opened to him when he was alone, and particularly when he was stretched on his bunk.

There was one bleakly hopeless thing that he might do, Lew decided. When the bottle was empty, Pete would sleep soddenly. If Lew could catch him, just when he awakened with the fires of thirst burning hotly in every nerve, Pete might be persuaded out of it. Lew had little hope of this, but he awakened at dawn and went at once to Pete's cabin, but Pete was gone.

It was a gray, chill day, and presently rain began to tumble out of the overcast sky, splashing the wharf and the packet. The *Swallow* remained tied up, with mechanics working below on the engines. An hour later, as he watched from his cabin, Lew saw

Pete come across the dock, a carpet-cloth valise in one hand but lurching because of more than its weight. It was worse than usual this time, and Pete had quenched his fires ashore, and it was again too late.

Lew was in the shore office that afternoon, working on the packet's paper, when Ollie came in to see Bill Seymour. He heard Seymour say: "Where's Pete?"

Ollie replied in the calmest way: "Busy."

"Well," Seymour said, "tell him he's taking the *Swallow* out in the morning, and I want him to be fit for it."

"Sure," Ollie said, as mildly as if there was no doubt that Pete would be.

Lew hated his brother at that moment, seeing the cold thoroughness of Ollie's plans. Dropping no hints, covering up for Pete just as Cap had done, laying himself open in no way. Ollie knew that Pete would never speak of how he happened to get started this time. He knew that his kid brother would never speak of it. Objectively, Pete Wilmot was bringing about his own downfall, and who would question it if this also meant a windfall for Ollie Vail?

Finished with his clerical work, Lew went back aboard the packet, going immediately to Ollie's cabin.

"Why don't you go ahead and move into

Cap's cabin?" he asked harshly.

Ollie looked at him for a studious moment. "Listen, kid, I'm getting tired of your talk."

"You're going to hear more of it." All night Lew had wondered how to say this, and now all his carefully rehearsed words slipped from mind, and he was saying in a breathless rush: "You know I'm grateful for what you've done for me, Ollie. Anyhow, I can pay you back the cash. I meant to pay you back another way, but I know I can't do it now. You figured you were helping me to cut a big corner when you sent me to school, and probably that was right. We cut another when I signed on as an officer, without coming up from the deck force or from the engine room. I don't want it that way, Ollie. It's not making me a river man, even if I can wear a uniform and eat with the passengers and cuss out a deckhand if I feel like it. I want to learn the river, and I'm going to start on another packet as a deckhand, if I can."

He saw that it was even more of a slap to Ollie than he had expected. There were stains in Ollie's cheeks, but not from anger. Then Ollie made it easier for him. "A fine thing, when I've given you a start that might put you in Bill Seymour's job some day!"

"Do you want me there for my sake or yours, Ollie?" He knew it was the cruelest thing he ever could have said, yet, even as he spoke, Lew knew that it had some basis of truth. Grimly he continued: "You've cut a lot of corners yourself, Ollie. Maybe you were long enough in each job to be a river man now, maybe not. Sure you've taken the *Swallow* up the river, and you've brought her down. But you always had Pete Wilmot and Cap aboard. If you take these two jumps at one time, you'll be on your own, and are you sure you can cut it?"

Ollie was getting genuinely angry now. "I know damned well I can cut it." Yet there was more than ruffled temper. For years Ollie Vail had known that he had been his kid brother's hero. He knew that he was no longer that. He knew that he was despised. He did not like this, but it was patent that his determination was not one whit diminished.

Pete Wilmot was still in his cabin when the *Swallow* slipped her lines the next morning and stood out into the Willamette. He had not emerged when later they were on the Columbia, heading eastward toward the great gorge in the Cascades. Lew Vail knew grimly that Ollie was going to have to earn every iota of his promotion. He would have to keep at the wheel the entire trip.

The deck force was buzzing now about Pete, and this was true down in the engine room. They all liked Pete Wilmot, and Lew doubted that one of these would talk out of turn. The trouble would come when they were again in Portland and Ollie again took care of the master's port details. Bill Seymour would know the truth then. He would realize that his own tolerance of Pete had been imposed upon. He would be angry that Pete's long record for strict sobriety on duty had made it seem unnecessary to check to make personally sure that he was in shape for work. That would be Ollie's hour.

They nooned at the Cascades and received passengers and cargo coming down from the upper flights, portaging here around the fierce rapids. The rain fell hard all morning, but for a time at the Cascades it slackened. When the *Swallow* stood down-river again at two in the afternoon, it seemed to Lew that the overcast sky had dropped, cutting off the tips of the vaulting, green-conifered mountains. Cloud wisps were floating nearly motionless across the faces of the cliffs, lending strangeness to the familiar panorama and the feeling of con-striction. They would be lucky not to be slicing fog with the jackstaff by the time they reached the Willamette. Then his purser's duties claimed him, and, a careful man, Lew gave them his full attention.

Two hours later Lew looked out across the river to see a definite milkiness in the air that masked the Washington shore, and he noticed by the throb of the engines that they were moving at a slackened speed. When he emerged onto the deck, he saw that neither shore was visible, that visibility held for only a few hundred feet on the channel ahead. At that moment the *Swallow*'s whistle cut loose, on a sweet, rising chord, then abruptly ceased. In a couple of seconds the echo rebounded, and Lew knew that this was telling Ollie, up in the wheelhouse, the distance to the nearest shore.

Lew climbed to the roof and stepped into the wheelhouse. Without taking his eyes off the limited channel ahead, Ollie said: "It just closed in like this. Damn it, I was sure hoping it'd hold off until we're out of the gut!" There was a tightness in his voice that was not usual to him.

Lew knew that they were in no danger, even as Ollie knew it. A good river pilot knew his headings as intimately as a man knows his way around his own house in the dark. Ollie had done this before and with ease, but now he had tightened up. Ollie was not unmindful of the scores of passengers on the deck below or the extremely expensive packet for which he was solely responsible. Lew thought he knew what Ollie was missing. It was backing, the backing of a more seasoned head.

It grew worse, and Lew could not tell if they had passed Crown Point and Rooster Rock and emerged from the gorge. Once Ollie said: "Did you mean it about transferring to another boat, kid?"

Lew said: "I guess I did, Ollie."

Then they were boring on through the fog.

Abruptly rain began to fall through the fog, needling the water. Lew could see Ollie growing tenser, and he said: "What if you can't find the Willamette? If we keep going, we'd wind up in Astoria."

He heard Ollie swear under his breath. "What're you trying to do?" Ollie snapped, and there was a hint of panic in his voice.

Lew regretted his efforts then, and reassured himself with the thought that he hadn't really believed that Ollie could be panicked by this. He thought of the passengers whose safety was in Ollie's hands.

They raised a small, midchannel island then, and Ollie heeled her over so fast that Lew had difficulty in keeping his feet. That was bad, dangerously bad, and if this feeling kept building in Ollie, it could only end in serious trouble.

Lew was thinking only of the passengers when he hurried back to the texas. The door to Pete Wilmot's cabin was not locked, and Lew shoved it open. The close, reeking air of the cabin hit him as he stepped inside. Pete was stretched out on his bunk, fully clad, snoring loudly, and there was a half-empty bottle of whiskey on the deck beside the bunk.

Lew shook him. "Pete! Pete! Wake up!" Caught after sleep and restrained from further drinking, Pete might be sober enough to be of some use. He kept shaking the man.

Pete stirred presently. "What d'you want?"

"Pete, there's a tule fog, and Ollie's getting rattled. You'd better stand by!"

After a moment Pete grumbled: "To hell with it. Ollie wants to be captain. Let him be captain."

Lew's eyes fell on the gear locker at the foot of the bunk then. Without thinking, he said: "Pete, your wife and little girl are aboard. They come aboard at the Cascades."

Pete sat up, staring at him. Then he said flatly: "You're crazy."

"I'm not, Pete. I've never seen them, but Missus Wilmot has blonde hair, doesn't she? And a dimple in her left cheek? And she's kind of shy and proud, isn't she? And the little girl's just like her. I happened to hear somebody call her Missus Wilmot."

Pete's eyes gradually lost their look of incredulity. "It could be. She's got an uncle in Dalles City. They could've been up visiting him." He reached instinctively for the bottle.

"Cut it out!" Lew said harshly. "Come down to the galley, and let's have some coffee."

Ten minutes later, when they stepped into the wheelhouse, Ollie only glanced over his shoulder. It was an awkward moment.

"You sober?" Ollie snapped at Pete.

"Did I ever come in here when I wasn't?"

Lew could see the tension running out of Ollie, and this was what he had hoped for. With his rival half sober again and standing by, Ollie would not dare let himself go to pieces.

Ollie knew this, and it was Ollie who took her on down the Columbia, then up the Willamette to Portland. And Ollie's little game was not spoiled, for anybody coming within feet of Pete Wilmot would catch the reek of whiskey.

As the deckhands made her fast at the wharf, Ollie turned to look at Pete. He said: "Pete, I wish you'd kick me hard as you can make it. You've got a right to hate me, but I hope you'll keep me on as your first."

There was only a mild wonder in Pete Wilmot's voice. "I'm not fit for the job, boy. It's yours, and no hard feelings."

"Uhn-uh." Ollie stared at him. First of all, he was a river man. "The minute you stepped in here, I started to get hold of myself. It wasn't that I didn't want you to see me scared. It was because I suddenly knew everything was all right." He paused a moment, then said: "Brother, I want to practice a while yet before I take that onto my own shoulders."

"You got to smell it a long while to really know the river," Pete agreed, and stepped out.

Lew did not follow him immediately. Nearly an hour had passed when he knocked at Pete's cabin and stepped into it at the mate's invitation. He was only half surprised that Pete was sitting quietly in a chair, and that the picture had come out of hiding and now was openly displayed on the standtable. The partly empty bottle of whiskey was where it had been before, and now Lew saw three full ones under the standtable. At first Lew could not tell if Pete had touched it after he came back.

Lew said: "Pete, I've got to admit that I lied to you. I saw that picture one day, and I knew how to describe them. But they weren't aboard."

Pete nodded. "I wasn't sure. It's all right, kid." Then he added: "Do you know that's the first time I ever broke one right in the middle? They've always had to run themselves out before they'd let go of me."

"But why, Pete? Why do you always do it?"

"There's no reason. It's a disease."

Lew was angry then at Mrs. Wilmot. Pleading wasn't what Pete had needed, or censure, or shame. He had needed to be shown that Pete Wilmot was stronger than anything that could be poured out of a bottle. Without thinking, Lew said: "Pete, you couldn't let the passengers down, could you? It's because of them that you broke it in the middle, isn't it?"

"I reckon so."

"But you did let your family down, didn't you? In another way they were strictly in your hands, too."

"I been thinking about that. I come back here because I needed a drink, but I ain't taken it yet."

"Why don't you take the job, Pete? Bill Seymour doesn't know about this, and I don't think anybody's going to tell him. You've been drunk on duty before, and Ollie tricked you into it. I've got a feeling that, if you took the job and kept this thing busted, Missus Wilmot would be happy to have you back again. It's worth a try, isn't it?"

"I reckon it is, Lew." There was a hard tension in Pete Wilmot's homely face.

Like a sigh, Lew said: "All right. Now, do we have a drink on it?"

After a long moment, Pete grinned. "We do. Coffee, kid. Come on, let's you and me go down to the galley."

And Lew went with him for, like Ollie, he wanted above all else to be a real river man.

A Bridge to the Future

Kermit did not use the letter. Instead, he rode the bus into Snyderville, then caught a Halvarsen truck out to the bridge job like any toughened construction hand confident of getting on. Only young Kermit Shrock was not seasoned, and he was anything but confident. He had come out of the mist-sprayed coolness of a vegetable stand in a big chain store in the city to plow into the lapping heat waves of this Catjaw high desert country.

The letter was in his scuffed, old suitcase with the new, work clothes, his father's gold, hunting-case watch, his mother's Bible, and the old snapshot from the days when the family had been together. It was only something that Kermit valued but probably would never do anything with. It was just something to keep.

He had never been east of the Cascades before, and the bare, rugged, burning vastness of the brown land roused a deep disturbance in him. Savants explained that once a more violent Pacific had laid claim to the continent, pulling itself inland as far as the Rockies, only to be defeated by crust spasms and hurled back. Vast inland lakes had been left behind by it that, in the young turbulence of the earth, had rolled and scoured for æons. Surely its marks remained here and the sense of old and massive conflicts.

A state highway was going across the desert now, but the Hell High Cañon bridge contract was only one of many Halvarsen Construction Company jobs. Kermit had no idea where big Charlie Halvarsen was, at present. Certainly he would have forgotten the letter he wrote, twelve years before, down on the coast. A letter the big, tow-headed engineer had addressed to the future — his own, Kermit had come to realize. Halvarsen had caught up with that future. Since then he had become one of the biggest bridge contractors on the West Coast. Kermit guessed that the letter might embarrass him now.

Alkali dust boiled up around the flatbed truck on the battered, temporary road to the cañon. In the hollows between the rearing escarpments of rimrock that stretched for unending miles, it was unbearably hot and frightening to a valley man. The road climbed gradually onto a plateau that was split deeply by the raging, white river. The Halvarsen camp stood on the lip of the river cañon, unsheltered, dusty, slowly burning in the beating sun, graced only by scrub juniper and sage and rabbit brush.

Sweat and dust had muddled Kermit's face by the time the truck clattered into the camp. The driver pointed out a shack that was the site office. "You'll find Vic Loos in there, likely, kid. If he's in a good humor, you'll probably get a job. But you must need one bad to come to this stink hole."

Kermit thanked the man and went into the office. There was a big room, with a couple of smaller ones opening from it. An office man was footing a stack of timecards. He looked at Kermit, seeing a big, raw-boned youth, and nodded vacantly.

"What's on your mind, kid?"

"Who'd I see about a job?"

The clerk jerked a thumb toward one of the side doors. Kermit went in what must be Vic Loos's office. A man was tilted back in a swivel chair there, paring his fingernails with a jackknife. He was in his mid-thirties, a slat-bodied man with curly brown hair that was short and parted precisely in the

312

middle. His lean face showed the weathering of any construction man, but was petulant. He kept on cutting his nails, seeming unaware that anybody had come in.

There was patience and a quiet dignity in young Kermit Shrock, and he continued to stand silently even when he became aware that he was being ignored with a subtle kind of contempt. Yet a prickling sensation had crawled into his temples. Loos finished one hand and went to work on the other. All five fingers, cutting and scraping and cleaning, then he snapped the knife shut.

In the calmest way Kermit said: "If you want to fix your feet while you're at it, mister, I can wait."

Loos shot him a quick, puzzled glance, then dislike began to seep into his eyes. "What do *you* want?"

"A job."

"What kind?"

"Anything."

Loos tapped the edge of the desk with the knife, scowling. "Good, as well as smart, are you? You don't look dry behind the ears."

"I don't mean I can do anything," Kermit said mildly. "I mean I'm willing to. I'd like to get a start in the bridge game."

After a long moment, Loos nodded. "All right. Tell Dunkel to fill out the papers."

Kermit went back to the outer office. Murray Dunkel looked at him with hard interest, then got some mimeographed forms out of a desk drawer. Loos came out of his office with his hat on, snapping at Dunkel as he passed: "Send him down to Harry Wister. He wants to build a bridge." He went on out, smiling grimly to himself.

Dunkel slipped a form into a typewriter and looked at Kermit again. The clerk was young, too. In a lean, hard way he was good-looking. Now his lips formed a soundless whistle. "You set him back on his tail, kid."

Kermit grinned. "For a minute I didn't give a hoot if he hired me or not. How come he did?"

"If you'd been sent packing, you'd never learn you can't do things like that, kid. But let's fill out this application."

Kermit answered a lot of questions. He was twenty-one, weighed a hundred eighty-three, stood six-one. Dunkel wrote "light" and "fair" in the hair and complexion spaces without asking and put down "blue" for Kermit's gray-green eyes. Kermit divulged that he had completed eight grades of school, had no next of kin, that his main experience had been selling papers, carrying a route, and working in a chain grocery store. There were a lot of other questions, to which he dug up answers. Then he put his name on a line at the bottom.

Dunkel said: "Here's a tip, kid. Some guys've got a foot you got to kiss every day if you don't want it in your pants. Loos is one of 'em. But if you ever say I said that, I'll call you a liar. Me, I just try to get along."

Within a week young Kermit Shrock knew exactly what Dunkel had meant, and why he had been hired instead of sent packing for giving the job engineer the lip. It was a tough camp, shot through with political influence. Vic Loos had a hand-picked cadre cut to his own egotistical pattern. The rest of the outfit truckled, or suffered the consequences.

The cañon that the bridge was spanning was over three hundred feet deep and much less than that across, two rises of basalt rock that, at the top, burned through the soles of a man's shoes. A cantilever bridge was going in, with massive, arched concrete-and-steel footings to be bonded to either wall. The bases had been hewn out and forms were being built. A concrete-mixing plant was being constructed. The campsite of the big cut was littered with lumber, sand, and gravel, sacked cement, and equipment. The camp shacks sat unprotected, slowly browning in the eternal sun. A huge gantry stood on the lip, and a suspension walk had been built across the cañon. Jackhammers and air compressors chattered and panted through the long days.

When he first looked down at the river so far below, a tight sickness had filled Kermit's stomach. There were cables and ropes everywhere, and scores of men worked up and down the faces of the cliffs around the footings. As a common laborer, Kermit found that he was assignable anywhere the extra help was needed. Harry Wister, the job foreman, proved to be a big, burly man who fawned on Vic Loos and, as compensation, rode roughshod over the crew. The first morning Wister divined that young Kermit was afraid of the big gut, and the game was on. He was totally inexperienced and so was wide open for abuse. They gave him the most dangerous chores on the project, time after time, working on the high cat-walks, swinging in bosun's seats, retrieving tools and materials from high, rocky eminences, toting dynamite for the powder man.

At first, Kermit thought it was a matter of getting used to it, but he couldn't. He never dared look down, when he worked around the forms, and his nights were filled with sweating, terrifying dreams. He realized that he was being given the more dangerous work than would be his normal run of luck. They wanted him to quit, to show yellow, and pull out. Yet Kermit carried out every task they assigned him with a patience and dignity that was maddening to his taunters. He saw Vic Loos's enmity deepening.

At the end of the first week, Kermit knew that he was close to finished. The heat remained, constant and torturous, and his suffering was only a little abated after someone troubled to tell him to take the salt tablets kept by all the water coolers. The temper that had prompted him to speak up to Vic Loos that first day crowded close to the surface. Loos would never give up until he had broken the boy's spirit. Kermit knew it and despaired. He fought down his terror of the cañon, and he carried out their risky chores. He came to the end of his rope.

He would have nailed Vic Loos and given him what he had coming had he not dreamed one night of big Charlie Halvarsen. The dream remained vivid when he wakened and lay spent and miserable in the dawn. His mind went back then to the cool bay and the huge bridge the W. P. A. was building across it.

★ ★ ★

Kermit Shrock had been living with his widowed mother then, on the little coast ranch that was mostly salal and salmonberry. They had kept a few cows, and every evening the nine-year-old Kermit had gone to the town to deliver milk. He never failed to pause on his way home to admire the new bridge, the pure strength and beauty of it as it looped across the wide mud flats.

Charlie Halvarsen had been a minor engineer on that project. He had once headed his own company, but the Depression had wiped it out, and he had been forced to go to work for somebody else. Kermit had not realized that anybody had noticed his own rapt interest in the bridge until one evening when Halvarsen stopped beside him.

"What do you think of it, son?"

Kermit had been unable to express himself for a thoughtful moment. "There's nothing purtier," he had breathed, at last. "Nothing could be any purtier."

Often, after that, he would see Halvarsen, and they would talk for a while. The engineer had explained a lot of the technical details. At that time Kermit had not guessed the deep discouragement that was in the man. They were good friends by the time the bay bridge was finished, and, the last time they met, Halvarsen had given Kermit the letter. Though he had read it a thousand times since, the photographic impression of that first reading, as he sat beside the road on his way home, would have lasted for Kermit's lifetime.

The unsealed envelope had been addressed simply to a Halvarsen Construction Company of the future, and the letter was very brief.

This is to recommend Kermit Shrock for employment as a bridge-man. A man needs no better qualification than his belief that a bridge is a "purty thing."

It had taken Kermit a long while to understand that his boyish enthusiasm had fueled lagging fires within the big man. That Charlie Halvarsen must have learned to see bridges again as the boy had seen the bay bridge. So Halvarsen had got on his feet again. Now he was known everywhere.

Even so, Kermit did not take the letter out of his suitcase when he rose to dress that morning. He had never had the chance to study to become the big engineer he had hoped to be. His mother had married again, and his stepfather had moved them to the city. He had not cared for his stepson, and finally had deserted them both. The burden had become Kermit's until finally his mother had died from overwork and discouragement. Even then, it had been several months before Kermit realized he was free and decided to go to work for Charlie Halvarsen's company — on his own and not daring to use the letter.

As he tramped out to the job in the morning's rising heat, Kermit knew that he had to stick. Even this bridge, in what all the men called a hell hole, would be a beauty when it was built. He was having a part in it, and this was something that Vic Loos and all his toadies could not touch. So Kermit once more dared the scaffolding in the cañon.

Kermit gained a friend shortly after that. Murray Dunkel, the office man, had been sharing a two-by-four shack with an engineering aide Loos fired for insubordination. Dunkel had been good friends with the man, and the incident seemed to put a bit of starch in his spine. He invited Kermit to move in. Kermit accepted, and he quickly grew to like the clerk. Dunkel was cynical and frankly self-seeking, but somewhere in him was a sense of sympathy. Dunkel heard things in the office, and Kermit finally learned exactly what he was up against.

"Loos hates you worse than the day you made him feel foolish," Dunkel told Kermit. "He expected to have you scared out long before this. If you're smart, you'll clear out, fella. But I know you won't. You're a funny kid."

"I want to work for this outfit. I'll get over being scared, and then it won't matter."

"Boy, you'll never get anywhere till you play ball with the powers that be. You'll never get a promotion. You'll never get anything. Loos has got this outfit in the palm of his hand. He can even fix it so you can't go to work for another unit."

"What's Charlie Halvarsen thinking about? He's not that kind of man!"

Dunkel grinned. "Maybe not. I've only seen him a time or two. But he's got too much on his mind to know what's going on everywhere. That's why the little big-shots can get away with murder. Tell you something that's got Loos nervous, though. Halvarsen expects to be up here next month."

Kermit's last resolution vanished. He wanted to see big Charlie again, though he knew the contractor would neither recognize nor recall him. He wore out the weeks, but he did not grow less frightened of the cañon. Vic Loos did not hate him less.

Then Loos decided to wind up the business summarily. At his vantage point in the office, Murray Dunkel began to perceive and report the plot.

"A man like that not only hates the man he can't break. He gets scared of him. The boys in camp here're afraid to get friendly with you, but they know what's going on. If Loos don't break you, he'll know he's slipping. Two things have always happened before. Either they knuckle down or they spout off and get fired. A man or two's tried to whip Loos, but he won't corner. So he can't figure it out. You just take it, when everybody knows you're scared to death of the gut."

"I'll whip him before I'm done with it."

"He don't mean to give you the chance. I heard him and Harry Wister talking about you. He wants to get rid of you before Charlie Halvarsen comes up. He's afraid you're one man with the guts to spout off about things."

"Think he'll just fire me?" Kermit asked. He was proud that he hadn't been scared out.

"They don't dare, now. They've got to make you quit or frame cause, so anything you say'll sound like spite. Just watch it, kid. Loos got a letter from Halvarsen. He'll be up here about Monday."

Saturday arrived with nothing new being introduced into the now familiar pattern. They finished the lower forms on Friday, and pouring was to start on the bases the following Monday. Kermit was helping to clean up the litter left by the carpenters, and in mid-morning followed the foreman to the lip.

Wister pointed down into the gut to where the white waters of the river boiled eternally. "Look, kid, it's low water. We want to get a stage gauge painted on that bluff down there, big enough to read from the top. All it takes is a big white line on the rock every foot for about ten feet. Get a bucket of paint and a brush and something to use for a straight edge. Pete'll let you down with the gantry."

Kermit stared at him, the old sickness souring his tight stomach. He did not know whether the work was really necessary or not. But he could tell from the wicked gleam in Wister's eye that the foreman expected him to beg off. Kermit looked down once more along the three hundred feet of bulging cliff, and could not help swallowing. But he forced himself to say — "OK." — and move off toward the supply room.

As long as he had been on the job, nobody had ever descended the cañon in this wise, and for an instant, before he slid into the bosun's chair on the line swinging from the gantry crane, Kermit almost rebelled. But scores of eyes were watching him now, some in sympathy, others in amusement. They had seen things of this nature so many times before.

Then a man growled: "What do we care what the river stage is? It'd take another Noah's flood to reach the top!"

Wister turned on him savagely. "Since when did you start questioning what we do around here?"

Kermit was in the seat, a gallon of white paint, a brush, and a short length of one-by-four hanging from it. The gantryman lifted him and swung him over the lip. It took every ounce of Kermit's strength to keep from shutting his eyes until he was out of sight. Then they glued tight, his sweating hands clamped to the rope sling fastened to the singing cable, and all his fear of his weeks here was less than now.

He knew that he was dropping far faster than was safe. Once he brushed the rock, and after that he kept his eyes open, watching the bulges below him, missing them by a hair's breadth, swinging himself into the clear with his feet. It grew shadowy as he dropped into the earth. Then the growling, white-frothed river seemed to leap at him.

Kermit knew he was going to hit the water. Instead of halting him twenty feet above, finishing the descent in delicate drops, the flagman only dipped his flag for slow. Kermit hit the boiling water and went under, and but for the safety belt he would have been washed from the seat. He clawed to the surface, the line slack around him, then it tightened with unnecessary roughness, swinging him out of the water and letting him arc wildly from one cliff to the other.

Rage forced the last bit of fear from him. It was coldly, cruelly deliberate. They expected him to be in such a state of nerves when he reached the top again that he would like nothing better than his time. He got the swinging stopped. He knew that they never expected him to last this long. He was certain now that there was no real need for gauge marks on the cliff. But they would get them!

His equipment had survived the submersion, and Kermit pried the lid off the paint bucket. In water to his waist, he measured the first twelve inches, steadied the board he had brought for a straight edge, and painted a line. Then he measured the next and painted it, and signaled the rim for a slight lift. One by one he painted the ten lines, with the gantryman occasionally giving him a jerk that sent him swinging crazily, certain he was going to have his brains dashed out against the rocks.

Yet the arresting fear of weeks did not return to him. A fierce determination came to him with the knowledge that he had taken their worst, unless they actually were prepared to murder him. He wasn't even afraid of that, in his deep anger. He finished his lines, threw away the straight edge, and signaled to be brought up.

The gantryman put everything he had into that rise. At times Kermit was certain he would be flung from the swinging seat, belt or no, and again a bulge above him seemed certain to crush his skull like an egg shell. Yet his eyes were open when he came up over the lip and the crane operator swung him in and dropped him roughly to the ground. They had licked the fear they themselves had fostered. He could be a bridgeman.

Kermit's knees were weak as he staggered to his feet and unfastened his safety belt. Most of the crew had gathered here by now, and there was a new look on their faces. Kermit did not take time to interpret it. He plunged straight for Harry Wister.

The big foreman was prepared for it. He bent as Kermit charged, and he got it in the first swing, a clipping punch that made a ringing sound in Kermit's ears. Wister grinned, sure of himself suddenly as Kermit staggered.

Kermit shook his head. His first surge of rage quieted, and the coldness of pond ice was in his eyes. He moved in lightly, deliberately. A smoking left fist sank into Wister's belly, bringing a grunt. A right cross clipped his jaw. The foreman's eyes glazed, his knees slacked. He fell like a sack of cement.

A man said softly: "That does me more good than a month in town."

Kermit headed for the office, which was out of sight of the lip. He did not notice a strange, dusty coupe parked in front. He plowed through the door and ignored the alarmed, wild shakes of Murray Dunkel's head. He surged into Vic Loos's private office.

Loos had been talking to somebody, but he looked up, and his eyes went wild. He clawed up out of his chair, backing. There was clearly no fight in him. Kermit seized him by the shirt front and began slapping the man. He slapped him until the man fell down on the floor and refused to rise.

A deep voice said: "That's enough, pup."

Kermit looked around. "Charlie Halvarsen!" he gasped.

Vic Loos struggled to his feet. He looked wildly at the big contractor. "The man's been a troublemaker from the start. You're fired, Shrock! Get out!"

"Just a minute, young man." Charlie Halvarsen's booming voice sounded exactly as it had twelve years before. "I'd like to know why you did it, before you go."

"I did it, and I got my money's worth. I'm ready to quit." Kermit had no charges to make. He knew they had never expected him to last long enough to paint those unnecessary markers at the bottom of the cliff. Now let them try to erase them!

Halvarsen looked at Loos. "I've been learning a lot of things by showing up on a job a day or two ahead of schedule. This kid isn't a troublemaker. No man who thinks a bridge is the 'purtiest thing on earth' would try to gum up the works."

Kermit stared. "You remember?"

"I sure do, but I didn't place you till he said your name. Why didn't you ever use that letter, boy? I went down to the coast once to look you up, but you were gone."

"Yeah, we moved away."

Halvarsen grinned at Loos, who was shifting position uneasily. "It's something you wouldn't understand, fellow. I was ready to get out of the game once, until a young shaver reminded me that a bridge is a thing of beauty. I think you might as well start packing, Loos, and take your sidekicks with you. I'm only sorry he isn't ready to take your job. But maybe he will be, before long. He meets the basic requirement . . . give me a man who loves a bridge, and it's easy to build the engineer."

Miracle of Starvation Flat

I

Clinging to the stormy top of the pile drivers, Cal Larimore caught a glimpse of Kim Nagel through the rain-spattered windows of the office shack. The old time-keeper was footing up a stack of invoices that could not be paid, his bald, gray head bobbing in emphasis as his pencil climbed a discouraging column of figures. Cal's lips tightened. Wind beating his face, he looked at Ole Jensen, his rigger.

"Well, Ole, what's it going to take to make it work this time?"

Jensen made a mumbling sound. He was trying to investigate the rigging at the top of the pile-driver tower while holding a pipe stem in his teeth and making frequent grabs at his hat, which the wind seemed to want. The combination garbled whatever he said in reply. When Cal strained to hear, Ole removed the pipe for a second.

"I say it'll take a new sheave."

Cal shrugged, having absorbed too much news of this nature in recent weeks to be surprised. From the tower he could see most of the project under his charge. With only a few days' rain, big Rampage Lake was running its feelers across the narrows and spilling into the stinking, half-dry bed of Drip Pan. Cal could see the mile-length span of completed trestle that came within two hundred feet of meeting here at the dry connection between the two lakes. Rolling, high-desert country, reminding him of his native eastern Oregon, swept to the horizons. It was the same strange, lake-dotted waste.

A pair of laborers moved furtively around a distant sand dune toward the tents of the construction camp. Not realizing it was the big boss perched on the tower with Ole Jensen, they were sneaking off work early to get ready for a Saturday night's fun in Christmas Springs, for today had been pay day. Dropping down the cleated rungs of the ladder, Cal grinned wryly. They didn't know it was probably the last pay day that the Larimore Construction Company could meet.

On the ground, Cal turned toward the office, a big man, still young, with a surprisingly light and springy step. As he opened the door, wind puffed into the office, scrambling the papers on the drafting table Kim Nagel used as a desk. The old man smashed them flat as if he were killing mice, swiveled his skinny haunches on the stool, and got down. He went over to the hot stove where, due to a touchy stomach that kept his eating sparse but frequent, he always had a kettle of soup simmering. Cal found himself recalling again that Kim had tossed every cent he had saved toward a badly needed retirement into the bottomless well of Larimore finances.

Cal declined Kim's offer of soup but filled a granite cup from the coffee pot, simmering with the soup kettle. Taking it black, he turned toward a window and idly stared at the rivulets of water gradually turning the summer's dust on the pane into mud and washing it clean.

"How much did you say we'd have to raise to meet another pay day?" he asked Kim over his shoulder.

Kim's spoon plunked into the bowl, and there was a moment's silence while he looked at the piece of scratch paper. "About eight hundred to meet the payroll, but there's almost two thousand in overdue lumber and piling bills."

Cal nodded. It struck him that he was as

much concerned over Kim's future as his own. Kim's position in the company was only what his payroll designation said — timekeeper. Yet a few weeks back he had dug up a fistful of greenbacks he must have been hoarding for years and tossed it carelessly on Cal's desk. Cal's desperation had been greater than his reluctance, and he had accepted the money in exchange for a note.

"Well, the only chance is the bank in Christmas Springs," Cal said. While his gaze traveled over a long stretch of sage flats, frequently broken by high scarps, his mind's eye stared at a string of hard luck. "Maybe I should have doctored it up, but I gave Ira Fiddler an honest financial statement. It looked so sour there's no use hoping he won't turn me down. Anyhow, I can't see him till Monday."

Cal's troubles had started two years before with a railroad tunnel caving in just when it was ninety percent complete. It had left him strapped. Then had come a little road building on which Cal had made a modest profit. Following that was a grain elevator that had burned three days before he was ready to turn it over to its owners. Then came a track-laying job on which he had managed to hold his own.

It had forced him to bid desperately low

on this narrows bridge job, simply because he had to keep working to hold his outfit together and because he had to have a fighting chance to get on his feet again. But it had been a sour project from the start, with nothing really disastrous happening as yet but with an endless run of small, but money-draining, setbacks and delays, such as the pile driver having to shut down this afternoon for unexpected repairs.

Financial stringency had forced Cal to the most dangerous of contracting resorts. With materials, and whatever else he could, he had been required to operate on credit, from one contract to the next, getting in deeper month by month. The job was nearly finished and ready to be turned over to the Narrows Toll Bridge Company, but Cal had long known that the final payment on the contract would fall far short of cleaning up his outstanding bills — even if he could meet his payroll till then, for which he had to have cash. He clenched a fist and shoved it into his pocket.

"Cal, why don't you sound out the bridge company about an advance?" Kim asked.

"Never!" Immediately Cal regretted the sharpness of his reply, but the thing Kim had suggested was completely out. In the first place, no contractor liked to admit financial insolvency to the other principal to the contract. In the second, Johnny Van Dyke's new toll bridge company had already strapped itself in raising what capital it had. In the third, Cal didn't have enough still coming to do more than carry his payroll to the finish, which would still leave him with creditors ready to tie up his equipment. And, finally, he didn't want Johnny Van Dyke's sister to know how things stood with him.

"They got sense, and they got guts," said Kim. "Don't know as I'd be so touchy about it, Cal."

"That's out, Kim!" But Cal admitted that the men who were backing the project had both sense and guts. Johnny Van Dyke ran a store in Tuckerville, northward across twelve miles of flat desert. He freighted for himself, and, when his outfit wasn't busy, he brought in winter feed for the nesters and stockmen above the supply point. But there had been a lot of people besides Johnny who had seen the advantage in the narrows bridge. The grangers were hauling a lot of produce to the railroad at Christmas Springs now. The stockmen, who drove to railhead in summer when the narrows had emerged from the lake, were the only ones who had bucked the toll bridge.

Even so, there had been very few willing to back a bridge financially. Johnny Van Dyke had managed to organize half a dozen nesters into a company. The state legislature had given them a franchise to build a bridge across the narrows and charge a toll until it had paid for itself, after which it was to become a public thoroughfare. It was a selfless public service.

Old Kim, who was a quiet, restrained man, had a way of clearing his throat so that it sounded like a hearty curse. "Well, if you can't warm Ira Fiddler's heart, it looks like Neb Judkins wins his little argument."

Cal nodded. Neb Judkins had been the only open agitator against the toll bridge. For one thing, he claimed that Lake Rampage would buck the structure a mile in the air when the first real winter storm hit it. Lake Rampage and Lake Drip Pan were actually one lake in the winter, two in the summer, with spring-fed Rampage being the only true lake and Drip Pan its overflow. As a result of centuries of evaporation, Drip Pan now had a strong alkali stench.

This continual process of uniting and separating had created a road problem for the Starvation Flat country. For many years the summer road to Christmas Springs had run across the narrows. When it disappeared in winter, there was only the long road that swung east of Rampage, then made a long loop back again. A single, hard day's travel could put a Starvation Flat man in Christmas Springs in summer. In winter, using the longer road, he had to spend a night at Neb Judkins's tavern each way.

Because a year-'round, direct road to Christmas Springs would rob him of a good deal of his patronage, Judkins had bucked it with all he had. And he got a lot of backing from the cowmen beyond Tuckerville by pointing out that their summer drives across the narrows would thereafter cost them a toll. To which the drovers had reacted characteristically. But it had been a matter of hot-headed argument, with no actual violence thus far.

A violent flare-up was all it would take to finish him, Cal thought grimly. But for some strange reason even Neb Judkins had stopped shooting off his face about the bridge for the last several weeks, as if he had resigned himself to the inevitable. Or else believed, as he had claimed, that no one could build a bridge across the narrows that would stay there in dead winter, with a norther shoving six feet of water off Rampage and dumping it on Drip Pan with the soggy, mile-long bottom of the narrows, into which Cal had driven countless piling, an unknown quantity when inundated, with the whole thing a gamble anyhow. Thinking of that, it was less discouragement than irritation that began to grow in Cal Larimore.

It took a desperate turn when, two days later, he sat across the desk from Ira Fiddler in the Christmas Springs bank as soon as it opened for business Monday morning. A gray-faced, shriveled man, Fiddler kept his sharp eyes on Cal's face while cutting the ground out from under him.

"For the past three, four months I could tell from your bank balance what kind of shape you're in, Larimore. I didn't need to see your financial statement. It don't matter if you bid too low on the job. You're legally required to deliver a completed bridge, according to contract specifications, for the amount you bid. The bridge company's been paying you once a month for the work you accomplish. And I've noticed that you've been depositing their checks one day and drawing the money out the next."

"Great Scott, man, I've got my own bills to pay!" Cal had written a bank loan off as impossible and was in no mood to wheedle Fiddler. He climbed to his feet.

"Just a minute," Fiddler snapped. "I'm concerned about the bridge company.

Johnny Van Dyke, Mike Epstein, and the others're all good customers of my bank. In fact, I know they all mortgaged themselves to the hilt to form the company."

"With you carrying the paper?" asked Cal in sudden interest.

"I hold the paper," Fiddler admitted impatiently. "What I want to know is, are you going to get that bridge finished?"

"Supposing you leave it to the company to ask that, fellow," Cal told him softly. He turned toward the railing and strode out through the lobby. A harassing, hemmed-in feeling was turning him reckless.

II

The feeling nearly broke out of him the next morning when he saw Neb Judkins, the tavern operator, riding his roan horse over the long, newly planked trestle leading to the big suspension sections in the center, coming from Christmas Springs. Judkins had never before visited the job, and it was possible that he was only on his way through to Tuckerville, since the starting fall rains had not yet stopped light traffic past the project. Yet the sight of the man who had treated the bridge with opposition and ridicule served to raise Cal's hackles.

Judkins turned off the bridge at the far side of the break and forded the shallow channel connecting the two lake bodies. As he splashed up on the near side, his gaze traveled slowly over the campsite, picking out the office. Work was shut down for the time being, waiting on new parts for the pile driver, and Judkins seemed to find this pleasing. He rode up to the office shack and swung down, a short, pot-bellied man with cool, calculating eyes. He opened the door with a heavy shove of the elbow and came inside.

"Well?" asked Cal with no warmth, while Kim refused to look up from his pretended work.

Judkins let his glance settle on the old man. "Gran'pa, why don't you go take a snooze? I wanta talk to your boss."

Kim bristled but, at a signal from Cal, rose and wiggled into his slicker, yanked on his rain hat, and left. At the stove, Judkins pulled off his soaked, buckskin gloves and warmed his red, pudgy hands.

"Larimore, I been hearing about your troubles. I want to let you have enough money to pull you through."

Cal had been expecting anything but this, and he stared frankly. But his wariness had by no means been put down. His eyes narrowed. "There's only one place you could have heard about my troubles, Judkins. That's from Ira Fiddler. And what business he's got telling you private matters I'll find out."

Judkins was undisturbed. "Seen Ralph Erman, from the piling camp. He told me that him and that fellow who's got the sawmill over on Sterns Mountain're fixing to attach your equipment. They aim to get their time for the timbers they've hauled down to you."

Pouring himself a cup of coffee to cover his confusion, Cal digested the statement. He had expected something like that from his creditors eventually, and it didn't matter much who started it. But he wasn't satisfied.

"What makes you think I can't borrow money at the bank, if you haven't been talking to Fiddler?" he asked bluntly.

"I know Fiddler's got too much business sense to loan you money."

"Then how come you want to?"

Judkins grinned a little. "Who said anything about a loan. I want to give it to you."

"Speak out."

"Look, Larimore, you're bested. Once they start throwing attachments and garnishments at you, you're thrown, pig-tied, and hamstrung. You just ain't gonna finish anybody any bridge unless I help you, and there's no use in trying to bluff. I'm willing to advance you what you need till you're through with the bridge and out o' here."

"Where's the hook?"

"I want to see the bridge finished. It's like this, Larimore. I found out quite a spell back that I can't stop it from going in. The legislature's authorized it, and most of the country's for it, except for a handful of cowmen. The cowmen still don't want it, but so far they ain't been willing to do anything that might get them into trouble with the State. They'd rather work it smarter than that."

"Blast it, get to the point."

"All right, here it is. They'd a sight rather see this bridge finished up right and proper, and then see it go out this winter. If you know how to build a bridge that'll ride this wild lake, you sure oughta know how to build one that won't."

Cal's eyes were dangerous. "Are you trying to bribe me?"

"Simmer down, Larimore, till you come to your senses. If the bridge should smash up in a storm, would the bridge company have the money to fix it? Could they raise it when some of us've maintained from the start that you could never make a bridge stick here?"

Cal had heeled around, and now he said angrily: "Judkins, you'd better get out before you're thrown out!"

Judkins found a cigar in one of his pockets and lighted it unhurriedly. "Go ahead and do what you gotta to salve your conscience, then listen. Nobody'd blame you. It'd just be another of them ideas that looked good but didn't work. Moreover, you ain't got any say in the matter. The bridge is coming out. The men backing me'd rather see it wash out, but, if it don't, it'll come out some other way. Them cattlemen ain't paying tolls to drive their herds where they've always drove 'em for free."

"Then let 'em drive past. There's still room enough."

Judkins shook his head. "That'd be a damned nuisance for every herd. The cowmen aren't going to do that, especially when it's a bunch of pesky nesters causing the nuisance."

"Too thin, Judkins," Cal said flatly. "You're making a smoke screen out of those cattlemen. I've heard them griping about the nesters' gall, but they aren't anxious to promote what you're suggesting. Who're are you working for?"

"Me, most of all," Judkins admitted. "That bridge is going to ruin my place, Cal. It ain't anybody in particular. It's the combination you're hurting that you're up against." He grinned in a placating manner. "Could be we might throw in two, three extra thousand, Larimore, to help you get on your feet again."

"It's not worth that to you and the

cowmen put together, Judkins. It's the man holding mortgages on the bridge company's private property back of you. He's the only one I see who could afford to do what you say. Ira Fiddler, the Christmas Springs banker."

"Why do you care, Larimore? Shucks, you got every reason to listen to my proposition and none not to. No matter what you do, this bridge ain't going to be standing here come spring. What say?"

"This." With a sweep of his arm, Cal put down his coffee cup and his fist crashed into the man's face. Judkins staggered back, clawing for his gun. But Cal's fist sank into his flabby belly, and he grabbed the gun.

"I'd beat the stuffing out of you, Judkins, if you weren't such a soft thing," he growled. "I'll just keep your pop gun, but you'd better ride."

Pure hatred spat from Judkins's eyes, then he pulled himself together. "You're making a mistake, Larimore. You sure are. On account of I ain't told you half of it, yet. But it looks like you'd rather wait and find out."

Judkins strode toward the door, yanked it open, and stalked out.

When he saw Judkins ride angrily out of camp in the direction of Tuckerville, Kim

345

Nagel came back to the office. He shucked out of his rain apparel, asking no questions, and when Cal volunteered no information, he went to the stove and poured a little soup into a bowl. The routine, a necessary habit in the old man's life, reminded Cal forcefully of the money he owed Kim. If Judkins had told the truth about the piling and timber people seeking to attach his equipment, Cal would be unable to move it to a new job until his bills were paid. It added up to bankruptcy, which meant, in turn, that Kim Nagel's retirement had gone down the drain.

It struck Cal then with moving impact that Judkins had offered to throw in two or three thousand extra. That would pay Kim what he had coming. Cal closed his eyes for an instant, shaking his head. It was a lot easier to build a bridge that would collapse or wash out in storms such as Rampage knew in winter than to build one to stay. A few sudden changes in design for the uncompleted sections would keep even the men who did the actual work from understanding. The design had been left solely in Cal's hands, and he had introduced a number of masterly innovations to solve special problems. All he had to do was fail to supply the proper answer to a suspected but easily overlooked stress some place. If the main section collapsed, it would be enough to ruin the bridge company and probably any prospects of the bridge's being repaired. At least it would satisfy Judkins and who-ever was behind him until Cal Larimore was out of the country.

Cal's thoughts were broken by Ole Jensen, who came dripping through the door with a rather pleased look on his leathery face. "I got her patched up enough, Cal. I reckon we can finish the job before we have to give her a real overhaul."

He was referring to the pile driver, on which he had been working since Saturday. "We'll hit it again in the morning," he added.

Cal exchanged a slow glance with Kim. If work started up, his payroll commitment would begin again, and he had no money to meet it. For ten years, from the time he was fifteen, Cal Larimore had been on other men's payrolls, and he saw the viewpoint of those who had been on his crew for the five years after that. In fairness to them, he should lay them off at once and cancel their board bill at the company commissary for the two days he had kept them here idle.

He saw that the same worried consider-ations were taking place in Kim's mind.

This seemed to be it, the point where Cal had to admit defeat. Yet, hot rebellion rose in him. Cal Larimore knew but one way to go, which was straight ahead. He had to keep going that way until his luck changed. He had to redeem Kim's faith in him.

At least he couldn't face it yet, and he said: "I'll let you know what time to begin in the morning, Ole."

His own crew seemed to be the only ones in the country who did not fully realize the Larimore Construction's shaky financial position. Ole Jensen stared at Cal in wonder.

"Thought you were in a sweat to get this thing wound up so we can get out of this stink hole."

"I sure am, Ole." Three weeks or a month more should see that accomplished. Abruptly Cal's mood changed, energy whirling up in him, sharpening the point of his jaw. "Okay, fella. Tomorrow morning, and give it hell!"

There was a relieved look on old Kim's face as he lifted another spoonful of soup.

Leaving the office, Cal ploughed down the muddy camp street to his own tent. He washed and shaved in cold water and donned clean clothes. He was going to ride up to Tuckerville for a pow-wow with

Johnny Van Dyke, though he had no clear idea of what he would say to the young storekeeper. It was just that the two had cottoned to each other from the start. It was time for Cal Larimore to swallow his starchy pride and put his cards on the table. From the talk that seemed to be going around, it was probable that Johnny — and his sister, Lucretia, Cal remembered painfully — had already been hearing things and wondering.

It was good to be lined on action of any sort. Cal pointed his saddle horse north, leaving the vicinity of the two lakes and riding up through a break in the distant rimrock that the road penetrated. The same desert of sage and bunch grass extended beyond, but six miles farther north he splashed across Cougar Creek and came into the greener, rolling country that the nesters had taken up.

Cresting the first fringe of hills, Cal saw a rider far below, coming his way. As he dropped down, he lost sight of the figure and forgot it. Tuckerville was four or five miles ahead, and the thought of seeing Lucretia Van Dyke again for the first time in several weeks was pleasant to Cal. He rode his horse at an unrushed jog, as the wheel-churned road swung at a distance past a volcanic cone lifting out of the rolling prairie. He was abreast of it when his hat sailed off, with the report of a heavy gun instantly following.

III

Swinging down on the offside of his horse, Cal pulled his gun. It was mostly a reflex, for he knew that the range was too great for his .44. He had no idea how close the bullet had come to lethal velocity, but he knew it had been fired by a saddle gun of some sort. Muscles pulled tight, he waited for a moment; then the beat of a fast-ridden horse came to him from beyond the knoll, growing fainter.

Cal swung aboard then, knowing it had only been a warning. Recalling the blobbed image he had seen on the road far below only a few minutes before, he guessed that it was Neb Judkins who earlier had ridden this way. Judkins could have recognized Cal's flat-topped Stetson or the white-faced saddler he always rode. It had been a chance encounter, but evidently Judkins had decided to warn Cal against making dangerous talk in Tuckerville. Neb Judkins was going all out now that he had declared himself.

Haphazard little Tuckerville was an old cattle town, but these days it catered mostly to nesters. Wagons coupled to dejected horses stood on the rain-swept street as Cal jogged into its environs. He racked his horse before Johnny Van Dyke's store and, going through the door, saw that there were no customers for the moment and that Lucretia was there alone.

She was straightening out and replacing some goods that she apparently had just been showing to some nester's wife. She looked up with a mechanical smile, but, when she saw Cal, the expression changed, giving way to genuine pleasure.

"Why, Cal!" she cried. "I didn't know but what you'd drowned in the lake."

He grinned at her, his warming eyes taking in her slim, supple figure and the heavy, copper-colored hair that curled around her pretty face.

"The rain's been hard enough to drown a man, for that matter. Where's Johnny?"

"Over getting a haircut." Lucretia put a bolt of pink, polka-dot gingham back on the shelf behind the counter, and, when she looked at Cal again, she was frowning. "So it's only Johnny you wanted to see."

"And you, Lucy. Been running into trouble out at the job." Cal knew that his excuse sounded lame. At the start of the job he had ridden into Tuckerville once or twice a week, and Lucretia and he had ridden together several Sundays during the summer. He was both surprised and pleased that she had missed him. On impulse, he added: "What would a man have to do to get an invite for supper tonight?"

"Why, just show up with a good appetite." Lucretia's close scrutiny passed over his face, and there was a new, troubled look in her gray eyes. "Cal, you'll be leaving pretty soon." Her slight frown punished him again.

He caught the import of her words, and it did not strike him as bold. Lucretia was like Johnny — and himself — in seeing her objectives clearly and, with impatience, brushing aside the conventional complexities with which most folks surrounded things.

"I know, Lucy." He saw that another decision had been forced upon him. She apparently had not heard much about his financial troubles, and it was something else that was bothering her. She had a natural desire — and a right — to know what was to come of the friendship he had carefully sought, now that he logically would be leaving the country in search of his next job.

The honest candor and warmth in the girl's expression stirred him. He knew now what he had sensed and hoped before, that Lucretia would marry him when he asked her. Yet, what had he to offer her? He wouldn't even get out of the country with the equipment to tackle another job. He had worked for himself for five years under steadily deteriorating conditions. If that didn't add up to complete failure, his arithmetic was no good. He couldn't say what Lucy wanted him to say, and it was with pronounced relief that he heard the door open and turned to see Johnny coming in.

Cal saw at a glance that Johnny knew more than he had told his sister. His greeting was friendly, but Cal sensed a guarded reserve in it. Recalling that Neb Judkins had visited Tuckerville, Cal wondered for the first time what the man's business here had been.

"Anything special on your mind, Cal?" asked Johnny. He had some of his sister's slightness, but there was good breadth to his shoulders, a half-pugnacious jut to his jaw, and a fine clarity in his level gray eyes.

"Why, no," Cal said. "I come over to

accept the invite to supper I had a hunch I could wheedle out of Lucy."

Johnny got into his apron, and Lucy left for home, animated, Cal saw, because she had a supper to cook for him. When they were alone, Cal waited for Johnny to speak out, if he had anything special on his mind, but Johnny stuck to casual talk.

"Seen Neb Judkins lately?" Cal asked finally.

Johnny nodded. "He was in this afternoon to buy some makings." Then he put Cal somewhat at ease. "You know, I don't trust that cuss an inch. He had a look on his face like he'd stole somebody's wife. Even joshed me about the bridge. That's funny when it had him ringy for so long."

Cal felt a little relieved. Yet, he saw now that he could not spill ·his troubles to Johnny, much as he wanted to share them with a friend. It looked as if Johnny still trusted him to deliver a completed bridge, lock, stock and barrel, and there was no use adding to the man's worries.

On impulse, Cal said: "What do you reckon's going to happen next summer when the first driver hits the narrows with his herd and your gatekeeper demands a toll?"

Johnny grinned. "Hell'll be raised so high

you could run a load of hay under it. But, dang their hides, they can help pay for the bridge. That's all the tolls are for. It'll belong to the public after that. If everybody does his share, three, four years ought to make it a free road."

"But what if some old mossyhorn up and blows the bridge out on you?"

Johnny Van Dyke's gray eyes went cold. "They'd better wear their dodgin' shoes the day they try that. There'll be lead flying. I was a nester before I set up storekeeping, and I'm still a nester at heart. We took a lot off them cowpokes before we got strong enough to sass 'em. No, sir. They better think twice before they try anything like that." He looked at Cal closely. "What made you ask?"

"Just got to wondering." Cal grinned and shrugged in dismissal. Yet it had been slowly dawning on him that, while the cow interests had far less stake in the plot against the bridge than Judkins made out, the tavern owner might manage to enlist them in it as a general blow against the hated and growing nester colony. The cowmen were naturally proddy enough to be continually irritated by the obstruction in their habitual driving route to Christmas Springs. In any event, Judkins seemed determined to make them appear to be the bridge's main enemy, and he would try to make any dirty work seem to come from them.

Cal hated to mention his suspicions of the Christmas Springs banker until he had some proof, for Johnny and his friends were completely at the man's mercy and would be terribly worried. They would go on the prod themselves, and, conditions being what they were, bloody trouble would follow. It was up to Cal Larimore to get to the bottom of it and avoid that. Either he could do business with Judkins and make a disaster to the bridge seem so natural that there would be no such trouble, or he could buck Judkins himself and face ruin.

It was a hard decision to make, for Cal Larimore was very human. Independent contracting had been the dream of years for him, and he wanted to go on with it. He wanted the right to claim his girl. He wanted prosperity and prestige and the things that success can give a man. Yet, he wanted honor and peace of mind.

The wind had come up strong again, as Cal rode back to the camp, while black clouds rolled across the sky. Rain beat under his streaming hat and rolled down his neck, and, by the time he dropped down through the broken scarp toward the twin lakes, he was cold to the bone. He saw the sleeping camp stretched below, dark save for a single lantern that probably belonged to Walt Fink, the night watchman, and the standing light in the office where Fink warmed himself and ate his midnight lunch. As he studied the layout, a fierce pride rose in Cal, and he knew that he wasn't going to go down, no matter what.

As he jogged up the streaming camp road, Cal saw that Fink was working at the pile driver. The man did greasing and other maintenance work at night, yet it struck Cal as odd that the pile driver — under Ole Jensen's personal care these last three days — should still require attention. Cal dismounted, left his horse, and climbed the ladder to the trestle.

The howling wind, he saw, covered his approach until he was almost on top of Fink, and the man straightened as if he had been jabbed with a sharp stick. His next reaction was to kick the pail of grease by his foot so that it rolled into the shadows. He had been filling a grease cup on the steam donkey, and he straightened and looked at Cal intently. Suspicion flared in Cal's mind, for the man's manner was more a matter of surprise at having been come upon unexpectedly.

Cal passed Fink in a fast stride and caught the grease bucket before it rolled off the trestle. Holding its bail, he turned to look at Fink.

"What's the matter, fella?"

The man laughed nervously. "Why, I just didn't know anybody was stirring and you startled me, Mister Larimore." He reached for the bucket.

Cal held it out of the way. "Must be midnight, Fink. Time for your lunch. Let's go down to the office."

"Why. . . ." Then Fink shrugged and picked up his lantern.

Inside the office, Cal dropped the bucket on the floor with a careless gesture and shucked out of his wet slicker and hat and stripped off his soaked gloves. With an elaborately unconcerned movement, Fink opened his lunch pail and perched himself on a drafting stool beside the stove. He fished out a big sandwich.

Then Cal ran his finger into the grease in the bucket. He rubbed his thumb and forefinger together thoughtfully, then looked at the watchman again.

"Just as I thought, Fink. This cup grease has got grits in it. Iron filings, likely. How long've you been working for Neb Judkins?"

A sullen, defensive look climbed into Fink's face, as though he had been expecting this. "If there's anything wrong with that grease, I never noticed it."

Cal laughed harshly. "If you'd been bright enough to brazen it out up there, instead of rattling and trying to hide the stuff, you might have made it work. It's too late now. You've been back of a lot of little breakdowns and setbacks we've had around here, I guess. I'm going to whip the hell out of you, Fink, and you'll get it light or heavy, depending on how willing you are to talk."

"I don't even know what you're driving at." The watchman bit into his sandwich, gathering his wits again. "They's sand got in that grease, I reckon. Somebody must've left the lid off, and the way the stuff blows around. . . ."

"Not in this weather. Listen, fellow, you're Judkins's man. And you've had a free hand all through the job. But Judkins must've done your thinking for you, keeping your dirty work small enough that I didn't get suspicious. If you want to sign a statement to the effect that you've been working for the man, I'll let you walk off the project. Otherwise, I'm warning you, you're going to need plenty of help."

Fink got down off the stool, pulling his

blocky figure straight. He was about Cal's age but heavier, and a grin flitted suddenly across his whiskery mouth. "Mister, you'll have to make that good. I don't know what you're talking about and. . . ."

Cal nailed him.

A wild sort of joy flared in Cal, for he was facing a tangible enemy after a score of half-shaped worries. He put the flat of his hand on the man's heavy shoulder, jerking him forward, then the other fist rocked Fink back. The boss-employee relationship was broken with the act. A light leaped into Fink's eyes as he staggered back, balanced himself, and got his big arms up.

It was a bloody and violent thing. As it dawned on the slow-minded watchman that he was reaping a whirlwind he had himself sown, he fought desperately. He lacked Cal Larimore's light, easy co-ordination, but he had more steam in his punches. Half a dozen times he rocked Cal back on his heels. Yet with calculated method, Cal whittled him down, bruising and cutting his heavy, bearded face and punishing his flabby belly. Then, when he had vented his paroxysm of rage, Cal dropped him.

The lamp that had been rocking on its base was smoking, and Cal turned it down, chest heaving. He eyed the watchman's inert body with complete indifference now, for the man had been only a cheap tool in a game he probably didn't understand. If he still didn't want to sign a confession, when he came to, he would get another mauling.

Cal's own nose was bleeding, and he held a handkerchief against it while he explored a swelling eye. He had drawn a card, and whether he could take a trick with it depended on himself. He had not suspected dirty work on the job for it had been done very slyly and there had been no reason to look for it. This was probably the first time gritted grease had been tried, for the donkey puncher was a good man and would eventually have noticed if it had been responsible for other breakdowns. Fink had worked first one way and then another in the countless things a traitor can do when he has free access to a project.

A lantern bobbed across the dark yard, then Kim Nagel rushed into the office, only half dressed. "What the devil's going on here?" He eyed Fink's prone figure. "You do that?" He looked at Cal's bloody handkerchief. "Who jumped who?"

Cal grinned. "I climbed him. Take a feel of that cup grease, Kim, and tell me if you think what I think."

The oldster did so and looked up with a

scowl. "Well, what do you know? That's why he was always so anxious to have little jobs to do out on the works at night. Whatcha gonna do with him?"

"I'm going to bust out some more teeth if he doesn't make a clean breast of it. I want it on paper."

Kim nodded, grunting. "Get it and you're fixed. Whoever's been paying Fink can danged well pay us some damages for lost time."

"Right, and I'm not exactly unhappy that it hasn't all been my own fault."

Fink let out a groan presently and tried to lift himself to a sitting position. He spat blood on the floor. Awkwardly getting his knees under him, he looked at Kim, then switched a cowering look to Cal. "Whatcha going to do with me?" he whined.

"You ready to talk business?" demanded Cal.

"I'll talk." The watchman got unsteadily to his feet and turned toward the drafting table that was Kim's desk, balancing himself. Then, with a quick movement, he tipped it, and the desk and lamp crashed to the floor.

IV

Cal jumped toward him, but the man spun and charged through the door, as the room plunged into blackness. Cal hurtled after Fink and slammed hard into the edge of the door as the man tried to pull it shut behind himself. Cal staggered back, his head reeling for a second. He heard Kim curse, as the old man fumbled a match alight.

Racing out the door, Cal saw through the darkness that Fink was making toward Cal's own horse, which still stood where Cal had left it. Cal reached for his gun as the man swung into saddle, and found his holster empty. He cursed as he watched Fink pound down the camp street and disappear into the darkness at its end.

A bitter anger held Cal through the next morning. Ole Jensen and the donkey man had to take down the pile driver machinery and go over it piece by piece to wipe away the last bit of tampered grease that the treacherous watchman might have put there. Since it was the only machine being used on the job, it was the extent of Cal's worries, but that much more time had been lost, and he cursed himself for letting a good card be ruined. It left him more dejected than he had been before for, no matter whose fault it had been, he was still helpless.

The previous night's storm did not abate that day. The wind was building a high chop on Rampage Lake, and, as the springs in its bottom drew freshet water from their huge subterranean veins, it filled with astonishing rapidity. Already a heavy stream was pouring through the narrow channel at the waist into Drip Pan, with the lesser lake growing by the hour. Cal had only a few more bents to put in on this side to complete the underpinning, and the piling now would have to be sunk into water. Then would come the more difficult feat of swinging the stringers for the suspended section that would close the gap over the connecting channel. But, when the planking was spiked down and the railings raised, the job would be finished.

It was this closeness that maddened Cal. He prowled the project, scarcely caring if the whole thing toppled into the water that would eventually broaden across the narrows until it was three quarters of a mile wide.

He was in this mood when Neb Judkins arrived in the company of three hard-faced men, late that afternoon. The work was still shut down, and Cal was in his own tent, getting into dry clothes for the third time that day because of the soaking rain. When they saw Cal, Judkins stepped down instead of riding on to the office, and came to the lifted flap of the tent.

His wet face wore a pleased look as he stepped in without invitation. His companions remained mounted, crowding their horses at the front of the tent. Judkins swept back his slicker in a careless gesture, making a point of showing his gun.

Cal faced him with rising hackles. "Well, your man made his report, did he?"

Judkins laughed lightly. "Keep your shirt on, boy. I've got good news for you."

"Nothing you could say would sound good to me, Judkins, but spit it out."

"My backers want to get it over with, Larimore. They're ready to sweeten the kitty a little. We'll pay your bills and meet your payroll and toss in five thousand for you, besides."

Cal scowled at him. "You don't need to

get so damned generous. I didn't get anything I can use out of your man."

Judkins dried his face with a bandanna. "I'd say you did, Larimore. Experience. What you've had ain't nothing to what you could get. We're set to make it real tough for you, if we have to. Should anything happen to your bridge before you turn it over to the toll company, it's your responsibility, you know. Maybe you're a friend of Johnny Van Dyke, but he'd owe it to his associates to hold you liable. They could get judgments against you that you'd be the rest of your life paying off."

"Why not another bullet from the rimrock?"

Judkins was unabashed. "I hoped you'd guess who that was. But we don't want to kill you, Larimore, though if you play balky, we might have to now to keep your mouth shut. Look. We'd like to make it all nice and smooth and quick. Supposing you finish that job and pull out of the country in shape to stay in business. Then this winter this nice bridge falls in the lake, and everybody agrees it's tough luck, but that it was a fool idea trying to build it in the first place. We'd rather do it that way. A lot rather. And, Larimore, I think you're commencing to feel the same way about it." Judkins chuckled. "If you ain't, you will be in a few days."

Cal took a quick step toward Judkins, then the starch seemed to run out of him suddenly. He turned half away, staring at his bunk. When he spoke, his voice was dispirited. "Get out of here, Judkins. I'll get in touch with you in a day or two."

Judkins's chuckle was louder this time. "I thought so, Larimore. I'll be waiting to hear from you."

"And have the money ready when you do. Currency. Five thousand."

"You betcha!" With an easy laugh, Judkins stepped under the tent flap, mounted, and his group whirled away.

When the pent-up crew piled from the sodden tents the next morning, work was resumed with energy. With its heavy beat resounding over the lakes, the pile driver's heavy hammer rose and fell, forcing in the last bridge bents. The acrid smell of the reheated creosote tank tainted the still high wind, and peeled piling, glistening blackly, rose upright at the end of a chain to swing into the driving tower. While the driving crew narrowed the gap between the two, long, trestle sections, the bridge carpenters, working with adzes and augers, finished and bolted the last big stringers together.

Working with his men, Cal Larimore felt the poisons of frustration run out of him. As if a symbol, the black overcast rifted at noon, followed shortly by an abrupt halt in the rain. The wind was dying, and both swollen Rampage and growing Drip Pan began to lose their running chop. When Cal heard a man whistling, he had a sense of a crisis having been passed, though the thing he knew he had to do still lay ahead.

In mid-afternoon the next day, the pile driver completed its work and pulled itself to one side by its own power. The bridge carpenters took over then, in the ticklish proposition of joining their long, heavy, prebolted stringers across the gap to prepare for the decking. Now disaster beyond man's planning and control could strike at any moment.

Cal motioned Ole Jensen, idle for the time being, to follow him to the office. There he grinned thinly at Jensen and at old Kim Nagel. "Ole, I wish you'd saddle up and ride over to Neb Judkins's tavern. I want you to tell him to be here in my office exactly at seven o'clock this evening. Tell him to bring Ira Fiddler. Tell him that unless he meets those two conditions, there's no use in his coming at all."

Though he did not understand, the rigger

nodded and left. While it would be a long ride, he had little to do from here on, and it would give him a chance to buy a drink or two at the tavern. He left, heading toward the big tents that served as the company stables.

A question rose in Kim's eyes, but he did not ask it. Cal smiled.

"If you're up to it, Kim, I wish you'd ride to Tuckerville and tell Johnny Van Dyke I want to see him here at seven. When you get him to camp, take him to my tent, and keep him there till I move the lamp on my drafting table directly in front of the window. Then get him to the office as fast as you can, and the more surprise you put in it the better I'll like it. Can do?"

The old man's leathery face flashed back a grin. "Can do, will do, and as good as done." He got his slicker and hat and headed out through the door.

Cal smoked a cigarette, letting it burn unnoticed until it almost scorched his fingers. He tossed the butt into the stove draft, frowning slightly, lost in thought. Excitement rose in him, and with it a tension that he did not welcome.

V

While the cast-iron stove crackled cheerfully, Cal Larimore waited in the office after supper that evening. Though his plans were carefully laid, he had been unable to loosen the tightness in him. Yet, his decision was made, and any amount of worried reconsideration would not change it. Three weeks more would see him finished here, he was confident now, with what at least looked like another first-rate bridge behind him. If Judkins and Fiddler showed up, Cal could very likely go from here to another job, one on which luck would run better. And he could take Johnny Van Dyke's pretty sister with him as his wife.

He watched the hands on the clock on Kim's desk crawl past six o'clock and continue their maddeningly slow progress. At six-thirty it began to rain again, pounding harder than ever on the shack's flimsy roof. It didn't worry Cal, for if Judkins and

Fiddler were coming at all, they would already be on the road. And old Kim with Johnny.

At a quarter of seven, Cal could not resist the temptation to check the loads in the six-gun belted to his thigh. He noticed that his fingers trembled slightly, and he frowned at them.

Then, ten minutes ahead of time, he heard the sucking sounds of horses' hoofs in the deep mud of the street outside the shack. The riders drew up, but he disdained going to the door to satisfy his curiosity. After a moment the door opened from the outside, and Neb Judkins came in, followed by Ira Fiddler. Cal's relaxed, impersonal greeting completely covered his inner turbulence.

It was patent at a glance that Judkins was in good spirits, though Fiddler had pulled a careful reserve onto his pinched face. The banker carried a small bag, Cal noticed. Then something moved past the window, and he saw that there were other men waiting outside. Once more Judkins had brought a bodyguard. Cal shrugged to himself. It didn't make much difference, one way or the other.

"Well, Larimore," said Judkins jovially, "it's a rotten night you called us out in. Why didn't you come over, instead of sending a man?"

Cal shrugged. "No sense in me taking a chance on anybody seeing me at your place. Besides, you're the one who's been pushing this deal, and you can do the traveling."

"That's what I figured. It's all right for you to play it cagey, as long as you play."

So far Ira Fiddler had said nothing, and Cal looked at him. "Did you bring the money?"

Fiddler nodded but still did not speak, and Cal noted a wariness in his eyes. The banker hadn't liked this summons a little bit, he saw, but had come in his eagerness to pull off his scheme with a minimum of trouble.

"Five thousand," said Judkins expansively, "and you just check out for your payrolls and bills. Fiddler'll see there's enough in your account to cover 'em."

Cal nodded, a new anxiety growing in him. He had instructed Kim to have Johnny Van Dyke in his tent by seven o'clock, and he had no way of knowing if they were there yet, or even if Johnny had been able to come. If the thing jumped the track at this point, Cal was on the spot. He had to stall for time. He rose and went to the stove, filling three cups from the coffee pot.

373

"You men must be cold. Since we've got to deal with each other, you might as well be comfortable."

Judkins and Fiddler accepted the coffee and drank it, for they were cold and wet, but they refused more. It was the alerting of a man, whose form he could vaguely see through the window, that informed Cal that somebody new had ridden into camp. Or seemed to have. He wasn't sure, but he couldn't stall much longer without rousing suspicions. Mentally shutting his eyes, he jumped.

"Well, Fiddler, you might as well count it out."

The banker spoke finally with a trace of eagerness in his voice. "Yes. Let's get away from here, Judkins." Putting the black grip on the table, he opened it. He lifted out several bundles of currency, and Cal noted that they were of large denomination. With a banker's methodicalness, Fiddler moistened a finger and started to count through each bundle for Cal to watch.

While Fiddler was so engaged, Judkins turned squarely toward Cal, giving him a long gaze. "There's a little point before we hand it over, Larimore. What kind of proof can you give us that you're doing what this pays for?"

While Cal seemed to ponder that, he idly twisted the base of the coal oil lamp, moving it a short distance meanwhile, so that it stood in front of the window by the drafting table. It illuminated the slickered back of a man outside, but Cal knew that it could be seen from across the street and farther down. He held his breath until he saw that this seeming fiddling had not aroused Judkins's curiosity.

"What kind did you have in mind?" Cal asked, still playing for time.

"That's where you pinched us," said Judkins with a candor that showed it to be a problem he had already solved. "We don't want nothing to happen till you're gone from here, or it won't look natural. Otherwise, we just wouldn't pay you till the bridge is in the lake. But we got an idea there's a marriage a-making between you and Johnny Van Dyke's sister. If nothing happens to that bridge by spring, then something's sure gonna happen to her brother. I kind of figure that'll be enough to make you come through, fellow."

"I reckon it would," agreed Cal, listening intently. Somebody's boots sounded on the steps then, and the door opened, and Kim Nagel came in. Looking puzzled when he saw Judkins and Fiddler,

Johnny Van Dyke followed.

Fiddler was Johnny's banker, and since Johnny suspected nothing of what the man was up to, he greeted him in a friendly manner. "What're you doing out on a night like this, Ira?"

There was dismay in Fiddler's face. He cast a nervous eye at the money neatly stacked on the drafting table, ten bundles of five hundred dollars each.

It was Cal who answered. "Glad you showed up, Johnny. Fiddler and I've just cooked up a little deal. I've been sort of pinched, and he's letting me have a few thousand. But mostly he's beginning to see he should've shown more public spirit about the bridge."

There was a snarl in Judkins's quick voice. "What're you talking about?"

Cal gave him a wide grin and started to roll a cigarette. "This deal I'm trying to tell Johnny about. How Fiddler wants to buy up the bridge company's franchise by canceling the mortgages he holds. He figures his bank can better afford to finance a public improvement like that than you and your nester friends. And he's right."

Johnny Van Dyke was not being deceived, though he did not understand what was taking place. Though Neb Judkins had turned dangerous-eyed and defiant, there was guilt and confusion all over Ira Fiddler, who was not accustomed to deals such as he had tried to force on Cal Larimore. And Cal saw that the man was regretting his greed plenty, for the moment. It was what Cal had hoped for, to rattle and frighten Fiddler into compliance. Neb Judkins was the unstable element, and right now he seemed ready to start trouble.

Fiddler looked down at the money on which his skinny hand still laid, and he gulped. He seemed to realize it would be ridiculous to deny any connection with it. And his handing money to Cal Larimore could have but one of two meanings, the loan Cal was implying it to be, or the bribe attempt that it actually was.

Neither Fiddler nor Judkins was sure that Johnny's arrival wasn't a simple matter of coincidence, but they knew that a face had to be put on this thing. They were slowly digesting what Cal had said, seeing the neatness of it, floundering mentally while they tried to figure a way out.

Cal knew that he had to crowd the moment. He had to force Fiddler to comply or admit openly to Johnny Van Dyke that he was out to break the bridge company for his own profit. The growing sardonic grin on

Johnny's face showed that he was glimpsing at least the general idea.

In his easy drawl, Johnny said: "Why, that's sure white of you, Ira, because if the thing don't work like we hope, we've been worried about how we can even pay the interest on our mortgages. Some of us even worried about what you'd do in that case. You sure surprise me, man."

Fiddler sighed, a new slackness showing in his already flabby face. Cal Larimore saw in that moment that Neb Judkins must have done most of the plotting in the scheme and that, denied the ability to talk to Judkins confidentially, Fiddler was at a total loss. Cal picked up a paper that had been lying inconspicuously on the table.

"In fact, I've worked out a little tentative agreement here," he remarked. "Your agreement, Fiddler, to purchase the Narrows Toll Bridge Company by simply canceling the mortgages. And I've also got my own note ready for five thousand dollars, to . . . shall we say . . . cover the losses I've suffered because of a man I had hired who had a bad habit of gumming up the works." He began to move the sheaves of money into a drawer. "I'll just clear space so you and Johnny can sign. Judkins and I'll witness it."

Even Neb Judkins saw that Fiddler had

collapsed. The banker sagged against the table, then nodded.

Judkins strode to the door and flung it open, motioning to his men. The three of them came inside, and they were all armed. It was a silent threat.

"Might as well get in out of the weather, boys," Judkins said, and cast Cal a baleful glance.

But this support failed to put the starch back into Ira Fiddler. Johnny Van Dyke picked up the agreement Cal had prepared and read it, nodding his head. Then he picked up a pen, dipped it, and signed. He held the pen toward Ira Fiddler, who stared at it.

Cal saw Judkins nod to his men. The tavern keeper was not going to accept a development that would render valueless everything he had so carefully done. Ira Fiddler sensed this, too, and, fearing gun play, grabbed the pen and hurriedly signed the document. Johnny, grinning broadly now, swept up the agreement and stuffed it into his pocket.

"That's sure a nice thing, Ira," he declared heartily.

"By Satan!" breathed Judkins. "I've only got two men to kill to put it right back where it was. You, Larimore, and you, Van Dyke."

The moment was freighted with danger, for his three men stood ready to go for their guns. Johnny had a gun on his hip, but he didn't look as if he even expected to have to grab for it. There was a glitter in Judkins's eyes now, the ghost of a smile on his lips.

"Don't play the fool, Neb," Fiddler bleated.

"You're the fool, Fiddler. What's to keep us from claiming you got suspicious of these smart jiggers? You're everybody's banker and see things nobody else sees. For one thing, Larimore's paying for a lot more commissary provisions from Van Dyke's store than he's getting, with them splitting the difference. Larimore's other creditors are holding the sack when he goes broke. Van Dyke's getting a lot more out of the bridge than he'd get the other way. Everybody knows how thick they've been."

"I don't know what you're talking about!" Fiddler screamed.

"Oh, yes, you do, and I'm talking plain so you can't slide out of it so easy. You were honest enough when you loaned the bridge company money, but you sure went for it when I showed you how easy it'd be to clean up big. Now, we gotta kill this pair, don't we, Ira, and that old turkey, over there? It's like this. We met them here for a showdown and had to gun it out. They got the worst of it."

Cal had almost forgotten Kim Nagel, who had pressed into a corner and remained there unobtrusively. Kim glared at Judkins's reference to him, then shuffled slackly to the stove where the eternal kettle of soup was bubbling. Setting a bowl on the stove top, he lifted the kettle to fill it.

While his hardcases watched Cal and Johnny, Judkins kept his eyes on Fiddler. Nobody was paying any attention to old Kim when he heaved suddenly, throwing the scalding contents of the kettle into the tavern keeper's face.

It touched off a bedlam. As surprised as Judkins's men, Cal stepped back against the wall, watching Judkins claw at his eyes. The gunmen, uninstructed previously because this development had not been foreseen, hung in indecision. Ira Fiddler let out a groan and dropped behind a second drafting table. Grinning, Johnny laid a foot on the banker's rump and shoved him on under.

"We don't want you hurt till you've carried out your bargain, fella!"

Cal saw then that Johnny had his gun in his hand, that it must have been there since Kim had thrown the soup. Which was why

Judkins's tough hands hadn't moved. Judkins looked at them finally through stinging, burned eyes. He stood apart from the gunmen. Cal saw the man take a measuring glance, then Cal's own hand shot gunward as Judkins drew, taking advantage of the fact that Johnny could not cover him and the henchmen, too.

Both guns spoke sharply, the one a second ahead of the other, and for a split second more Cal didn't know what had happened. He had felt neither jar nor pain, then Neb Judkins lifted his shoulders, raising on his toes, his head sagging, and pitched forward. The henchmen glowered, but none of them dared to challenge Johnny Van Dyke's steady gun.

The two shots roused the camp, and in a matter of a minute men were pounding toward the office. Cal turned the three gunmen over to Ole Jensen to be run out of camp, but kept Fiddler in the office with himself and Johnny. While he explained the whole situation to Johnny, old Kim threw a tarpaulin over the body on the floor. He looked at Cal, finally, and grinned.

"Dang it, that was good soup, too," he grumbled. He went out, heading for the cook house.

"Well, Fiddler," said Johnny, "I reckon

your main crime was in what you intended to do and not in what you done. You've always been a greedy man, but as far as anybody knows an honest one, up to now."

"It was Judkins," Fiddler said weakly. "He came to me like Satan and tempted me." He looked at Cal pleadingly. "I owe you that five thousand in damages, and we'll burn the note. I'll take over the bridge and carry it till it pays out."

"That sounds like another bribe offer," said Cal, shaking his head. "You'd have gone ahead with a dirty, rotten crime if you hadn't been stopped. I want damages for the delay you've caused me, and I want your bank to take over the project it tried to ruin. But beyond that, you've got to answer for your part in this, though the judge might be more lenient if you do your best to make amends."

After a long moment the banker nodded in agreement. "I guess you're right. Anyway, everybody here knows you shot Judkins in self-defense, so there won't be any trouble over that."

Old Kim came up from the cook shack with a fresh pot of soup shortly after Fiddler and the others had departed in Ole Jensen's charge. Its appetizing aroma filled the room, and Kim poured some into coffee cups.

"Better warm your gizzard before you start home, Johnny," he suggested.

"Fill me one, too," said Cal. "I'm riding home with Johnny. We're going to be out looking for another job pretty soon, Kim, and I've got some important talking to do up Tuckerville way, first."

Johnny grinned at him. "Man, it won't take nowhere near the talking you seem to think," he said. "In fact, I danged near could give you her answer right now."

"Get on with you, man. You can't give me all I hope to get with it."

About the Author

Giff(ord Paul) Cheshire was born on July 27, 1905, at Cheshire, Oregon — a community near Junction City named for his grandfather who had crossed the plains from Tennessee by wagon in 1852. His first professional sale was made in 1934, to a Western pulp magazine, and he became a professional author of short stories and novels until his death on January 6, 1973. Cheshire's strongest novels are those that are solidly based on historical events and include THUNDER ON THE MOUNTAIN (1960) and STRONGHOLD (1963) by Giff Cheshire as well as RIDE WEST FOR WAR (1961), ROGUE RIVER (1962), SNAKEHEAD (1965), and MIGHTY BIG RIVER (1967) by Chad Merriman.

About the Editor

Bill Pronzini was born in Petaluma, California. His earliest Western fiction was published under his own name and a variety of pseudonyms in *Zane Grey's Western Magazine*. Among his most notable Western novels are STARVATION CAMP (1984) and FIREWIND (1989). THE BEST WESTERN STORIES OF BILL PRONZINI was published by Ohio University Press in 1990. He is also the editor of numerous Western story collections, including WILD WESTERNS: STORIES FROM THE GRAND OLD PULPS (1986), THE BEST WESTERN STORIES OF FRANK BONHAM (1989), and THE BEST WESTERN STORIES OF LES SAVAGE, JR. (1991). He recently edited UNDER THE BLAZING SUN: WESTERN STORIES by H. A. DeRosso for Five Star Westerns and is currently preparing a second collection of H. A. DeRosso Western stories. He is married to author Marcia Muller. They make their home in Petaluma.

"The Bad Year" first appeared in *Blue Book* (2/49). Copyright © 1949 by McCall Corporation. Copyright © renewed 1977 by Mildred E. Cheshire.

"A Mug at Charley's" first appeared in *Adventure* (5/46). Copyright © 1946 by Popular Publications, Inc. Copyright © renewed 1974 by Mildred E. Cheshire.

"Strangers in the Evening" first appeared in *Zane Grey's Western Magazine* (10/49). Copyright © 1949 by The Hawley Publications, Inc. Copyright © renewed 1977 by Mildred E. Cheshire.

"Man Breaker" first appeared in *Blue Book* (8/51). Copyright © 1951 by McCall Corporation. Copyright © renewed 1979 by Mildred E. Cheshire.

"Whistle on the River" first appeared in *Argosy* (7/46). Copyright © 1946 by Popular Publications, Inc. Copyright © renewed 1974 by Mildred E. Cheshire.

"Stagecoach Pass" first appeared in *Blue Book* (1/50). Copyright © 1949 by McCall Corporation. Copyright © renewed 1977 by Mildred E. Cheshire.

"Renegade River" first appeared under the title "Fighting Castaways of Renegade River" in *Dime Western* (3/47). Copyright © 1947 by Popular Publications, Inc. Copyright © renewed 1975 by Mildred E. Cheshire.

"East Ain't West" first appeared in *Western Story* (4/47). Copyright © 1947 by Street and Smith Publications, Inc. Copyright © renewed 1975 by Mildred E. Cheshire.

"The Road to Jericho" first appeared in *Blue Book* (4/50). Copyright © 1950 by McCall Corporation. Copyright © renewed 1978 by Mildred E. Cheshire.

"Know Your Headings" first appeared in *Short Stories* (4/10/47). Copyright © 1947 by Short Stories, Inc. Copyright © renewed 1975 by Mildred E. Cheshire.

"A Bridge to the Future" first appeared in *Adventure* (1/47). Copyright © 1946 by Popular Publications, Inc. Copyright © renewed 1975 by Mildred E. Cheshire.

"Miracle of Starvation Flat" first appeared in *Western Story* (7/47). Copyright © 1947 by Street and Smith Publications, Inc. Copyright © renewed 1974 by Mildred E. Cheshire.

"Giff Cheshire: Oregon Man" by Bill Pronzini. Copyright © 1998 by Bill Pronzini.

The employees of Thorndike Press hope you have enjoyed this Large Print book. All our Large Print titles are designed for easy reading, and all our books are made to last. Other Thorndike Press Large Print books are available at your library, through selected bookstores, or directly from us.

For information about titles, please call:

(800) 257-5157

To share your comments, please write:

Publisher
Thorndike Press
P.O. Box 159
Thorndike, Maine 04986

NEW HANOVER COUNTY PUBLIC LIB.

3 4200 00506 9121

LH CB
8/00

NE 3/01

MG
6/99

2/99

NEW HANOVER COUNTY PUBLIC LIBRARY
201 Chestnut Street
Wilmington, N.C. 28401

GAYLORD S

ML